The Fine Art of Pretending

RACHEL HARRIS

Spencer Hill Press

This book is a work of fiction. Names, characters, places, and
incidents are products of the author's imagination or are used
fictitiously. Any resemblance to actual events, locales, or persons,
living or dead, is entirely coincidental.

Contact: Spencer Hill Press, PO Box 247, Contoocook, NH 03229,
USA
Please visit our website at www.spencerhillpress.com

First Edition: June 24, 2014
Rachel Harris
The Fine Art of Pretending: a novel / by Rachel Harris – 1st ed.
p. cm.

Summary: A girl decides to change her image and gets her best
friend to agree to be her pretend boyfriend to raise her profile, but
when the time comes to end the charade both of them are surprised
to find their feelings aren't pretend anymore.

The author acknowledges the copyrighted or trademarked status
and trademark owners of the following wordmarks mentioned in
this fiction: Ben & Jerry's, Barbie, Big Mac, BMW, Cadbury Adams
USA LLC (Trident), Canon, Cartier, ChapStick, Charlotte Russe,
Chuck Taylor, Chunky Monkey, Clinique, Coke, Crown Royal, Diet
Mountain Dew, Disney, Dr. Pepper, Dumpster, Etch A Sketch, Evian,
F-150, Facebook, Forever 21, Google Hangout, Grease, Hulk, iPod,
Jeep, Jenga, Juicy Couture, Kanye West, Kleenex, M&M's, Mad
Dog, McDonald's, Nike, Oreo, Quarter Pounder, Rack Room Shoes,
Raisinets, Red Bull, Reese's Pieces, Sephora, Sprite, Seven Up, Sevens,
Sugarland, Super Swamper, Taco Bell, Taylor Swift,Twitter, Twix,
UFC, US Weekly, Wii, Wizard of Oz, YouTube

Cover design by: Kate Kaynak
Interior layout by: Jenny Perinovic

ISBN 978-1-939392-28-2 (paperback)
ISBN 978-1-939392-27-5 (e-book)

Printed in the United States of America

For everyone
who has ever chased a dream,
dared to try something new,
or found beauty in their own skin,
this one's for you.

SATURDAY, AUGUST 7TH
Exactly 8 weeks until Homecoming ♥

ALY
FAIRWOOD CITY MALL, 12:20 p.m.

The cleavage popping out of my scandalously low-cut halter top heralds the beginning of Operation Sex Appeal. I turn sideways and adjust the neckline, alternately slouching and straightening as tall as my five-foot frame can go, but the fidgeting doesn't make a bit of difference. After three and a half years covering my horribly disproportionate chest as much as possible, there's just no hiding the girls now.

I take a deep breath and silently repeat my new mantra, the words of wisdom that Kara quoted when I agreed to this makeover.

If you want to recreate yourself in a new image, you must embrace your inner vixen.

But as my teeth worry my lower lip and I scan the piles of halter tops, miniskirts, tiny shorts, pushup bras, and anxiety-inducing bikinis around me in the dressing room, I ask myself the million-dollar question: *Do I even have an inner vixen?*

Shaking the urge to grab my oversized volleyball camp tee, I close my eyes and try to imagine the male population's reaction to the girl staring back at me—Alyssa Reed 2.0. A vision of the packed assembly hall at Cypress Lake campground materializes in the darkness. Across the room, a blurry-faced guy with messy dark hair turns toward me, shock registering as he *really* notices me for the first time. The rest of the room quiets as he glides through the mass of bodies, slow-motion style, to take me in his arms, thread his fingers in my hair—

"Incoming!"

My heart jumps into my throat. I twirl to meet Kara's overly enthused hazel eyes peeking over the slatted half door, and twin surges of heat blossom in my cheeks.

"This batch has jeans and shorts for the camping trip next week, and I got a ton of dress options for the back-to-school dance." She stands on tiptoe, scans my outfit, and smiles in approval. "That's hot. Who would've believed you were hiding such a killer body under all those hideous man-shirts and baggy pants?"

I roll my eyes and pull at my neckline again. As the self-declared fashion guru of Fairfield Academy, Kara considers my relaxed style a personal affront, and as my best friend, she's made it her life's ambition to *reform* me. Somehow, whether by fierce will or pure stubbornness, I managed to deflect her obsessive makeover attempts for the last three years, only to succumb last night in a moment of pure, unadulterated desperation.

To say her elation rivaled that of a five-year-old on Christmas morning would be a gross understatement.

As if my change of heart weren't enough, Kara ensured her success by showing up at practice just over an hour ago, shoving me first into the shower and then into her death mobile, and then stopping only to drag our friend Gabi out of bed before flooring it to the trendiest mall in town. I'm stunned she didn't drive all the way to Houston.

"You know, those baggy pants happen to be Juicy Couture." Granted, that's as stylish as my current wardrobe ever got, but I still think it should count for something.

According to Kara's snort, apparently not.

"Yeah, Aly, you're a total label-whore." Blowing me an air-kiss, she pulls open the door and shoves about six pairs of jeans and at least a dozen dresses onto the closest overstuffed rack. She fluffs her bangs and surveys the hanging options with a concentrated gaze. "Too bad Brandon's working today. I could really use a male opinion." She tosses a quick glance to the corner of the room and adds, "And some help, since *somebody*'s not doing crap."

From her sprawled position on the dingy threadbare carpet, the third member of our glorious trio lifts her hand and gives Kara a one-finger salute.

"I'm in here for emotional support," Gabi says dryly. She grabs a red-dyed strip of her long black hair and intently studies the split ends. "Besides, I'm not sure I fully support this Project Hot to Trot thing anyway."

I release a breath and turn back to my reflection. My two best friends couldn't be more different, as evidenced by the emotional tug-of-war they've put me through ever since we set foot in Forever 21. I know Gabi doesn't have a problem with the clothes—she changes her style like people change their Facebook status. And while I'm normally lucky to pull off jeans and a T-shirt, she fluctuates between all of them with ease. Gothic black, flowing hippie, dominatrix leather, chilled-out jeans...it all works. Which means she's stewing about something deeper, and knowing Gabi, that could be just about anything.

"It's Operation Sex Appeal," I clarify. "Hot to Trot makes me sound like a race horse." I tug the revealing halter top over my head and slip on a floral print dress with a tiered bubble hem, enjoying the feel of the fabric. It's a far cry from the worn-out cotton of my favorite tee, that's for sure. "And you don't have to support what I'm doing—but you should support me. I believe I've earned that after living through all *your* schemes."

Back before Kara moved to Texas and Gabi and I were still a twosome, she was actually the more *reserved* member of our duo. The shift didn't happen until her dad left in seventh grade and Gabi placed full blame on her mom. But when that shift happened, it *happened*.

In the mirror, she lifts her dark-lined eyes to mine and frowns. "I just don't get why you're letting Kara do this. You worry too damn much about what other people think."

My hands clench around the foreign material. Her words, as truthful as they may be, cut just the same. I draw a deep breath and meet her reflected gaze as I try and find a way to explain something I'm still figuring out myself.

"Gab, I'm not doing this to get Kara off my back or to get her to shut up about my clothes. I'm doing this for *me*." I look at the strange vision of myself decked out in a dress, of all things. "This is something *I* have to do. I've spent the last three years feeling like I'm watching life from the sidelines, Gab. Don't get me wrong, you guys rock, my grades are good, and my family's amazing, but isn't high school supposed to be the best years of our lives? I thought I'd have scrapbooks filled with pictures of boys and kissing and mementos from dates. But I don't have that stuff. *I* have volleyball trophies and pictures from training camps and group pictures at dances with the girls."

The space between Gabi's eyebrows scrunches together. I'm not surprised she doesn't understand. Gabi never gives a flip what other people think of her. But then, she doesn't need to because I care enough for the both of us. For a while, it was enough to be friends with the cute guys and have them smile and wave at me in the hall. But over the past year, things changed. Now I want those same guys to see me as more. To see me as someone who is actually dateable. And last night, packing my same old comfortable, cotton wardrobe for the senior camping trip, I realized that the time to make a change is now or never.

But convincing a rebel like Gabi of that is going to take some finesse.

I twist the end of my long auburn ponytail into a bun and decide to go the comedic route. "Besides, can you honestly think of anyone better than two hot divas like yourselves to help me attempt this mission impossible? Transforming *this*..." I sweep a hand over my goober self like a deranged game show host. "...into someone *sexy*?" I strike a smoldering pouty pose for full dramatic effect.

Kara snickers as Gabi throws her head against the rickety wall and bangs it repeatedly. She's never been one for holding back her feelings. Or for being *subtle*.

"I *so* don't want to be a killjoy," Gabi says, lifting her head and leveling me with a pointed look. "Do you know how much it pains me to be the voice of reason? But, Aly, you've always run from anything that would single you out—and I gotta tell ya, being 'sexy'? That's kinda gonna entail some attention."

"Experimentation in adolescence is healthy," Kara interrupts, sounding exactly like her psychiatrist mother. "Besides, I'll be there to guide her through the testosterone-crazed havoc she's going to create. Aw, Gab, don't ya see?" She puts her hand over her heart, tilts her chin, and pretends to hold back tears. "Our little Aly's growing up."

"Thanks a lot," I say, lobbing a discarded shirt at her head with a mock-scowl.

Kara sticks her tongue out and tosses the shirt back. I duck. Before I can grab another random garment, a series of tinkling bells erupts from her purse, and she squeals. Gabi and I exchange a look as Kara tugs out her phone, gives her shoulders a shimmy, and says in a decidedly lower voice, "Hey, baby."

"*Daniel*," Gabi mouths. The current love interest. If the squeal wasn't enough to clue us in, the sexy, purring quality to Kara's voice sealed the deal.

With my personal shopper otherwise occupied, I squat down next to Gabi and squeeze her hand. "Please understand. I need this."

She studies me for a moment and sighs. "Listen, you're my best friend. No matter what, I'm here for you. If you say this is what you want, then this is what we'll do. Even if I don't understand it." She plucks the shirt off the floor and starts folding it, pausing to shoot me a smile. "So I guess I'll shut the hell up and actually make myself useful."

With a grateful grin and renewed passion for the mission, I stand and strip, ready to throw on whatever offending item Kara placed next for me on the rack. The sea of colors in the room makes me feel like I'm playing dress-up in an Easter egg and none of this stuff is *me*, but I guess that's the point. To be different. Shake things up. At this point, it certainly can't hurt.

My gaze lands on the item hanging on top, a skirt barely long enough to cover my butt, and my eyes pop in shock.

She cannot be serious.

Where would this even land on a person of normal height?

I hold the glorified belt up to myself and stare at Kara for confirmation of her insanity, but she's too busy twirling a strand of cropped brown hair around her finger to notice.

"Sounds good. I'll be ready at six." Pause. "Maybe. If you're lucky." Suggestive giggle. "All right. Bye, baby." Kara hangs up the phone and falls against the door in a mock-swoon. "Daniel's sooo hot! He's going to do quite nicely in this year's Homecoming picture, don't ya think?"

The wannabe skirt flutters to the ground. "*Homecoming?*" Noting the slight manic quality to my voice, I press my lips together and then smile, attempting to tone down the crazy. "I mean, are you serious? Aren't you the one who said any relationship over a month is a waste of perfectly good dating time? Homecoming's, like, two months away."

Fifty-six days to be exact, but who's counting?

Kara stoops to pick up the skirt, shrugging like it's no big deal, and I force my fists to unclench. I have to remember that not everyone is as fixated on this dance as I am. Accepting the garment, I push past the topic of my secret obsession and focus back on my shared—and now group-accepted—plan.

One thing at a time.

I step into the skirt, which is every bit as horrible as I'd imagined, and then pull on the white sleeveless top Kara pairs with it. The braided straps require the strapless bra I have on, which even after hours of wear still feels like it's going to fall around my waist at any moment. I discreetly run my hands over my butt—making sure the scrap of fabric she considers clothing is at least covering it—wiggle the cups of my bra, and exhale slowly. My reflection looks like a stranger, and I feel like an imposter. Clearly, this isn't going to be as easy as I originally anticipated.

My phone buzzes, and I motion for Gabi to check it. She roots around in my purse, muttering, "It's like freaking Grand Central Station in this joint."

As I lean over to adjust "the girls" again, I smile, waiting for Gabi to relay the text message. The total lack of privacy is one of my favorite things about having best friends. I know everything about Gabi and Kara, and they know all my dirty secrets, too.

Well, if I had anything remotely juicy to share, they'd be the first to know, at least.

"Your place tomorrow, five thirty," Gabi reads in a monotone voice. "Let's eat after. Your choice: La Cantina or Carmela's." She hands the phone over and I text back, *Brandon, remember what happened last time we ate @ L.C.? Definitely Carmela's. See U then.*

"Sounds like a hot date."

Spinning around, I bonk foreheads with an over-the-shoulder-reading Gabi. "Ow!" Gabi ignores the collision and widens her eyes expectantly. "Yeah," I mutter. "Totally hot date."

Kara cocks her hip, and I pinch the bridge of my nose, hoping to hold off the oncoming headache. "Guys, seriously. Brandon's meeting me to talk strategy. Coach Connelly roped us into coaching the junior high volleyball team our sisters joined at the rec center. Seems my mad skills on the court, paired with Brandon's past coaching experience and, well, the fact that I don't want to do it by myself, makes us the perfect—and only—choices this year."

Kara narrows her eyes. "And how do you think *he's* gonna react to your new look?"

"Who, Coach Connelly?" I ask innocently. Kara smiles patiently, and I groan, pulling off the belt/skirt. "He probably won't even notice. Or care."

Gabi snorts. "Aly, you do realize Brandon's a guy, right?"

"A very popular, very gorgeous guy," Kara adds in a weird tone of voice.

I lift my head with one leg in a new pair of Sevens. My gaze darts between my two suddenly suspicious best friends, and I stand from my stooped position. "Why are y'all looking at me like that?"

Kara folds her arms. "Not that I'm not stoked you're finally willing to accept help, but is this makeover really about Brandon?"

Should've known.

Hiking the jeans up my short legs, I silently lament designers' inability to realize women with butts can also have a slim waistline and say aloud, "For the bazillionth time, Brandon thinks of me like a sister." Which, of course, only feeds Kara's hunch, so I quickly add, "Not that it matters because I'm not into him anyway. We're *friends*."

A smirk twitches the corner of Kara's lips, and I exhale in frustrated defeat. We've been over this topic so much that I may as well shut up now and save my breath. A platonic male friend is a concept Kara finds inexplicable, and believe me, I've tried to explain. She just doesn't get that some things are easier to talk about with a guy or that, with Brandon, no topic is ever off-limits. Except for maybe the massive crush I had on him a few years ago, but that's ancient history.

Gabi grabs a top that actually appears to have more than an inch of material and says, "Hey, if this isn't about Brandon, and you say you're not into him, that's cool. I believe you."

"Thank you," I tell her, reaching out for the shirt. At least one of them seems to get it. Then Gabi's grip tightens on the fabric and I'm forced to lift my gaze.

"But I promise you, come Monday, when the camping trip starts and guys' eyes start bugging out? He *will* notice." She grins sweetly. "And he's definitely going to care."

Yanking the soft cotton shirt from her hands, I turn away and pull it on, fluffing my hair as I survey the result.

Regardless of what they think, I doubt Brandon will ever see me differently—but other people will. The cute and funny girl who's "just friends" with all the popular guys is gone. That girl the guys think of when they want to shoot hoops or need an ear to listen, but never when they want a date, has left the premises. The Aly staring back at me has on spanking new clothes that actually show her shape, and wears a determined smile.

This is going to work. It has to. I'm not doing this for Brandon, or for Kara, or for anyone else.

I'm doing it for *me*. The senior camping trip starts Monday, the kick-off to my last year at Fairfield Academy. And this year, everything's gonna change.

In two months, when Homecoming rolls around, a new and improved Alyssa Reed will walk into the twinkle-lit ballroom. One with a new look, a new reputation, and a new *man*.

BRANDON
TEXAS SPRINGS CAR WASH, 12:45 p.m.

"*Who's* coming out tonight?" Justin asks, shouting to us from inside the minivan.

I look over from my perch, scrubbing the rear driver-side tire. "Don't think I can, man. Mom's off and wants to have a family dinner." I toss the brush into a bucket and grab a clean towel. "She'll probably crash early though, so give me a call before you head out."

Carlos and Drew are under the red canopy next to ours, vacuuming a Lexus with the radio blaring. Carlos stops singing off-key long enough to say, "You know I'm there."

Drew catches my eye as he shrugs. "Sorry, guys."

I shake my head as he ducks back down to wipe the interior. He's spent the entire summer dragging ass because his girlfriend is heading to Austin for college. Now that she's actually leaving, I can only imagine how much fun he'll be during the camping trip next week.

If I learned anything from Dad's death, it's that life's short. Our senior year should be spent having fun and hanging out, but Drew doesn't get that. He keeps wanting me to ask out one of Sarah's friends—as if I need to be chained down like him. Between school, baseball, work, looking out for Mom and Baylee, and now coaching with Aly, a relationship is the last thing I need. That would just add stress and I have enough of that shit already.

My phone beeps in my pocket, and I pull it out, laughing as I read Aly's text about La Cantina. I'd forgotten about the last time we went there—and the mysterious "secret ingredient" in the restaurant's queso.

Carmela's it is.

"Yo, Brando." I pocket my phone and glance up to see Carlos smirk. "A customer needs your *assistance* out front."

Great. Wiping the sweat off my forehead with the back of my hand, I saunter to the front of the car wash prepared for battle. Half of the Fairfield Academy baseball team works here, and as captain of the team, I'm the unofficial manager on duty. The title sounds more prestigious than it is because, really, I have one role: handle problems and irate customers.

Squinting through the waves of heat radiating from the pavement, I see a metallic blue BMW idling.

Shit.

Over the summer, Lauren Hays started bringing in her brand-new car a few days a week, dropping unsubtle hints and flaunting her tight dancer's body. Drew's already taken, Carlos is an ex who refuses to go back to her, and Justin is a regular hookup who doesn't require maintenance. That leaves me. And the girl's yet to take a hint.

Lauren's essentially the female version of Justin. She likes to have fun, loves being caught having it, and always needs someone new on her arm. It seems I'm her latest victim, but I'm not interested in spoiled brats who throw Daddy's money around. Mom works too hard and I bust my ass too much to have patience for princesses. Lauren's a genuine pain in my ass.

But she *is* smoking hot.

As I get closer to her car, the driver-side door opens. Lauren steps out in a tight white T-shirt stretched over a black string bikini top, cutoffs so short they're practically pointless, and tall shoes that make her tan legs go on for miles. She lifts her dark sunglasses on top of her light blonde hair, and when she steps in close, coconut wafts off her skin like she took a bath in sunscreen.

"Hook me up, Brandon?" she says. "I was on my way to get a new bikini for the camping trip, but then I saw how dirty my car was." Her mouth curves into a flirty smile, knowing she was here just a couple days ago. The car's so clean you could eat off the damn hood. I take the keys from her outstretched hand, and she curls her fingers around mine. "Just give me the Taylor special. You know what I like."

Gliding past me on her way to checkout, she stops when she reaches the main door to blow me a kiss. The second the door closes, the laughter begins.

"Brando, that chica wants you bad."

I look back to see Carlos, who apparently followed me to the front, shake his head. Glancing at the door Lauren disappeared through, he throws his arm around my shoulder, and says, "Trust me, you ain't seen nothing yet. Just wait 'til the camping trip starts. Four days of uninterrupted game play? You best be bringing your garlic, crucifix, and holy water, cuz that girl's vicious."

ALY
FAIRWOOD CITY MALL FOOD COURT, 2:40 p.m.

I topple into my chair in the crowded food court, arms laden with bags from Charlotte Russe, Forever 21, Rack Room Shoes, and Sephora. Fresh from Kara's salon, my hair bounces around my shoulders like a freaking Pantene commercial. It's a good thing I rarely spend any money, saving instead for my nationwide road trip next summer, because my pathetic checking account has definitely taken a beating.

Gabi plops down across from me with our trays of food. She slides my chicken fajita nachos toward me, and the smell of jalapeños reinvigorates my tired brain.

Who knew shopping could be so exhausting?

"Our nail appointment is in twenty minutes," Kara says, setting down her tray of highly nutritious and tasteless salad. "So better eat quickly, girls."

Circling a finger over her tray, I say, "I hate to tell you this, Kar, but *that's* not food. That's what food eats."

I smile to show I'm teasing, and she glances at the pink Cartier watch on her slender wrist. "Nineteen minutes," she says, looking back up with a wicked grin.

I lift my hands in surrender. "Hey, as the daughter of a caterer and a lover of all things yummy, I'm just trying to do my civic duty." She rolls her eyes, and I pop a chunk of cheese-coated chicken into my mouth.

Shopping doesn't just make me exhausted—it makes me ravenous. And these nachos are seriously calling my name. I eagerly dive in, and after several minutes of blissful eating and watching brave power-walkers lap the food court in the face of such scrumptious temptation, I notice Gabi scowl.

I thought we'd moved past the drama for the afternoon.

Wiping my hands on a crumpled napkin, I ask, "What's going on in that multicolored head of yours, Gab?" She looks over in confusion. "I see that gloomy face. Is this still about my makeover mission?"

"No." She plucks a pepperoni off her pizza and wraps it in a long string of congealed cheese. "I don't love it, but I get it. The gloom and doom is because Lauren just walked in."

"Ah, that explains it."

Gabi nods and shoves the pepperoni in her mouth. I follow her gaze to where the captain of the dance team stands texting on her phone. Lauren Hays is the master of the fake smile when she wants something and the giver of the evil-eye when you fail to do it. She's pretty much ignored me since freshman year, but she and Gabi have a love-hate relationship. They're both on the dance team, so they tolerate each other. It's just that Gabi refuses to bow to the captain's every whim, and Lauren has zero patience for anyone with a backbone.

I pinch the ends of my freshly highlighted hair between my fingers and sink a little lower in my seat. This new look is barely an hour old. I don't think I'm ready to unveil it to the queen of the senior class *now*.

What if she hates it?

What if she doesn't even notice?

Honestly, right now, I don't know which outcome would be worse.

Kara narrows her eyes, seeing what I'm doing, but I don't care. I never claimed to be brave. Or sexy. Operation Sex Appeal is all about working from the outside in.

I glance back at Lauren and relax a smidge. Luckily, she keeps her nose in the air as she walks in our direction, which means I may be in the clear. I slowly release a breath, afraid to make any sudden movements—but then her dang phone beeps. She glances down to retrieve it from her purse, and when she looks up, her gaze lands right on me.

"Oh, how cute." I grit my teeth at the despised word as Lauren sidles up to my side of the table. "Has someone been playing dress-up?"

Blood drains from my face, and I see Gabi stiffen across from me. "Shut the hell up, Lauren."

"Oh, Gabriela, I'm just teasing her." Lauren's smirk morphs into one of the fake, plastic smiles I've seen her give a hundred others. Swiping a fry from Gabi's tray, she says, "I think it's sweet our resident tomboy wants to break out of her shell."

Her blinged-out phone beeps again, and she looks down. When she does, I attempt to regroup and rally...but the excitement, the hope, and the eager anticipation of the morning are gone. Now, all I feel is stupid. Like I *am* playing dress-up, in clothes and in a persona that I couldn't pull off in a million years, so why even bother?

Lauren huffs a sigh. "As much as I'd love to hear what on Earth brought *this* on, I have to run. As class president, there's much to do before the camping trip and all." She wiggles her fingers in farewell and adjusts her purse strap on her shoulder. "Tootles."

Kara watches her sashay away, then spears a chunk of lettuce with her spork. "Did she just say *tootles?*"

Gabi chuckles, but I'm too busy recalculating to respond. I've come too far to give up now, but Lauren just called my transformation *cute* and *sweet*. The same two words that have followed me my whole life. I don't want to be the same old Aly in a new designer wrapper. I want *real* change.

Clearly, a makeover is not going to be enough. If I want people to take me seriously, I need to add another layer to Operation Sex Appeal.

But what?

SUNDAY, AUGUST 8TH

7 weeks and 6 days until Homecoming ♥

ALY
ALY'S HOUSE, 5:45 p.m.

I sit at my vanity, staring at the free gift-with-purchase bag stuffed with makeup, and try to remember which products Kara used yesterday. The idea of a beauty regime is as foreign to me as losing a volleyball match, but desperate times call for desperate measures. After applying the coral blush to the "apples" of my cheeks (another new term for my vocabulary), I grab the berry-stained lip gloss I'm almost certain is right. I unscrew the cap, pump the wand, and raise it to my mouth.

A sudden rap on the door makes the wand skitter across my cheek, leaving a zigzag stripe of Blackberry Bloom in its wake.

"Lovely," I mutter, yanking a handful of tissues out of a crochet-covered box. Regardless of how often I've watched Gabi and Kara do this, obviously makeup application skills cannot be obtained through osmosis. I toss the balled-up Kleenex into the waste bin and bellow, "Come in, Kaitie!"

Instead of my younger sister, Brandon lets himself in, a notebook with sketched-out game plans tucked

weeks, but it's nothing serious, you know? But these girls don't mind because that's not what they want. They're in it for fun, too."

I nod, getting a decent picture of what he's talking about...and where he's going with this.

"A *Commitment*," he continues, "is the opposite. They're the ones who deserve and *want* an actual relationship. They're the type you ask to be your girlfriend and bring home to meet your parents."

"And where do I fit into these two groups?" I ask, although I already know.

"Well..." He clears his throat and runs his hand over the back of his head. "When we did this game, we all agreed you are a *Commitment*."

Of course I am.

I know, call me a traitor to my gender, but while the chauvinistic ranking system sucks, that's not what annoys me the most. What *does* is being lumped into the *Commitment* group.

On some level—like deep, deep, *deep* down—I get that it's probably a good thing. If a great guy came around who wanted me to be his girlfriend, I'd be all for it. And it's sweet that the guys supposedly think I deserve a relationship, whatever that means. But really, what I hear Brandon saying is that they all think I'm boring. Unattractive. Not worth the effort.

Casuals are obviously the confident, exciting, sexy ones. The kind of girl I wish I was.

Brandon plucks his thumb over my pursed lips. "You're disappointed in me?"

"No, not in *you*." At his confused look, I explain, feeling the heat of blood rush to my face. "Honestly? I'm annoyed with myself! I know you probably think being in the *Commitment* group is some sort of compliment—"

"It really is—"

"—*but* all I hear is that the *Casual* group is the fun group. The hot group. The group that guys actually like!" I take a breath and lower my voice. "The type of person I want to be seen as for once."

"Aly, you're totally missing the point. The group thing is stupid. It's just a thing we did one night that took on a life of its own. But it's not real." Brandon's quiet for a beat, then he shifts his weight, adding, "And Aly, hotness had nothing to do with what group you were put in."

I roll my eyes, not believing that line of bull for a second, and mentally run down the list of senior girls. The *Casuals* are easy to spot. Girls like Lauren Hays and even Kara. The girls who not only invented the social order at Fairfield Academy but control it. The ones who will look back at high school and not see a wall of just-a-friend dates and a solitary ex-boyfriend, but a long list of flirtations and adventures. The confident girls. Cheerleaders, dance team members, maybe even a few of the jocks.

Just not competitive volleyball players like me.

"You okay?" Brandon cups my shoulder and shakes me a little. "Aly, I promise you, the group thing is fucked up, but you being a *Commitment* is a good thing. Really."

I absently nod in response as a new dimension to Operation Sex Appeal comes into focus. Thanks to my lunchtime run-in with Lauren, I know an external makeover isn't going to be enough. If I want to get out of the perpetual friend zone and experience how the other half lives, I'm going to need a total life overhaul. I have to get the guys to see me differently, as someone confident, exciting...*Casual*.

But I'll need proof.

The last piece of the puzzle arrives in the form of a handsome face. The holy grail of my quest. The only guy at Fairfield Academy more popular than Brandon, and by far the biggest player. If I can get him to be interested in me *and* ask me to Homecoming, I'll know for sure I've successfully crossed over into the land of the *Casuals*—and break the curse of my Wall of Shame.

A slow smile creeps up my face. I may not have figured out all the ins and outs yet, but Operation Sex Appeal definitely just got a new finish line. It started with a new wardrobe, and it will *end* with Justin Carter.

BRANDON
ALY'S HOUSE, 7:05 p.m.

As Aly and I walk down the narrow sidewalk to my truck, I watch her from the corner of my eye. She's still wearing that secret pouty smile of hers, the one that says she's up to something. It always makes me nervous. For the last hour, she's been distracted and quiet, which on a normal day is bad enough, but when the topic is volleyball, it's downright scary.

Obviously, telling her about the groups wasn't the best idea I've ever had. But I had to. When she looked up at me with those watery blue eyes, I had to try to fix it. If I could, I'd make it so Aly never frowned again.

She stops at the passenger door, and I step in front to give her a boost. The six-inch lift kit and Super Swamper tires on my F-150 may be necessary for mud riding, but they make it impossible for her to get in by herself. The girl is short. Even with the ridiculous new shoes she's sporting.

Wrapping my hands around her tiny waist, I lift her up and catch a whiff of the familiar sugar-cookie scent clinging to her skin. She scoots across the leather seat, and I watch her black skirt ride up her toned thigh.

I don't know where to look. Or how *not* to look. Walking into her room earlier, I literally did one of those stupid double takes you see on TV. I'm used to Aly lounging around in baggy clothes and messy ponytails with her only makeup being ChapStick. *That* Aly I know how to act around. But this one in a short skirt and tight top showing off an impressive rack? This Aly is seriously messing with my head.

I clear my throat and look away from her bare legs. "If you're aiming for attention, that skirt's a good first step to getting what you want."

Her white teeth sink into her bottom lip, and she glances down. "Is it overkill? Too *sexy?*"

The way she says it, and even just hearing the word come out of her mouth, is just too weird. Smiling at her familiar bout of discomfort, I chuckle and say, "Nah, you're fine."

I shoot her a wink and close the door, unable to stop myself from laughing as I round the hood. The new clothes threw me, but the overthinking, constantly worrying girl in my truck is definitely the Aly I know.

My amusement dies when I yank open the door and Aly nails me with a glare. "People could find me sexy, y'know. Obviously no one *we* know, but it's not that outrageous a concept." Crossing her arms, she sinks lower in her seat, and I cough into my fist to keep from laughing again. She's so damn cute. The scowl on her face is so out of place that it's like being annoyed with a grumpy kitten. I like hanging out with Aly for a lot of reasons, but her laid-back attitude is definitely at the top of the list. She's fun and drama-free. When I'm not accidently offending her, that is.

Revving the engine, I glance over and say, "Aly, of course you can be sexy." *Exhibit A: those legs.* "That's not what I meant. I just don't think of you like that."

Or at least I didn't until you wore that skirt.

She makes a sound that's a cross between a groan and a sigh and shakes her head. "Exactly, and that's why I'm doing this."

I stop with my hand on the shifter.

Seeing the look on my face, Aly throws her head back against the seat. "That came out wrong. It's not because *you* don't think of me that way. It's that *none* of the guys at school do."

I reverse out of the driveway, hoping she'll elaborate, and she twists toward me, tucking her legs under herself. "See, once I had my epiphany about the Wall of Shame, I got this idea. You're probably going to say it's stupid, but whatever. I'm just tired of being invisible, Brandon. Of guys always seeing me as a friend. This is senior year. My last shot. If I want the male species to finally find me dateable, I have to do something drastic."

"Drastic?" I ask, waving my hand in her direction. "As in letting Kara turn you into her own life-size Barbie doll?"

Aly playfully bats my arm but nods. "Yeah. I'm calling it Operation Sex Appeal."

I cough and look over.

Oh, she's serious. Okay.

"And you telling me about that chauvinistic ranking system sealed the deal," she continues. "Guys see me as a *Commitment.* I'm too much work, too serious. For once, I want to see what it's like to be a *Casual.*"

Aly bites her lip in excitement, and I groan. Yep, she totally missed the point. She was supposed to see that her lack of exes isn't a bad thing. It boils down to respect. Some guys know she deserves more effort than they are willing to give.

But clearly, my confession in her room only made things worse.

Time for damage control. "So does this mission of yours have an end goal?" I have a feeling that it involves more than just a wardrobe change, and I tighten my grip on the wheel. I can't help feeling protective of Aly. We practically grew up together. And with a name like Operation Sex Appeal, I can imagine the kind of guys she'll attract. But Aly's smart. I'm sure she's not planning anything *too* crazy to become this other person.

"Well," she says, scrunching her nose. "Before, it was getting a new look and a new guy by Homecoming. But now, I'm thinking the only way to show I've really changed is for that guy to be Justin."

My foot hits the brake, and I swerve to avoid hitting the curb. Waving a hand at the pissed-off driver behind me, I shake my head and clutch the wheel with both fists. "Aly, you can do a hell of a lot better than Justin."

Her voice pitches in confusion. "But I thought Justin was your friend."

"He is." I take a breath and change lanes. "Which is how I know you can do a lot better."

For some reason, Aly seems surprised, but I have no idea why. She's seen the girls Justin usually dates. There's not a chance in hell she can get involved with him and *not* get her heart broken. And then *I'll* have to break something on *him*.

No way. I have to get her focused on someone else.

"It doesn't matter anyway," she says, trying to pull down her skirt. With all her fidgeting, it's ridden up even higher on her tanned thighs. If she keeps dressing like this, she'll get more than Justin's attention. "I realized the clothes aren't going to be enough. Unless I can get everyone to take my transformation seriously, I'm destined to stay invisible and single for the rest of my life. I have to get people to start seeing me differently..."

Aly's voice trails off, and her body stills. She tilts her head to stare at me, and from the prickle on my neck, that can't be a good sign. I catch her eye before looking back out at the road. "What?"

She opens her mouth and closes it. Several times. Then she shakes her head and says, "Nothing. It's stupid." After only a few seconds, she continues. "It's what I said about getting people to see me differently. It reminded me of all those dumb Hollywood movies—you know, where the makeover actually works? But in those movies, it normally takes that one popular guy asking the girl out for the rest of the school to realize how awesome she truly is."

My eyes cut to her, but she's staring straight ahead. She leans forward and adjusts the air-conditioning vent, refusing to look back in my direction. "I was just thinking, hypothetically, that if you pretended to hook up with me—just pretended—and helped sell the whole *Casual* thing, that the guys would be more likely to buy it. And then maybe they'll find me dateable, too." As soon as the words leave her mouth, she hides her face in her hands. "*God*, that sounds stupid. It was like I could hear how it sounded out loud and, just...Never mind. Forget I said anything. I'm a dork, and it's stricken from the record, okay?"

Aly squirms in the seat beside me, fidgeting with her fingers, her hair, her skirt, and the neckline of her top. I keep glancing back, hoping she'll turn toward me so I can see her face, but she's looking anywhere but in my direction.

I've seen the dumb movies she's talking about, mostly with *her* when it was her turn to pick. They're dumb because the plots are completely bogus, just like her idea. But I know Aly. She honestly thinks her crazy idea could work. And, though she'll never admit it now, she was completely serious.

Aly is on a mission, and I know from experience she won't stop until she gets what she wants. Her fierce determination is what I admire most about her. She's convinced she wants to be a *Casual*, and nothing I say will change her mind. Hell, I'm the one who put the idea there to begin with. But maybe if I step in and join her in the crazy, it'll keep wolves like Justin away.

"What, exactly, would the pretending involve?" I ask.

Her head snaps up, and her jaw drops. "Um, I—I guess it wouldn't be much different than what we do now. We'd just call it something else. Maybe add holding hands in public or something?"

I park in front of Carmela's and turn off the engine. She's probably right. Even when I'm going out with someone, I normally see Aly more than the other girl anyway. People always get the wrong idea about us or assume we're hooking up on the side, so it won't take much to get them to believe we're together for real. And with the camping trip starting tomorrow, it'll be easy to spread it around quickly.

Shit, the camping trip.

I scrub a hand over my face, picturing a Lauren-sized shadow for four days.

"See, it's stupid, right?" Aly says, her cheeks pink with a blush. "Forget I said anything." She yanks off her seatbelt and throws open the door. I put my hand on her arm to stop her.

"Actually I was thinking it might be nice not to worry about girls for a while."

Her blue eyes flare with hope, and I jump out from my side of the truck. I'm not ready to say yes to her crazy-ass scheme yet, but I'm close. I round the hood, and as I help Aly down, I can practically hear the wheels turning in her head. The door to the restaurant opens, and the familiar sound of the mariachi band wafts outside. One of the guys leaving stops to check Aly out, hungry eyes devouring her legs, and she steps back, stumbles in the new shoes, and latches onto my arm.

There's no way I can let her do this alone.

Why can't she see what I do? She's a *Commitment* girl, and that's not a bad thing. I just need to help *her* realize it. I throw the guy a look to back off and pull her back to my truck.

"Look, if you're serious and you really think this'll help you get what you want, I'll do it. We can start telling people tomorrow that we're hooking up."

Her mouth opens in shock. I reach out and gently close it.

Aly blinks and shakes her head as if to clear it. "On your word?"

On your word is an expression Aly started using years ago. She normally uses it whenever she knows something is bothering me and I don't want to talk about it. I've never used it because Aly always tells me exactly what's on her mind. Even when I'd rather she didn't.

"On my word," I promise, stooping down to look her in the eyes. "If this is important to you, then count me in." I squeeze her hand and tease, "But when this plan of yours works and you have guys crawling all over you, you better not forget about me, all right?"

Aly laughs and jumps up, throwing her arms around my neck. She kisses my cheek, and the scent of sugar cookies fills my head.

"Holy cannoli! Brandon, you're amazing!" She hops down, wobbles, and beams up at me. "And it won't be for long, I promise. After people buy it and stop seeing me as a *Commitment,* we'll just say we're better off as friends and go back to regularly scheduled programming. Except I'll be the new confident, *Casual* Aly." Her smile widens as she waggles her eyebrows. "And I'll have Justin Carter to prove it."

little longer, I say, "It's only a year, man. You'll be with her at UT in no time."

"I know. It just sucks. But it's not like I didn't know this was coming or anything." Drew drags a hand across his face and groans. "Get my mind off it," he says. "Any chance I missed something crazy in the last forty-eight hours?"

And there's my opening. *Dammit.*

I glance at Adam leaned back in his parked car. "Actually, yeah. You could say that." Drew's body shifts forward as I take a stalling sip of soda. "Aly and I..." I snap the pop-top from my can and pitch it. "We're sorta dating now."

"Wait." His eyes bug out, and he shakes his head as if it's defective. "Did you just say *Aly*?"

I nod, and the audible gasp from his direction is pretty much the reaction I expected. Guilt hits me like a punch to the gut. Honesty is important to me. Girls always know the score, and friends know where they stand. I don't have time for lies or liars. But loyalty matters more. If anyone finds out this hookup with Aly isn't real, she'll be embarrassed.

And I refuse to let Aly get hurt.

"We went out last night," I explain. I start drumming a beat on my legs to give my hands something to do. "We got to talking...and decided to try going out." I realize the drumming is making me look nervous so I stop. "Just see where it goes and have fun, y'know? No *commitment* or anything."

My skills in lying suck ass. It's a good thing I never do it. There's not a chance in hell Drew, one of my best friends who knows me better than anyone except for Aly, bought any of that. I glance over and wince at the look of pure stupefaction on his face.

"You're serious?" he asks.

"Yep," I say, popping my lips around the word. An eternity seems to pass. It's probably more like thirty seconds. Dust from the gravel road flies in the air from arriving cars, and I count the sounds of slamming doors. I watch Aly's ex sitting in his car and wonder if he's been listening. I steal another look at Drew and brace myself for the call-out.

What he says is, "It's about damn time."

My body goes still, then I jerk my head around, sure I heard him wrong. "Huh?"

Drew pushes to his feet, suddenly all smiles. "Dude, Aly's perfect for you. Call it casual all you want, but the two of you have been in denial for like three years now. Sarah and I had a bet on how long it would take you to wake up, and it looks like I just won." He shoves my shoulder. "I still feel like shit, but I'm happy for you, man. It's about time you got your head out of your ass."

♥ ♥ ♥

"Gentlemen, I have an announcement."

The second Carlos and Justin enter the room, Drew hops off the top bunk. At this rate, the whole campground will know by dinner. He already told people in the parking lot, including Adam, which was awkward, to be honest, and Lauren, which made it all worth it. And now, without giving the guys a chance to ask what the news is, he announces, "Brandon and Aly are going out."

"Hooking up," I clarify from my mildew-infested bed. Based on their reactions, it falls on deaf ears.

Carlos stops in the center of the cabin. "Say what?" he asks, setting his guitar on the floor.

Justin tosses his bag on an empty bunk and sits next to me. "You're joking, right?"

I look him in the eye, then look to Carlos, and feel the blood begin to boil. I'm not really with her, but two of my closest friends acting as if the idea is impossible pisses me off. "And what the hell's wrong with Aly?"

"Nothing, man," Justin says, throwing his palms in the air. "Aly's incredible. Hot, too." He smirks like the cocky son of a bitch he is, and it takes everything in me not to remove it from his face. "But what happened to her being a *Commitment*? You say you don't want a relationship, but then go and ask out their damn spokesperson?" Justin glances over at Carlos, who nods in agreement. "What gives?"

Behind him, Drew subtly shakes his head.

We've been friends long enough for him to know me. To sense the anger I keep bottled up raging just beneath the surface. I draw in a slow, controlled breath and let it out.

I get what my friends are saying. After my dad died and I saw what that did to my mom, I vowed I'd never fall in love or lose myself in a girl. And other than Justin's one failed relationship freshman year, he's always lived by the same creed. Together, we pretty much wrote the book on dating fast and furious, and Carlos is far from a serial monogamist. It's not that they have anything against *Aly*, just what me being with her represents. I get it. Their reaction makes sense. And it's the truth because Aly and I aren't *really* together.

But I still don't like it.

"You're right," I say. "We did decide Aly is a *Commitment*, but this summer she changed." Getting through that with a straight face takes a fucking miracle. "She says she just wants to enjoy her senior year and keep things casual. We have fun hanging out, so we decided to go with it and see what happens."

Drew beams like he's a proud father at a championship game. He's still not buying the "casual" part. Carlos nods rhythmically, an impressed smile crossing his face, and Justin tugs on his ear, his expression a weird mix of confusion and anger. But it's clear they all buy the story. I lean my back against the wall and exhale.

Carlos leans over and punches my shoulder. "Never would've guessed Aly was a closet *Casual*, but hey, what do I know?"

"Yeah, if you know what you're getting yourself into, that's great." Justin gives me a thin-lipped smile. "Aly's awesome."

"I know." It's the first truthful thing I've said all day.

Justin stands and heads for the door. "I'm gonna go check this place out. I'll catch y'all later, all right?" He pushes open the door without looking back, and Drew raises his eyebrows. If I didn't know better, I'd think Justin was jealous.

Fine, let him be. But he's not going anywhere near Aly when this experiment is over.

I check my watch, wondering if she's here yet. If my friends are any indication, this week is going to be interesting.

ALY
KARA'S DEATH MOBILE, 2:15 p.m.

Riding in Kara's car is a little like playing Russian roulette. You know it's a matter of when—not if—an accident will occur, but you're betting on it not being today. Or on your side of the vehicle.

My head rattles against the passenger-side window as Kara screeches across three lanes of traffic. From the backseat, Gabi screams over the music, "Spill it, girl!"

By the time Kara picked me up, after taking forever to pack her five color-coordinated pieces of luggage, we were already running late. But my friends didn't care. They demanded details. The only way to get Kara driving was by promising to tell all once we got on the road.

"Don't even tell us he didn't notice the makeover," Kara says, accelerating through a yellow light. "He's a guy with two functioning eyeballs. He noticed."

"No, you're right," I say, gnawing on my lip. "He did."

Brandon noticed the second he walked through my bedroom door, but not in the way Kara thinks. The big-brother vibe radiated off him all night, and I'm sure his protective Superman persona was the only reason he agreed to our fake hookup.

But hey, at least he went for it.

Gabi presses her face between our headrests and grins. "So did his tongue hang out? Did he go all googley-eyed? Spill it, girl, because if you don't, you know I'll just call Brandon."

The scary thing is I don't doubt that for a second. I twist in my seat, unable to look at either of them as I tell the lie. I went back and forth all night on if I should tell them the truth. Brandon said it was my call. But I just can't. Gabi and Kara were cool about my makeover, but pretending a hookup to get guys to notice me sounds like a teen movie gone bad.

"Actually," I say, focusing intently on the road ahead, "he asked me out."

Kara stomps on her brake twenty feet before the stop sign. "I freaking knew it! Didn't I tell you? Guys and girls can't be friends. The sex part *always* gets in the way."

When Harry Met Sally logic aside, a shiver rolls down my spine at the image those words put in my mind. I'm a proud, card-carrying virgin, but I'd be lying (and I've already had enough of *that* today) if I said I never thought about what it would be like to make out with Brandon. According to the rumor mill, he's quite talented in that department.

I shake my head.

Eye on the prize, Aly. Justin, Justin, Justin.

"Didn't I tell you Brandon would notice?" Gabi folds her arms on the back of the seat and smirks. "I bet he figured if he didn't scoop you up now, someone like Justin would."

I nearly choke on my tongue. Nodding, I dig through my empty purse, trying to hide my discomfort. I *hate* lying to my friends. But the alternative is the truth, and that's way too embarrassing. I probably should've driven with Mom. Her catering company, the Sassy Gourmet, is in charge of the kitchen this week. But getting a ride with Mommy definitely didn't feel very *Casual*-like. Plus, I'd have had to tell the girls eventually.

Now that I had, it's time for a subject change.

"You know, Gabi, with me and Brandon hooking up, we're gonna be spending even more time together. And, since Brandon's good friends with Carlos, he'll probably be hanging around a lot more, too."

Gabi leans back in her seat with a growl, and I glance over at Kara, who immediately jumps on the new topic. Gotta love that girl and her never-ending matchmaker ways. "Hey, that's right! Now, Gabi, do we need to go over the fine art of flirting again? Let's see, step one—when a boy smiles at you, it's okay to smile back."

I pull down my visor and see Gabi flip us off in the mirror. We've been trying for the last six months to get her to admit she likes Carlos. It's obvious they're into each other, and they flirt constantly. Unfortunately for Carlos, there's the pesky detail of Gabi refusing to date high-school boys. She says it's too expected. But she doesn't date that many college guys either. Gabi's comfortable being on her own—a concept that boggles my mind.

"Maybe I'm just not into him," she stubbornly says from the back seat. "You ever think about that?"

Kara adjusts her rearview mirror to see Gabi better. It's not like she needs it to see the road or anything. I immediately grab the buckle of my seatbelt, ensuring it's secure. "So you're saying you don't think he's hot?" she asks.

Gabi crosses her arms and slides further down in her seat. "I refuse to answer the question on the grounds that I may incriminate myself."

"He likes you, Gabi," I say, closing my visor and turning to face her. "And we know you think he's cute. His cuteness isn't actually up for debate—it's a fact. So when are you gonna give the poor boy a chance?"

"Never!" She slams her hand against the back of my seat. "Look, besides the fact that he's still in high school, his family goes to our church. Wouldn't that just make my mother's freaking day?"

Gabi and her mom are like oil and water. Ms. Avila rides Gabi about her clothes, her hair, and how she thinks a *young lady* should act, and Gabi loves finding creative ways to make Mom grab for the rosary beads.

Kara and I exchange a smirk but drop it for now. We switch to safer topics, such as how far Lauren Hays will push the rule against string bikinis, and all talk of me hooking up with Brandon is safely averted. Ten miles later, the sign for Cypress Lake comes into view.

"Fairwood Academy," I whisper, my insides starting to shake. "Prepare to meet the new Aly."

BRANDON
DINING HALL, 5:40 p.m.

My stomach rumbles as I eye the long table of food. I shift my gaze to the large clock on the wall, note the twenty minutes remaining until dinner, and curse myself for not packing a few protein bars. Clearly, the trip organizers do not understand the realities of the teenage male stomach.

To distract myself, I scan the crowded hall for Aly and end up spotting her mom. I forgot she was in charge of the kitchen this week. Mrs. Reed smiles and looks around, then points to the tray of cookies in front of her, motioning me over. I tell the guys I'll be back and stealthily cross the room.

It pays to have friends in high places.

"Don't tell anyone," she whispers, sliding me a handful of cookies under the table. "I swear I could hear that stomach of yours growling all the way over here. Now shoo before I get in trouble for playing favorites." I give her a quick hug and shove a cookie in my mouth. Pocketing the rest, I make my way back across the room.

"Aw, yeah! Using hookup status to snag us some food," Carlos says, snatching a cookie from my hand. "I knew being friends with you would pay off eventually."

I glance back at the table, but Mrs. Reed must have returned to the kitchen. She didn't treat me any differently, so Aly must not have told her about our upgraded *hookup status* yet. The term curls my mouth as I inhale another cookie. Everything about it feels wrong when it comes to Aly. She wants more, *deserves* more, than a casual hookup. I know it; now I just need to get *her* to realize it. Preferably before Homecoming.

As soon as Justin sees the new post-makeover Aly, his view on her being a *Commitment* is gonna go straight through the window. He'll be more likely to buy us hooking up, but it'll also put her on his radar. I'd prefer if that never happened.

I look at the cookie I was prepared to devour and hand it over to Drew, narrowing my eyes as I scan the crowd. At least for now, Aly is taken, and as strange as it is that it's by *me*, I'll be damned if I let Justin's hands get anywhere near her.

Shaking off the thought, I growl, "Let's grab a table." By now, almost the entire senior class has arrived and the room is filling up. Shouting over the mob, I tell Drew, "We need a table for eight. Kara has a new victim."

"Make that nine." Justin's voice carries across the room, and I turn and watch him saunter over with a tall, curvy blonde. "Guys, you know Lauren."

The arm wrapped around her thin waist says he's clearly over whatever bothered him earlier. There's nothing a little female companionship can't solve—that's Justin's M.O.

But for the first time this summer, I'm glad to see Lauren. Being glued to Justin's hip puts a major cramp in Aly's plan, and for that, I could almost kiss her. It's also good to see Lauren preoccupied. Maybe after Drew told her about Aly and me, she finally took the hint.

Lauren's mouth curves with a flirty smile. "Hey there, Brandon."

Guess not.

"Hey," I say, turning back to the door, looking for Aly again. Where the hell is she?

Our group takes their seats at an empty table. Carlos grabs the chair next to mine, spins it around and straddles it, and says, "So, now that you're dating Aly, you gonna lay some groundwork with Gabi for me or what?"

Justin reaches across the table and smacks him upside his head. "What's your deal with that girl?

She blows you off every chance she gets. She's not interested, and plenty of other girls are. Move on."

Carlos grins. "But that's just it. She's feisty. Listen, I know she acts like a hard ass, but I've gotten the girl to crack a smile a couple times, and let me tell ya, it's worth it."

Justin shakes his head in disgust. "I don't get you, man." He leans back in his seat and shifts his attention to the main entrance. "Whoa."

I don't need to turn my head to know who just walked in. Justin's frozen, and Lauren's sharp eyes are on mine. I shift around, and as predicted, word of our hookup has spread like wildfire. Pairs of eyes around the room lock on me.

But not Aly's. She looks at Justin.

Right.

A small grin twitches her lips as she worries the bottom one between her teeth.

I swallow hard.

She's beautiful.

When did that happen?

It's not the new clothes, although seeing she actually has a body is a nice change of pace. It's more than that. It's the whole package. Aly's always been hot, but now it's like she's starting to believe it. And her confidence is sexy.

Behind me, I hear a loud smack. "Ow!"

I glance back to see Justin rub his arm. Glaring at Lauren, he asks, "What the hell was that for?"

She shrugs, and my hands tighten into fists. I should be happy for Aly. She's getting what she wants. But if her plan works, she'll end up with more than Justin's attention—she'll have a broken heart. And I can't let that happen. Not on my watch.

Unclenching my hands, I look back, and this time Aly meets my gaze. Her entire face lights up in her signature smile—head tilts, eyes crinkle, and the tiniest of dimples pops out in her right cheek. The pressure in my chest goes away.

With the senior class tracking my every move, I get up and stride toward her. I pick her up in our usual hug and then, remembering the hungry eyes behind me, lower my head and give her a quick kiss.

Aly's mouth is soft and tastes like cherry. A strange urge to kiss her for real grips me, to part her lips and see if she tastes just as sweet inside.

Whoa, where did that come from?

I quickly lift my head and feel more than hear Aly's giggle. "Thank you," she whispers.

Clearing my throat, I shut down the crazy thoughts. I watch Gabi, Kara, and Daniel stroll toward us, realizing that pretending is going to be more awkward than I'd thought. But when I whisper back, "No problem," and see her smile again, I remember why I'm doing this. "You ready?"

Aly nods, and I turn to bump fists with Daniel. "We got seats back here," I tell them, reaching down for Aly's hand. As I lead the group back to the table, the curious crowd silent and scrutinizing, I bend close to her ear. "You look really good."

I mean it, too. She's wearing a short jean skirt and a dark green tank top that clings to her chest. Her heels show off the lean muscles of her calves, and with the ninja grip she has on my hand, she only stumbles once. Guys lining the aisle don't even try to hide their roaming eyes. Yep, this pretending thing is gonna suck.

When I return to the group, Carlos's mouth is open. He quickly scoots over, freeing the chair beside mine, and seats himself next to Gabi. No surprise there.

From across the table, Justin openly stares. "Hey, Aly."

Aly grins at the table and fidgets with her fingers in her lap. "Hi, Justin."

Principal Thompson steps onto the raised platform at the front of the room, calling for attention. I meet Justin's eyes as I slide my arm around the back of Aly's chair. His mouth quirks. I rest my hand on her bare shoulder, and after jumping at the initial contact, she scoots over and leans against my chest. Justin turns away, and I inhale her familiar sugar-cookie scent.

During the never-ending list of rules, from the corner of my eye I see Drew scratch the side of his jaw repeatedly. I look over, and he widens his eyes, nodding toward Aly. He drops his gaze to her low-cut shirt and lifts his eyebrows, indicating the obvious makeover. I shrug.

Guess I should have mentioned that.

Finally, Thompson gives the green light for food. Our group hustles to the front of the buffet line, where platters of chicken wings, pasta, brisket, and sandwiches are set out. Knowing it's from the Sassy Gourmet, I load my plate down with every intention of coming back for more. I make a stop at the dessert section, stuff another one of those delicious cookies in my mouth, and add several more to my plate. Aly grins happily. I know that smile.

Reaching around her, I take the tray from her hands like the good fake hookup that I am. "I've got that."

She tucks her hand under my elbow and grins. "Why, thank you, *baby*."

Leaning close to her ear, I reply, "Anything for you, *darling.*"

Aly laughs, and we turn to walk back to the table...just as Mrs. Reed exits the kitchen. She halts mid-step, head cocked to one side, and Aly falters in those damn shoes.

Her mom soaks in our cuddled state and grins widely. Aly gives her a sheepish wave and tugs on my elbow. As we walk back to the table, I lean close to her ear. "How long until she's on the phone with my mom, telling her about this?"

Aly laughs, and her shoulders visibly lower. "Oh, I give it thirty seconds, tops." When we sit down, the table is still empty, so I lean over and ask in a hushed voice, "How's it going so far? What did you tell Gabi and Kara—fact or fiction?"

Aly scrunches her nose. "The facts are way too embarrassing. I hate lying, but the truth is just so pathetic." I open my mouth to say that we can still back out, tell everyone tomorrow that we've decided just to be friends, but then she adds, "Besides, the end result will be worth it."

Her eyes zone in on Justin a few yards away.

I shove a sandwich in my mouth.

The table fills, and as we eat, conversation revolves around graduation and plans for college. We all plan to stay in-state, heading to either UT or A&M. I'm too busy stuffing my face to contribute much, so it takes a while to notice Aly picking at her food. She's not one of those girls who only eats salads either. She enjoys eating as much as I do, so I know something is up.

"You okay?" I whisper.

She looks up and then around the room. Her eyes pause on Lauren sitting in Justin's lap before swinging back around to me. "I just feel like I'm on display or something. People keep looking over here."

I scan the crowd, meeting a few people's eyes. "That's what you wanted, right?"

Aly fiddles with her napkin and shrugs. "Well, yeah, it is. But I don't know what to do now."

"You eat." To demonstrate, I wrap a thick portion of linguine around my fork. I lift it to her mouth, and, grinning, she opens for me to slide the fork inside. Pink lips close around the plastic, and as I drag it back out, it's impossible to look away.

"Funny." She rolls her eyes as she dabs the corner of her mouth, and I shift back in my chair.

"Look, forget about them," I tell her, ignoring the stares around us. We're definitely giving them a show. "We got their attention. The plan is working. Now, relax."

"Easy for you," she says before releasing a heavy breath. "But I can try."

Smiling up at me, she takes her own fork and dives into her food like the girl I know. Her plate has a decent-sized dent in it when the sound of a foodgasm rocks the table. I look over to see Gabi elbow Aly in the side. "Girl, holy crap. These cookies are your best yet."

"Wait." Carlos glances at his plate of crumbs. "You made these?"

A blush creeps up Aly's neck. She sucks at taking compliments as much as I suck at lying, but these cookies are *seriously* good. "It's my recipe," she admits. "Mom totally made them, though."

He steals a cookie from a disgruntled Gabi and garbles around a mouthful of chocolate. "Hot damn."

Stupid pride fills my chest. I had zero to do with Aly's dessert, but a smug smile tugs my mouth anyway. "I know, right?" I squeeze Aly's shoulder and say, "My girl's gonna be a pastry chef."

The words just come out. *My girl.* Everyone, including Aly, looks at me, and I stuff another cookie in my mouth. If I had said that before today, no one would've blinked an eye. Aly and I have been friends forever. But now the words sound proprietary. Like I'm really saying she's *mine.* And in their eyes, she is.

After dinner, we agree to meet back for the bonfire in an hour, then head off to clean up. Aly and I hold hands walking out of the building. It's weird how *un*weird that is.

We stop when the path forks between our two cabins, and in my best impersonation of a lovesick idiot, I say, "I'll see you in an hour, *honey.*"

Aly laughs and gives me a playful shove. She heads toward her cabin but, after a few steps, turns to wave with a happy smile that takes up her whole face. In the shadows of the trail, she looks like the Aly I've been friends with for years, sans makeover. She continues down the path, her laughter trailing behind her, and I feel the answering smile on my face long after she's gone.

ALY
BONFIRE, 8:00 p.m.

I stand at the edge of the raging bonfire in my pesky heels, balancing on the edge of an old log used for seating. I dart a glance at the crowd, pretending I don't notice the groups huddled in conversation around me. My heel slips, I lose my footing, and I stumble. I try to sit down and then shoot back up again.

Where's Brandon?

When the gawking happened at dinner, he was there to keep my usual crazy-hyperness at bay. He balances me out nicely that way. But now I'm alone. Gabi's back at the cabin, trapped on the phone with her mom in the latest Avila-family smackdown, Kara left before I did to meet up with Daniel, and Brandon's nowhere in sight. How am I supposed to act? Ignore the whispers? Smile and wave when people point at me? Act aloof and superior...if I can even pull that off?

Abandoned for the time being, I mentally go through my volleyball drills and pray for backup support to arrive.

Knowing Kara, she's probably discovered an amazing secluded spot to make out with Daniel and won't surface again until dawn. In fact, that's probably where Justin and Lauren are, too. There's a reason he's known as the school player, which is exactly why I need him to ask me out. If Justin gives me the *Casual* stamp of approval, I'll know my transformation is a success.

Strong arms wrap around my waist, and I jump. I twist in the embrace and look up into Brandon's life-saving green eyes. He glances around, notices the audience, and kisses the tip of my nose. "Miss me?"

"You have no idea." Taking a deep breath, I collapse against his hard chest.

Brandon tenses, and he lifts my chin. "Is something wrong?" He looks around again. "Did somebody mess with you?"

"No, nothing like that. I'm fine." I smile, realizing it's the truth now that he's here. "Actually, I'm more than fine. I'm great. Like you said, our plan's working. I think I'm just shocked at how quickly things are changing." I bite my lip to stop a sudden fit of giggles. "And maybe a little drunk on excitement."

I feel the rumble in Brandon's chest and know what's coming. I wince as he says, "Oh good, I love drunk Aly."

"Shut up!" I say, squeezing my eyes shut in embarrassment.

"As long as it isn't on Mad Dog 20/20, that is."

"Ugh, I knew you'd bring that up, you asshat!" I pinch him in the ribs and shudder at the memory of my first high-school party. "I vowed to never let anything that horrid cross my lips again. You just like bringing it up because you got to play hero, saving me from prying eyes while I tossed my cookies outside." I pause and scrunch my nose. "After my *seriously* ill-advised attempt to fight Nasty Angie."

Brandon grins. "Can't lie—two women fighting over me was pretty hot." I scowl, and he laughs.

"Guess our new status proves those exes right though, huh?"

I hadn't thought of that. Three years of being best friends, Brandon dating a new girl every week... that's a lot of girls. And every single one of them was mean to me, like Angie, too. They were jealous of my friendship with Brandon and constantly gave me the stink-eye whenever I came around. Now they'll think there *was* something going on between us all along.

I really didn't think through this plan very well. Luckily, I have Hurricane Gabi as a bodyguard.

"Whaddup, whaddup," Carlos says, appearing behind Brandon's shoulder. "What's going on, party people?"

I peer around him, wondering if Justin is there, too. No such luck. Sighing, I look down and notice the guitar in Carlos's hand. Gabi has a thing for musicians. Another cosmic sign they belong together.

As if the universe planned it, my phone buzzes with my rebel friend's ringtone. I laugh reading the message: *Traitor.* I scan the crowd and find her at the edge of the bonfire, signature scowl in place. I text back, *Frowning leads to premature wrinkles*, and she flips me off.

I motion her over, and with a visible grunt, Gabi ambles toward us, her frown deepening when she spies the instrument in Carlos's hand. "You play?" she asks when she stops a foot away. Her eyes narrow at me as if I'd somehow planned the whole thing.

"Nah," he says, lifting the guitar by the neck. "Carrying it around just looks good for the ladies."

Picking up the sarcasm—being a master at it herself—and then ignoring it, Gabi cocks her hip and says, "We've run in the same circles for years. How did I not know this?"

Carlos offers her an impish grin. "There's a lot you don't know about me, Gabriella. I'm a man of many talents."

She flicks her multi-hued hair over her shoulder and glances away, going for *bored*. But I know better. "Whatever."

Carlos shakes his head, chuckling to himself, and sits down on a log to tune his guitar. Brandon sinks onto the soft grass and kicks out his legs, and I plop myself in front of him. Gabi smirks, raising and lowering her eyebrows in a "told you so" gesture, and I sigh. Here I go again, confirming her theory about my long-held feelings for Brandon.

Another example of how I did *not* think this plan through.

Gabi's silly smile falls a few beats before I hear a familiar voice say, "Hey, guys."

The rock wall of Brandon's chest manages to grow harder as Lauren appears over us. Her plastic smile wavers ever so slightly when she focuses on me. "Y'all having fun?"

I don't know what the sudden tension is about, but beyond her, Justin is at the bonfire talking with our third baseman and his eyes are on me. He winks, and a surge of adrenaline hits my bloodstream, so I answer honestly, "Yeah, this place is great." Looking away from my future conquest, I grin at Lauren. "Are *you* having a good time?"

She lifts her shoulder in a half-hearted shrug. "The day's been filled with surprises, that's for sure. It'll be interesting to see how it all plays out." Lauren bounces on her toes and gives Brandon a pointed look.

Not fluent in cryptic, I blink. *Well, this is awkward.*

Brandon locks his arms around my waist, and Lauren smiles again. "I'm gonna go grab a bottle of water, but you guys have fun. We'll have to catch up later, Brandon."

She takes a step toward the dining hall and stops. Her gaze passes over our group until it rests on Gabi. Then, sliding a hand across Carlos's shoulder, she says, "He's talented, huh? I used to *love* lying on his bed and listening to him play." Gabi's eyes narrow into slits, and Lauren leans down, saying in a lower voice obviously still meant to reach the rest of us, "Play that song I love, will ya?"

With a final pointed look at Brandon, she walks off.

"Okay, so Lauren's a bitch," I whisper to Gabi, who is following the dance captain's progress with her eyes. Angry energy snaps around her. I don't know if she's furious on my behalf or her own, but metaphorical cold water needs to be poured on this situation stat. Gabi's like the Hulk—when she gets angry things tend to get messy, and from the squinty look of her eyes, we're about two seconds away from disaster. We need a distraction.

And that's when Carlos starts strumming. Either he understands Gabi better than I thought or the boy has seriously good timing, but he gives me a small nod as the music seeps into the air. He doesn't sing, but he doesn't need to. The soft melody, coupled with the raging fire and smoky haze, is mesmerizing. After a few bars, Gabi slumps down beside me, mumbling about airheads.

Crisis averted, I relax, too. I stretch my legs out and snuggle deeper in Brandon's arms, enjoying the moment.

Music speaks to my soul more than anything else. More than volleyball or even chocolate, which is saying something. I used to dream about joining the choir at church, but I could never bring myself to sing in front of other people. No one—not my parents, Gabi, Kara, or Brandon—know how often I lock myself in my bathroom, turn on the radio, and serenade my toothbrush.

I hum to myself, watching Justin from across the bonfire. Our eyes meet. Before today, I could count on one hand how many times Justin has looked in my direction, and they've all been a cursory glance or to ask a question. This look is different. I don't know exactly *how* it's different, only that it is. He raises his gaze past my shoulder, and my pretend date laces his fingers around my waist.

I gasp as the edge of Brandon's hand glides across a sliver of bare stomach where my tank top has ridden up. His chest rumbles with the strum of Carlos's guitar, and tingles radiate from the heat of his touch.

This is no big deal, I tell myself. I'd get tingly if *any* guy touched me.

But the problem is that same jolt happened earlier in the assembly hall. I close my eyes and force myself to relax against him. This is Brandon, after all. My best friend. My partner in crime.

This is just a sign of how well we're playing our roles. I'm even convincing myself.

After a few moments of deep breathing, my heart rate returns to normal. I open my eyes, but Justin is gone.

TUESDAY, AUGUST 10TH

7 weeks and 4 days until Homecoming ♥

ALY
ALY'S CABIN, 7:45 a.m.

I'm in the middle of a delicious dream. I know it's a dream because Lauren's nose has inexplicably doubled in size. We're out in the water of Cypress Lake, and from across the crowded space, Justin's eyes meet mine. I can tell he realizes what a fool he's been in overlooking me all these years. It's written in the thought-bubble above his head. Pushing Lauren and her honker aside, he starts gliding toward me. His eyes hungrily skim over my new bikini as if he wants to devour me as the rest of the class looks on, cheering. Except for Brandon. His thought-bubble is filled with overprotective, big-brother-like growly sounds. But it doesn't matter because now only a mere foot separates Justin from pulling me into his arms.

That's when Kara's obnoxious snore yanks me back to reality.

"No!" I squeeze my eyes tight, trying to grasp the final wisps of the fantasy, but it's hopeless. Then a wondrous thought occurs and my eyes fly open. Today, that fantasy could very well become a reality—well, minus Lauren's bizarre nose growth.

The look I shared with Justin across the bonfire last night still gives me chills.

Operation Sex Appeal is working.

With a giggle, I leap out of bed and rush through my *new* morning routine. I still can't believe I came up with this crazy idea in the first place. I'm Miss Play-It-Safe. Miss Unadventurous. This whole mission is so *not* me. If anything, it's closer to a stunt Gabi would pull. Satisfied with the *Casual*-looking girl in the mirror, I race to the assembly hall to meet Brandon for breakfast. We signed up for the beach volleyball tournament, and while that sport is the one area of my life in which I feel confident, I'll be no good to anyone on an empty stomach.

I skitter to a stop inside the door, searching the crowd for his familiar handsome face. Brandon stands up from the back table and waves me over, lifting a plate piled high with eggs and bacon. This is the first time we've been alone for an extended time since beginning the charade, and we easily fall into our teasing banter.

"You know, if I knew what a good fake hookup you'd turn out to be, I'd have suggested this a long time ago."

Brandon laughs. "Yeah, well, I need you fueled and ready to spike someone's head off."

I grin around a mouthful of eggs. The rush I normally get before a big match courses through my veins, and my muscles tense. I'm used to practicing at least six days a week. The past few days have been new and exciting, but I'm ready to get back on a court. Electric energy makes me bounce in my seat as I finish off the plate and down a glass of OJ. "Let's get to it!"

Out in the blazing Texas heat, teams gather together to check the lineup. I see the names matched up with ours and bite my lip to keep from smiling. This will be almost too easy. Brandon's good at any sport involving a ball, and I've made MVP of the girls' volleyball team the last two years.

Brandon and I fall into an easy rhythm, and the first match is over before it even begins. We totally own the slackers playing opposite us, who more than likely only signed up to stare at girls in skimpy clothing. I narrow my eyes in concentration as they leer over the net. I spike the ball, land it in the perfect spot between them, and adjust the strap of my new hot-pink sports tank that has a built-in bra clearly not made for a chest like mine.

Welcome to my *turf, boys.*

As our official historian, Gabi snaps a picture of our victory hug, and a hum of whispers rises from the crowd. I giggle, high off the win. "They think we're totally smitten," I say, playing up my Southern accent and batting my eyelashes like a belle.

Brandon rolls his eyes and picks me up, throwing me over his shoulder as he jogs to the sideline cooler. I squeal and bang my fists across his sweat-slicked back. Grains of sand stick to his skin, and when he returns me to my feet, I avert my eyes.

I take a long sip of Evian, relishing the feel of the cold water sliding down my parched throat, and swipe my arm across my forehead. A definite benefit of not wearing my usual clothes is the ventilation. I grab my towel and pat off a layer of sweat.

A prickly sensation creeps along the back of my neck, and discreetly, I turn to scan the audience, expecting to find Lauren nailing me with another one of those lethal stares. I have to say, having those things directed at me? Not a fan. But when my gaze lands on the person giving me the prickles, I freeze.

And my stomach flip-flops.

Justin's standing opposite me in black swimming trunks—and nothing else. His bare chest glistens with a sprinkle of sand dust. His eyes roam over my exposed skin, causing a slow-burning fire to spread throughout my body, and when his gaze meets mine, his mouth kicks up in that famous, lopsided grin.

Holy cannoli.

Just as I begin to think my dream is stepping into reality, a different muscular chest disrupts our contact. I step back, confused, as Brandon holds out a towel with a tight-lipped smile. I wave the one I already have in the air.

Brandon knows about Operation Sex Appeal. He knows it's my mission to get Justin's attention. You would think he'd be happy to see my progress. The sooner Justin gets interested, the quicker Brandon can go back to his string of adoring fans.

I circle my finger in front of his angry face. "Everything okay there?"

Brandon nods curtly.

"On your word?" I ask, still not getting the tension radiating from his shoulders and eyebrows. He has seriously annoyed eyebrows.

He blows out a breath. "Yeah, I just need you focused. We still have another team to kill, remember?"

That makes sense. I nod and take another pull off my drink, excitement over the next match already bubbling up.

"I'll be right back," I say, grabbing Brandon's empty bottle. "Last night I saw a recycle bin over by the bonfire." I alter my voice to a snooty tone, an echo of our science teacher, Ms. Burns, and say, "After all, everyone must do their part."

I get the laugh I wanted, erasing the creases of tension from his forehead, and I take off for the bin. On my way back across the uneven ground, the crowd parts and Lauren steps in my path. My foot rolls at the hatred in her eyes, and I trip, busting my ass in the dirt.

"Shit, that hurts."

Brandon runs over as I push to my feet, testing my weight on my ankles. "Are you all right?"

I take a moment to assess and then nod, dusting off my wind shorts. "I'm fine." Brandon's green eyes show concern, and I smile with assurance I don't feel. And pretend I don't hear the snickers trailing behind me.

Operation Sex Appeal was designed to get people to notice me, and I can honestly say I don't feel *invisible* right now. But I can also say that, for the first time since we arrived, I'm wondering if maybe being a *Casual* isn't all it's cracked up to be.

♥ ♥ ♥

Under the hot spray of the shower, I rinse off my favorite birthday-cake-scented shampoo. I'm still floating from my moment with Justin, and the bathroom is empty, so I start humming my favorite Sugarland song. I curl my lip and shimmy my shoulders, and somewhere during the conditioner, I start to sing aloud.

"All I want to do..."

Bopping my head, my jamming continues as I step out and coat myself with vanilla lotion. Between running and volleyball, I'm forever in the sun, and this is my attempt to keep my skin from looking eighty in ten years. Thoroughly covered, I wrap my hair in a fluffy towel turban-style, put on my new bright yellow bikini and a pair of jean shorts, and pad back to my bunk.

Arctic air-conditioning hits my damp skin, and I shiver as I toss my towel on the floor. Shaking out my hair, I sing, "Baby drive me crazy," as I comb my fingers through the snarls. Kara's radio sits next to my hair dryer, so I flip it on and scan the stations until I land on my favorite. Hitting the switch on the dryer, I begin belting the top forty hit over the loud *whir.*

Crooning into my hairbrush microphone and with the dryer humming in my ear, I *almost* don't hear the creaking sound behind me. But mid-head bob, swaying arm still outstretched, I freeze, then promptly spin on my heel.

Brandon is sprawled across Gabi's bed, hands behind his head, ankles crossed. The corner of his mouth twitches as he meets my horrified gaze. He winks, and I whirl back around, killing the radio. "What the hell are you doing here?"

God, if you're listening, please have mercy and take me now.

Brandon chuckles, and I shake my head, choosing to believe this isn't happening. I don't look back. I *can't.* With my breathing near hyperventilation, I continue drying my hair, hoping with everything in me that he'll be gone by the time I'm done.

Eventually, every strand is bone dry. I have no choice but to turn off the dryer, wrap the cord around the handle, and put it in my bag. Only then do I turn around.

Sure enough, he's still sprawled out, silently nodding his head, tongue tucked in his cheek. "That was awesome."

I throw my head into my hands. "I was supposed to be alone! Everyone's out at the lake." I peer at him through the slats of my fingers. "And why aren't you, exactly?"

He shrugs. "I got bored. I wanted to see if you'd go hiking with me, but after that performance, I'm thoroughly entertained."

Oh, God. I dive onto the bed and cover my head with my silk pillow from home. Gabi's bed creaks again, and I know he's on the move. When my own bed shifts under Brandon's weight, he tries to pry away the pillow but is unable to overpower my death grip.

He chuckles. "Aly, I'm sorry if I embarrassed you—"

"Ha!"

"Okay, I'm sorry *that* I embarrassed you. But there's nothing to be embarrassed about. The moves were quite hilarious—"

That statement earns him my pillow to *his* head, which he catches without missing a beat.

"But I had no idea you could sing like that. I thought we didn't have any secrets, but you go and hide something like this?" He *tsks* and from the corner of my eye, I see him shake his head. "Makes me wonder what other deep dark secrets you have. Relationships, even casual ones, are built on trust, Aly. I don't know if I can keep dating someone I can't trust."

Despite myself, I laugh at his teasing. I sit up but can't bring myself to look at him. Instead, I focus on a loose thread on the comforter and wrap it around my finger. "No one knows. I'd be literally scared to death to sing in front of anyone."

"You just sang in front of me and lived to tell the tale."

"Ah, but see, I didn't know you were there." I shift on the bed and slowly lift my eyes to study his face. He's smiling, but doesn't appear to be laughing *at* me. "Normally, I only sing in the bathroom. Besides you, only my toothbrush and hairbrush have been privileged enough to hear these pipes."

He tucks a strand of hair behind my ear. "You should broaden your audience."

His green eyes sparkle with sincerity, but I've never been good at taking—or believing—compliments. I clear my throat. "So, hiking, huh?"

Brandon's forehead wrinkles in confusion before a huge smile spreads across his face. "Oh, right, wanna go? I hear the trails in this place are awesome. We can swing by the lake after if you want."

Anything that gets us away from this moment.

"Sure," I say. "Let me grab my shoes."

I throw my hair up in a messy ponytail and step into abused Nikes. It's just Brandon right now, so I can be myself...or at least myself wearing a bikini. Then I follow him out the swinging cabin door, ready to explore. And, hopefully, forget all about my impromptu concert.

WEDNESDAY, AUGUST 11TH
7 weeks and 3 days until Homecoming ♥

BRANDON
LAKESIDE, 2:30 p.m.

A splash pulls Aly's attention to the lake, and I sneak another peek. Over the years, I've seen her in a bathing suit tons of times, but she's never worn anything like this—a tiny yellow bikini that leaves very little to the imagination. But mine is filling in the pieces anyway.

Post-makeover Aly is beginning to short-circuit my nerves.

Laughter rings out, and I gratefully turn to watch the chicken-fight. Kara on Daniel's shoulders and Lauren on Justin's. The match is at a standstill, each girl pushing yet neither budging.

Aly sits up beside me to scream, "Come on, Kara!" drawing my eyes to her again.

My fired-up imagination conjures a vision of the two of us taking on the winner, her tanned thighs wrapped tightly around me.

A dude in the water calls out to Drew, and, shaking the image away, I turn to see him walking toward us. Thank God. Although he's spent the majority of his time in the cabin texting Sarah, I could hug him for showing up now. I need a distraction.

Any distraction.

I bump his fist. "What's up, man? Anything changed in Sarah's world in the last hour?"

"Fu—screw you." Drew never curses in front of a girl, a trait that makes him exactly the kind of guy Aly should go after. Unfortunately, he's whipped. Drew plops onto the sand and squints into the sun. "She's alone on a new campus and sorority rush just started. She's freaking out, and I can't be there for her. I hate it."

"But you are there for her." Aly leans back on an elbow and adjusts her top. I avert my eyes, noticing Drew and Carlos do the same. "Don't listen to these guys. I think it's sweet you call her so much. Sarah's lucky."

Drew shakes his head. "I'm the lucky one. But thanks." Then he claps his hands and says, "Almost forgot, guess what I just heard? Tonight's karaoke in the main hall, baby."

"Now that's what I'm talking about," Carlos says. Picking up his guitar from the towel in front of him, he breaks out in a horrendous rendition of the country song "I've Got Friends in Low Places."

Aly laughs so hard she snorts. "I thought you were supposed to be a great musician."

Carlos smiles good-naturedly. "Nah, I play a mean guitar, but I can't carry a tune in a bucket."

Smirking, I lean close to Aly's ear. "Speaking of carrying a tune…"

"No." She pushes me away, her eyes wide. "Don't even think about it, bud." Sticking out her tongue, she stands up to stretch, and my eyes involuntarily trace the length of her body. She saunters to the dock and spreads her towel near the edge, dangling her feet over the side. She leans down to splash cool water on her heated arms and legs. My mouth goes dry.

Gritting my teeth, I force my gaze back to the chicken-fight in the lake.

This mission needs to end—the sooner, the better. For her *and* for my sanity.

Aly may *think* she wants to be a *Casual*, but she's wrong. Really, this whole thing seems to be about people seeing her differently, but she can get the same results without the sexy clothes. They are messing with my head, and they're just not *her*. If I can get her to realize that, maybe things can go back to normal. It's definitely worth a shot.

I walk over, and Aly scrunches her tiny face, squeezing her eyes shut. I squat down and, putting my years of girl knowledge to use, sweetly say, "Come on, do it for me?"

She shakes her head, keeping her eyes closed. "Uh-uh. Brandon, don't do this to me. I love you to death, but there's no way I'm getting up on a stage in front of all those people."

"But think of it as another step in Operation Sexy Clothes Makeover Thing—"

She huffs. "Operation Sex Appeal."

"Yeah, that. Listen, what better way to shock everyone's preconceived notions of quiet little Aly than by having her kick major ass at karaoke night?"

And then maybe we can call an end to this whole thing.

Aly's eyes open. A slow smile twitches her lips, and I'm sure I got her.

Then her hands shoot out.

I have just enough time to snap my arm around and bring her with me before we fall. We hit the surface in an ungraceful splash, the tepid water welcome on my sunburned skin. I pop up first, wipe the stinging sunscreen out of my eyes, and wait for her red head to emerge. A second later, she does, sputtering, laughing, arms flailing. Instinctively, I pull her close so she can catch her breath, but I should've known better. As soon as she's within arm's reach, she smiles wickedly and dunks me again.

Oh, it's on now.

Full-on war breaks out as we wrestle in the water, laughing and dunking. Aly nails me right in the eye, and I hear a distant voice say, "They're so cute together."

Aly looks at me, and we share a conspiratorial smile.

ALY
MAIN HALL, 8:05 p.m.

Relaxed against Brandon's hard chest, I feel calm. I'm confident that, despite anything he might say otherwise, I'll be enjoying the show from a safe distance at the back table, cheering on the brave souls who don't suffer from stage fright.

In the front of the room, our advisor directs a few football players to move the makeshift stage while the AV guys set up the sound system. Someone turns on a microphone, and the feedback screeches through monster-sized speakers. Wincing, I turn away and discover Lauren glaring at me.

She and Justin are standing next to the only two empty seats at our table, the ones that happen to be right next to where Brandon and I are sitting.

The seating arrangement is pure luck. My planned afternoon catnap turned into an extended siesta, thanks to forgetting to set the alarm on my phone. Brandon woke me up when he came to get me for dinner, and I ran around like a hamster on speed to get ready.

Judging by the way Justin's eyes skim over my black sleeveless top and dark jean skirt, I did all right.

"You look incredible, Aly," he says, his eyes meeting mine. Brandon clears his throat, and Justin lifts his chin. "Being with this chump obviously agrees with you."

He reaches over to fist-bump Brandon and lets the tips of his fingers graze my shoulder. The temperature in the already-warm building skyrockets. Lauren snatches his hand, wraps it around her waist, and practically sits in his lap.

The girl is messing with my plan. Operation Sex Appeal keeps adding layers. The newest dimension: annihilating Lauren Hays.

Our advisor calls a name over the audio system, and our nut-job of a wide receiver walks up to kick off the show. A familiar drumbeat rolls out the speakers as he begins a quasi-decent version of "Ice, Ice Baby."

I snuggle further into Brandon's chest, getting quite comfortable with the dynamics of our fake hookup, and feel his arms tighten around me. He leans close and whispers, "Please go up there with me."

Leaning my head back, I whisper-reply, "No."

Warm breath tickles my neck as he tries again. "Aly, I'm willing to make an absolute jackass out of myself because, unlike you, I really *can't* sing. But I want to do this for you. Please? Just one song? I'll be up there the whole time, I promise." He gently lifts my chin to meet my gaze. "You trust me, right?"

It may be the sincerity in his warm eyes. It could be the gentle pleading of his voice. Or maybe it's the inexplicable tingly sensation that spread over me when he whispered in my ear. But suddenly—and without checking with my brain first—a breathless, shaky voice comes out of my mouth and says, "Okay."

Brandon beams. He lowers his head to kiss my cheek, then—before I can call him back—runs at a full sprint to where the song lists and sign-up sheets are. Kara looks over inquisitively, but I can only shake my head. My eyes dart back to Brandon. My face is on fire, my heart is going a mile a minute, and with what sounds like the ocean in my ears, I realize I'm having a mini-panic attack.

What did I just agree to?

Brandon returns with a broad smile, and I concentrate on remembering how to breathe. He crouches in front of me, taking both my hands in his.

"I pulled some strings, and we're up next." His smile stretches up a bit on the left side, highlighting the dimple in his cheek. "I didn't want you to have a chance to change your mind and run off on me."

I can only assume my face displays what I feel inside: complete and utter terror. I'm about to inform him he'll have to go up there by himself, that I had an out-of-body experience when I agreed and there's no way in *hell* he's getting me up there, when the advisor calls our names. Gabi and Kara's expressions change from confusion to shock.

Tell me about it, I want to scream.

Brandon pulls me up, and our table cheers. He shakes his head at my freaked, bugged-out eyes. "Trust me. You're gonna be great."

Then he leans down and kisses me.

Okay, it's not a huge kiss. Barely more than a peck and probably completely done for show. But it's enough to send all thoughts of stage fright (or anything else for that matter) right out of my head. Numbly, I allow him to lead me to the stage.

In the space of a heartbeat, I'm there, on the platform. With no chance of backing out. At least not without looking like a bigger dork than I will for singing. Swallowing hard, I turn to face my classmates. The crowd seems to have doubled during my short walk from the back table.

In the spotlight, my shirt feels too tight, like a second skin. My skirt too short, too revealing. I tug on the hem, confident I'm about to lose the lasagna I just wolfed down all over the makeshift stage, and draw a shaky breath, waiting to see what song Brandon could've possibly chosen for this embarrassing spectacle. When the opening notes of "Summer Nights" from *Grease* begin, my mouth tumbles open.

Brandon grins, then silently mouths, "Trust me."

He goes first, and his unnecessary falsetto is so *off* that I can't help but laugh. Then, it's my turn. I sing the lyrics on impulse. He turns so he's facing me, not the audience, and sings the next line in a register so deep and opposite the first that I fight back another laugh so I can sing mine. And so it goes, me keeping my eyes on him, following his lead, and something—or someone—takes over.

Brandon's horrifically bad singing helps me relax. Soon it feels like it's just the two of us, alone and goofing around in my living room. He hams it up playing Danny Zuko, complete with *snazzy* John Travolta dance moves, and I do my best to match with my wholesome Sandy impersonation.

Talk about an original *Commitment* girl.

The audience cheers along from the very beginning, even joining in for the background "tell me more"s. Singing with Brandon is so much fun that, before I know it, the song is over, ending on the impossibly long note that he totally murders, but in the best way possible, grin on his face, eyes crinkled, finger extended high in the air.

For one short moment, it's silent. That short moment feels like a lifetime. Then, to my utter amazement, we receive a standing ovation.

We did it.

I stare at the crowd, stunned, unable to comprehend what just happened, and sense Brandon watching me. I look over, and he smiles. Grabbing my hand, he lifts it in victory, resulting in even more whooping.

My cheeks burn and I bite my lip, but nothing can hold back the smile splitting my face. I feel incredible, blissed out more than I ever thought possible.

Chin lifted a little higher than before, I take a step off the stage and feel my ankle roll in my strappy, platform shoes. A gasp comes from the girl in the front row, and a vision of me smacking my head on the cold, hard linoleum floor in the world's worst encore plays in my mind. But then Brandon's hands are there, circling me, halting the ground from meeting my face. Saving me like he always seems to do.

"Oops." I grab onto his elbow with a grimace, feeling the cords of my neck bulge out. "That was epically embarrassing."

Brandon shakes his head. "Don't worry about it. Barely anyone noticed."

I turn to the still-cheering crowd and realize he's right. Only a few of the girls in the front row are smirking at my almost wipeout.

Freaking heels. They are going to be the death of me.

Keeping a firm grip around my waist, Brandon leads me back to our friends. The second we reach the table, Gabi and Kara tackle me.

"How did I not know you could sing like that?" Gabi asks, pulling back from the three-way embrace. "And why in the hell didn't I bring my camera?!"

"Seriously, Aly, that rocked!" Kara wipes a stray hair from her wide-open mouth. "I can't believe you got up in front of all these people! I mean, I would in a heartbeat, but you?" She squeals again and wraps me in another tight hug.

She rocks me back and forth, and I grin, realizing I took a major step in the right direction. *Casuals* are defined as being fun and adventurous. A week ago, that would *not* have described me. But tonight, for the first time in my life, I abandoned myself in public to pure pleasure. I almost passed out while doing it, but hey, it's all about the baby steps.

But the question is, did Justin notice?

I gaze over Kara's shoulder. Brandon is standing in the middle of his friends, being not-so-gently ribbed, taking it all with a smile on his face.

"Powerful singing there, Brando," Carlos says, straight-faced. "Crazy moves, too."

"You know, it was chivalrous to try and help Aly sound better by sucking so badly," Drew adds. "But next time, I think she can handle the singing stuff on her own."

Justin crosses his arms, an eyebrow arched over a devastatingly dark eye. "Yeah, that was raw entertainment right there." He waits a beat, then his smile breaks free and he slaps Brandon on the shoulder.

They all join in, laughing and talking, and Justin slides his gaze toward me. He nibbles his lower lip and nods, giving me a slow once-over. A choreographed victory dance plays out in my mind.

Oh yeah.

He noticed.

THURSDAY, AUGUST 12TH
7 weeks and 2 days until Homecoming ♥

ALY
ALY'S CABIN, 12:35 a.m.

My heart is totally going to beat out of my chest. Gabi clears her throat—our signal—and I ease out of my bunk, hoping the ancient springs won't creak. I look at Kara's empty bed. She sneaks out every night, and Thompson hasn't caught *her* yet.

Everything will be fine, Aly. Chill out.

I tiptoe barefoot across the rough boards to where Gabi waits. She sticks her head out the door for a quick chaperone check and then waves me through. Clinging to the shadows cast from the cabin, we move stealth-like through the grass, avoiding the lampposts marking the trails, and creep toward the sand bank near the lake.

It's our final night at Cypress Lake. When Gabi suggested tonight's jailbreak at dinner, I completely balked. But my fake hookup whispered in my ear, reminding me that a true *Casual* wouldn't hesitate at an adventure like this, so I gritted my teeth and let them convince me it would be fun.

As I carefully step over a fallen branch, a twig beneath my foot snaps. I jerk back, wide-eyed, sure we're about to be busted. The worst that can happen is detention—we leave in the morning so it's not like they can send me home early or anything—but I've never been in trouble before. For the last three years, I've managed to avoid Gabi's nuttier adventures by claiming a mountain of homework or rigorous volleyball practice, but now there's no backing out.

Tonight, I'll prove I'm the *Casual* type. Even if it freaking kills me.

The moon's reflection on the water peeks through the trees as we near the deserted beach. Gabi and I are the last to arrive. Kara and Daniel had their own secret rendezvous scheduled, and Drew claimed a headache, so tonight it's the six of us. Justin and Lauren stand near the water, and as we approach, she slides her hands around his waist and into the back pockets of his jeans.

The display is typical and frustrating, but I'm determined not to let it affect me. It's not like the boy can make a move on me tonight anyway; he thinks I'm with Brandon.

Patience is a virtue.

I walk to where Brandon kneels in the sand, spreading out a blanket. He dusts his hands on the back of his pants and grins when he sees me at the cover's edge. "Wasn't sure you'd make it."

"Why wouldn't I?" I cross my arms. Sometimes I *hate* how well he knows me. "I said I'd come, didn't I?"

"Yeah, you did." He takes my hand and tugs me down beside him. "But I bet you're obsessing about being caught. Am I right?"

I scowl. "No." Normally I tell Brandon everything, but it feels important that he believe my transformation into a *Casual* is easy and natural. So I aim for blasé as I ask, "So what's the plan? Just hang out and stargaze all night?"

"Actually," Carlos chimes in, plopping down and hogging half the blanket. "How about Truth or Dare?"

Gabi rolls her eyes, squatting down between us. "Seriously?" She tries to look annoyed for Carlos's benefit, but really, she's a dare queen.

Justin and Lauren walk over hand-in-hand and kneel down. Lauren smiles her plastic smile at me and says, "I'll go first. I love a good dare."

This was why I avoided all those boy-girl parties in junior high. Truth or Dare, Spin the Bottle, Seven Minutes in Heaven—all different names for the same torture. I'm not fearless like Gabi or confident like Kara. I survived those games by a combination of avoidance and aptly timed bathroom trips. Yet here I sit—a senior in high school—and it catches up with me.

Effing jailbreak.

"Okay, Lauren," Justin says with a glance at me.

Uh-oh.

My stomach clenches, and I swallow hard.

"I dare you and Aly to make out for thirty seconds."

I stare ahead dumbly, positive I heard wrong. But from the grin twitching his lips, I can tell my ears are working just fine. A small *squeak* escapes my throat as Lauren shrugs like it's no big deal. When Justin looks away, she nails me with a look of challenge.

Where the heck's a bathroom when you need one?

Sliding her feet beneath her, Lauren leans forward, and I finally find my voice. "I'm not kissing Lauren!"

She sits back, grinning in triumph.

"What's the big deal?" Justin asks. "It's just a game."

I open my mouth, but no words come. A very small, very miniscule part of me considers doing it. Justin is noticing me. Refusing his dare will erase all the positive steps I've taken this week. But there's just no *freaking* way it's going to happen.

Now, how do I get out of it?

Luckily, Brandon speaks up. "It's not Aly's dare, it's Lauren's. She doesn't have to do it."

My knight in relaxed-fit jeans. I lean against his chest and smile in gratitude.

Justin glares at Brandon and says, "All right, Lauren, I dare you to flash everyone."

"Whatever." She grabs the hem of her shirt. "You know, you can just search YouTube. I did this at Mardi Gras last year."

Her eyes flick to Brandon, and she lifts her top.

Averting my gaze, I look to see if Brandon is watching the show. Thankfully, his eyes are on the sky. I don't know why I'm so relieved, but I am. Perhaps feeling my stare, he looks down at me and then away, clearing his throat.

Did I seriously risk getting caught for this?

"Okay, my turn!" Lauren says, adjusting her shirt. "Brandon, truth or dare?"

I can't even imagine the kind of dares this girl can come up with; truth has to be the safest choice. And since I know everything there is to know about Brandon, it'd be a lot less stressful to watch. Closing my eyes, I *will* him to say truth.

"Truth."

Another wave of relief washes over me. I give him an encouraging smile, letting him know I'm here if things get sticky. There's a lot Brandon doesn't like talking about, his dad's death being at the top of the list.

"Truth?" Disappointed, Lauren scrunches her forehead. I get the distinct impression she was hoping for a dare—and I have a hunch what that dare would involve. After a few moments of painful suspense, she says, "I don't know. I can't think of anything good." She huffs a breath and asks, "Brandon, are you a virgin?"

My head snaps up. Lauren acted as if it's the dumbest question in the world, but she inadvertently stumbled on the one thing Brandon and I never discuss. I've always assumed he's not, but he refuses to tell me how far he goes with the girls he hooks up with, not that I'm that eager to know.

Brandon looks at me, then back to Lauren. "No."

The truth hits like a punch to the gut.

My jaw hurts with the strain of keeping my face as neutral as possible, and I avoid looking him in the eye. Brandon places his warm hand on my shoulder, and I stop myself from flinching.

Why do I care if he's a virgin or not? Any girl he sleeps with is his business.

And we're not *really* together anyway!

This week of pretend hooking up has ended up feeling more like a week of being his pretend girlfriend. And it's the *pretend* part my head and heart are having the most trouble with.

With forced effort, I relax my spine and place my hand on his. This isn't his fault. It's my own brand of crazy. Brandon exhales, his breath fanning the hair on the top of my head. His thumb wraps around mine as he returns to the game. "Gabi, truth or dare?"

I look at my friend, not surprised to find her watching me with concern. I nod, letting her know I'm okay, and the dare queen surprises me by answering, "Truth."

"Good. Confession time." I hear the smile in Brandon's voice, and I'm pretty sure I know what's coming. "How do you feel about my man, Carlos? And no copping out with that 'I like him like a friend' bullshit either."

Even from across the blanket, I hear her breath release in a rush. Her body locks up, only her eyes moving as they slide from Brandon to Carlos and then to me, pleading for my help.

Hey, this was your guys' suggestion, I want to say, but instead I give her an encouraging smile.

"N-no," she stammers. She lifts her chin and glares over at him. "I don't like Carlos. He actually bugs the crap out of me."

Unfortunately, she wasn't able to control her *voice* as well as her face. Brandon and Justin chuckle, and I try my best to hide my smile behind my hand. *I so knew it!*

"Sweetheart, if you're gonna lie, at least try to be convincing," Lauren says, her voice dripping with false sincerity.

Carlos leans on one arm to whisper in Gabi's ear. I don't know what he says, but *whatever* it is, it magically stops her from climbing over the blanket and ripping Lauren's bleached-blonde tresses from her head. The two of them stare at each other for a moment, and then she sinks against him and actually smiles.

Well, what do you know? Maybe this game is good for something after all.

Gabi clears her throat. "All right, my turn." Her stare zeroes in on me as she says, "Truth or dare?"

Aw, crap. Is it possible to say neither? Gabi just got burned on truth, and I've been *far* from Miss Truthful lately. What would I say if she asks about Brandon? But then, a dare almost had me making out with Lauren a few minutes ago. I waffle back and forth, gnawing on my lip like a freaking rabbit, and then spit out, "Dare?"

Gabi sits up tall with eager eyes, and I immediately start wishing for a do-over.

"Since this trip started, I've seen the two of you," she says, motioning between me and Brandon, "give each other little kisses on the cheek and that chaste peck on the lips last night, but I've yet to see you go at it. I've spent *years* watching the two of you pretend you weren't hot for each other. So go for it already." Wiggling her shoulders, she says, "Aly, I dare you to make out with Brandon for a full minute."

Gabi smiles as if she's given me a present. Like this is an easy dare.

Ha!

Truth, truth, truth! I pick truth!

I turn to Brandon in alarm. We didn't plan for this. Rules from before still apply; he can back out, but how would that look to our friends? To *Justin?* We hold a conversation with our eyes, Brandon studying me under scrunched eyebrows, and then his teeth sink into his lower lip. Without thinking, my eyes follow the movement.

Has it always been that full?

I look at his upper lip and find he has a matching set. Model lips, that's what they are. No marks, no dry skin marring them. They look soft and wet and yummy, and I lick mine on impulse.

"Dude, what're you waiting for?" Carlos calls. "Plant one on her."

I lift my eyes and am shocked to see Brandon is staring at *my* mouth. He swallows audibly and flicks his gaze to mine. The emotions darkening the soft green color are too confusing to name.

Does he want to back out?

An exhale of breath leaves Brandon's lips, almost like a laugh, and he scoots closer to me on the blanket. I twist my legs under myself, sitting tall as I face him. He cups my chin and tilts it toward him, drowning me in the now dark-green depths of his eyes, the cologne I gave him for his birthday filling my head. It's woodsy and yummy and I always loved how it smelled on the store testers, but on Brandon, it's even sexier. My eyes flutter closed, and I inhale again, this time slowly. Goose bumps prickle my arms, and my head gets fuzzy.

Brandon slides his hand down the column of my neck and brings the other up, threading his fingers through the hair at my nape. His breath fans across my cheek, and everything south of my bellybutton squeezes tight.

When his mouth first meets mine, it's hesitant, questioning. But as I move my lips with his, he quickly grows bolder, coaxing them apart.

Desire, pure and raw, electrifies my veins as his tongue sweeps my mouth. A whimpering sound springs from my chest, and instinctively, I wrap my arms around his neck, tugging him closer. Needing more. My teeth graze his full bottom lip, and I pull it, sucking on it gently.

He moans and knots his fingers in my hair, and a thrill dances down my back.

Brandon is an amazing kisser, just as I knew he would be. I have no control over my body's reactions. I lose myself in his lips, his tongue, and his strong arms, forgetting time and space and even my surroundings—until Gabi's snicker brings reality crashing around us, reminding me we have an audience.

And that I'm kissing Brandon.

We break apart, out of breath, and stare into each other's eyes.

That was unexpected.

I search Brandon's face, wondering if he felt anything even close to what I did.

And still do.

His soulful eyes search back. The adorable dimple in his cheek pops, and I lick my lips, savoring the lingering taste of spearmint. I just kissed Brandon. And I liked it. A lot.

My stomach drops, my head spins, and my pulse races. Shaking my head, I turn to the group, trying to focus back on the game. But thoughts of the scorching kiss consume me, leaving me dazed and weak-limbed.

I inhale a shaky breath and attempt a smile. "Carlos, truth or dare?"

BRANDON
BRANDON'S CABIN, 4:24 a.m.

The second hand on the large fish clock makes its sixtieth trip around the dial, and I turn over to look at Justin's empty bunk. He's off with Lauren somewhere, as he's been every other night. Drew is knocked out. Carlos is snoring.

And I'm stuck awake, watching a damn clock and thinking about Aly.

Tonight did not go as planned. Not that I *had* any plans, but ending the night making out with my best friend wasn't exactly on my to-do list. Now that I did, I can't shake the memory of Aly's face when we stopped.

There was no way to get out of that dare without coming clean about our non-hookup, so I'd planned to give her a simple kiss. Just enough to shut everyone up, no tongue or groping involved. But I hadn't counted on her being so responsive. Or my body taking over the way it did.

Kissing Aly was fucking hot.

The only thing keeping me from running to her cabin now and picking up where we left off is figuring out what I'd say once I got there. Knowing Aly, she'd send me back anyway, telling me we should just pretend it didn't happen. But can we do that?

Do we even want to?

That girl can kiss. The whole senior class already believes we're hooking up; would it be so bad if we did it for real?

I punch my pillow and throw myself back onto the bed.

No, I can't even think about suggesting that. Aly deserves better. Whether she'll admit it or not, she's a *Commitment* all the way, and hooking up for real will only hurt her.

And our friendship.

Groaning, I shove the pillow over my head.

One thing's for sure. I'm gonna have to amp up my game plan. Either I need to get Aly to realize she's not a *Casual* or find her a target other than Justin. Because if things stay the way they are for much longer, we're going to ruin our friendship forever.

FRIDAY, AUGUST 13TH
7 weeks and 1 day until Homecoming ♥

ALY
ALY'S ROOM, 4:30 p.m.

Home, sweet, dirty home. I kick a mound of clothes out of the way and trudge across my bedroom floor, heaving my suitcases onto the unmade bed. I brought entirely too much crap on the camping trip. Pre-makeover, I would have had a bunch of tees, a couple pairs of shorts, and my worn-out one-piece. It would've all fit into one duffle bag. Instead, I got an extra cardio session in by lugging makeup, four pairs of shoes, three different bikinis, and enough wardrobe options to keep a Beverly Hills socialite happy.

Beauty truly is pain.

I glance at the dresser spewing clothes and consider turning on my laptop. Word of me and Brandon getting together has to have spread to the rest of the school by now. I take a step and then hesitate, imagining the "what is he doing with *her*" comments surely cluttering Facebook. I'm *so* not ready for that. Left with no other choice, I smile and flop onto my soft bed, close my eyes, and give in to what I really want to do anyway.

Relive last night.

Delicious tingles explode wherever Brandon touched. My lips burn, and my head gets delightfully fuzzy. I want to lose myself in the sensations, but I hear my doorknob rattle and force my heavy eyelids open.

Kaitie's strawberry-blonde ponytail bounces as she runs through the door and straight to my dresser. Amused, I prop my chin on my hand. She begins rifling through the drawers, tossing even more clothes onto the floor, and I scrunch my nose in wonder. But when my favorite baby-blue pajama set lands in a pile of dirty clothes, I decide it's time to intervene.

"Can I help you find something in particular?"

She spins around, eyes bugged out. *Busted.* Placing a hand over her chest, she exclaims, "God, you scared the crap out of me!"

I lift an incredulous eyebrow. "Uh, Kaitie, it's *my* room."

She winces and slides her back down my dresser, pulling her knees into her chest. "Sorry for touching your stuff."

I shrug. I don't really care if she borrows my clothes; she's just never done it before. Kaitie's five years younger than me and only just getting to the age where she cares about this stuff. "Is there something you need?"

"Tonight's the team sleepover at Baylee's," she explains with a defeated frown, "and I don't know what to wear."

Now I get the dilemma.

Brandon likes to tease that *I'm* a worrier, but honestly, my sister has that market cornered. She's an introvert, an extreme one, but while talking to people outside her family and friends is a challenge, Kaitie's biggest obstacle is her perfectionism. One small mistake or hiccup haunts her forever. That's why I pushed her to join the junior-high rec team and why I agreed to co-coach it, even though my schedule is utter chaos. Six games and a one-hour practice a week is nothing compared to giving my sister the confidence that I know sports can bring. I've experienced it, and I want that for Kaitie.

I climb out of bed, pausing to ruffle her hair on my way to the dresser. I scour through the mess until I find an old pair of Fairwood Academy P.E. shorts and a *Kiss my ace!* T-shirt.

Kaitie grabs them excitedly and hugs me. "Thank you!" Then she sprints for the door, calling over her shoulder, "Gotta pack!" She disappears into her side of the bathroom, but then sticks her smiling face back in. "I'm so glad you're home!"

"Me too, doodle-bug."

Alone again, I look at the mess and sigh. Since I'm up, I might as well begin the laborious task of separating laundry into piles. *Yay!* I make decent headway until a muffled Taylor Swift song begins playing from under one of the mounds and I mess them all up again, searching for my lost cell phone. I follow the music to a pair of jeans, singing along with the chorus, and pull the phone out. Brandon's face grins up at me.

I fluff my hair and smooth my shirt, then realize he can't see me anyway. Clearing my throat, I answer the phone before the second verse starts. "Hey, what's up?" Nice, casual, without a hint of any lusty, hormone-filled innuendo. Well done.

"Aly?" Brandon sounds far away, and I hear clattering on the other end. "I thought you'd never pick up. I need help. Baylee's hosting the team sleepover tonight—"

"I know, Kaitie already ransacked my drawer," I interrupt, still proud she's stepping outside of her comfort zone and going. "I don't envy your mom tonight, that's for sure."

He groans. "Yeah, well, Mom just got called to take over a night shift at the hospital. I'll be here, but I don't think the parents want a seventeen-year-old guy alone with a bunch of thirteen- and fourteen-year-old girls."

I snort. "Uh, no, I don't think so."

Silence on the other end.

"Brandon?"

He clears his throat. "So, yeah, I was thinking, maybe you can ask your mom if you can help chaperone? I mean, considering I'm now your man and all, I don't guess you have a hot date or anything, right?"

I laugh at his teasing tone, and then his words sink in.

I'd be alone with Brandon. All night. Unsupervised.

My stomach flutters. Normally I'd be on shift at the theater, but I got the weekend off to recover from the camping trip. "Um, I don't know. Let me go ask and I'll call you right back."

I disconnect and stare at the phone. A slow smile spreads across my face. Then I barrel through the door. "MOM!"

Not in the kitchen. Not in the living room, office, or laundry room. I plow through her bedroom and pull up short when I finally find her sitting at the vanity in her bathroom.

"Hey, Mom," I say, taking a seat on the huge, claw-footed bathtub. "You're looking good."

She meets my gaze in the mirror with a hint of amusement shining in her eyes.

Okay, it's about to get thick in here. There's no way she's gonna go for me having a co-ed sleepover with the guy she now believes to be my quasi-boyfriend. Maybe before she saw us at the camping trip, but not now. This is going to take a lot, *a lot* of sucking up.

"Seriously," I say, smiling big. "Dad's not gonna know what hit him. Sting either. He's going to take one look at you from up on that stage and pull you into his harem."

Dad is taking her to see Sting...again, a date-night tradition from back in college when they discovered their mutual love for The Police. And tonight, the thing that'll keep her from suggesting *herself* as the new chaperone.

Mom taps her blush brush on the makeup mirror and gives me a pointed look. "Don't think I don't see what you're doing with the flattery, missy. Though, I do look pretty hot if I say so myself. My men deserve nothing but the best." She picks up her eyeliner and, without looking at me, asks, "So what is it? You need more new clothes? You broke something? What?"

I sigh and fidget with the star sapphire ring on my finger. *So much for sucking up.* "You know how Kaitie's going to that sleepover thing? At Baylee's?" Mom nods, so I continue. "Well, Brandon just called. His mom was pulled into work at the last minute and can't stay to chaperone, and *nobody* thinks it's a good idea for Brandon to do it by himself. That's just asking for a lawsuit or a scandal of epic proportions."

She sits back from lining her eyes and folds her arms. "And?"

I clear my throat and convert my smile into sweet and innocent. "So we thought maybe I should go over there. Help watch the girls, show off my mad baking skills, keep the dragons of gossip away. You know, be a good big sister and bond with my team."

Mom rolls her eyes. She shakes her head, staring pensively at her reflection, and purses her lips. "Kaitie's really been looking forward to that sleepover. It's the only thing she's talked about all week." She pumps her mascara wand in the tube and makes the requisite mascara-face in her mirror. With mouth open and words distorted, she says, "And I know Sheila must be disappointed missing the sleepover, too."

I bounce my foot but keep quiet. My input now can only work against me.

After leaning in to comb through and inspect her eyelashes, Mom turns to me. "Okay." I sit there, flabbergasted, as she pauses, squints, and then nods. "I trust Brandon, and more importantly, I trust you. You can go."

I totally didn't see that coming. I mean, I was hopeful, but severely doubtful. Jumping up from my perch on the bathtub, I lean down, breathe in Mom's heavenly scent of roses and baby powder, and smile at her reflection. "Thank you!"

Her mouth says, "You're welcome." The look she gives in the mirror says, *You better not make me regret it.*

I nod to both messages and slink out the door, then dash back to my bedroom. I pull up my recent calls and tap Brandon's name. The moment he picks up, I blurt, "I'm in."

It's not until after we hang up, with me promising to be there by six, that nerves set in.

I touch my lips, remembering the feel of his mouth on mine. Our kiss sent *me* reeling, but I'm not naïve enough to think it affected Brandon the same way. He's hooked up with countless girls, girls with a ton more experience than me. For all I know, he could've thought kissing me was like kissing his sister.

Or air.

What if he was bored kissing me?

I let the horror of that thought sink in for about thirty seconds before squaring my shoulders. It's not like it matters if he was bored anyway because it's not happening again. This mission is about getting Justin. Brandon and I already had our shot, and he turned me down. My eyes flit to our Homecoming picture on the Wall of Shame.

It was freshman year, three years ago, but it still stings when I think about it. I can't let myself go down that path again. Brandon is my friend. And my *fake* hookup.

That's it.

Still, as I pick up my duffle bag and dump the clothes inside it onto the floor, I can't stop the butterflies from taking flight as I ponder what pajamas *I* should bring tonight.

♥ ♥ ♥

"They're here!"

I hear Baylee's squeal from behind the closed red wood door moments before it opens and an excited ball of energy envelops me in a hug. "Thank you so much for coming! Now it's really gonna rock!"

A deep, sexy chuckle comes from behind Baylee, and my pulse quickens. Brandon leans against the door and smiles. Despite my mental pep talk back in my room, and again on the drive over, my palms slick with sweat.

"Glad to be here," I say, stepping back from the girl's embrace. *Focus on why you're here, Aly.* "Now put me to work."

Kaitie and I came early to help set up, knowing their mom would be getting ready for her shift and Brandon is clueless. We walk through the door, and Brandon grabs the grocery bags and tote from my hands to look inside, brushing his fingers against the inside of my wrist. My eyes dart to his mouth.

How can such an innocent touch cause my insides to melt and my limbs to get all twitchy at the same time?

Baylee sticks her head into the closest bag. "What's all this?"

Blood rushes to my face as I wrench my eyes from Brandon's lips. I can't bring myself to look and see if he caught me. Tucking my hair behind my ear, I answer in an annoyingly breathless voice, "Every sleepover needs movies and spa stuff." I force a smile at Baylee. "And the right kind of snackage is essential to any party's success."

"Trust her, Bayls." I finally look up and see Brandon staring at me with an unreadable expression. *Could that touch have affected him, too?* "Aly's an expert on snackage."

We hold each other's gaze for an extended moment. I still have no idea what he's thinking, and

I pray I'm just as pokerfaced. Sadly, my sinking gut tells me different.

"Y'all okay?" Baylee asks.

That snaps us out of it. I nod, and Brandon turns around to walk into the family room. I notice our sisters exchange a strange look as I fall in step behind him, setting my overnight bag on the bench in the foyer.

Nope, this isn't awkward at all.

Baylee presses play on her "girl power mix," and I turn myself into Martha Stewart to keep the pesky thoughts at bay. I push the recliner and sofa back and have Brandon remove the coffee table to add more floor space. After laying out the spa products and stacking movies by the television, I set out the snacks in the kitchen. I'm pouring chips into a bowl when Miss Sheila comes down the stairs in her scrubs. She walks up, pulling me into a hug.

"Alyssa, you don't know how grateful I am for you bailing us out at the last minute like this. I *hate* missing the sleepover." Eyes the same soft green shade as Brandon's peer at me with sadness as she sighs, squeezing my shoulder. "But I know the girls are in good hands."

"I stole every stereotypical sleepover idea from every movie I've seen," I confirm. "The girls will have a blast."

She smiles, then darts her gaze to Brandon. "My shift's from seven to seven," she tells me, "so I want to catch up with you in the morning, okay?" The pointed look she gives me confirms my suspicions. Mom totally told her about that moment she saw at the campground. I squirm under her scrutiny, and the level of awkward rises.

She winks, letting me off the hook for now. Then, in a rush of energy rivaling her daughter's, she kisses her children and runs out the door with a parting, "Behave, you two," thrown over her shoulder.

The door closes, and Brandon and I share a look. We're officially without supervision.

I zip back around and snag a cookie from the counter.

When in doubt, pig out. That's my motto.

"Anything else left to do?" Kaitie asks, grabbing a chip.

I give the kitchen and family room a thorough examination. Satisfied that everything is ready, I shake my head. "Nah, just have to order the pizza. You girls head upstairs to clean up."

As they clomp up the stairs, I reach for the phone. I *feel* Brandon watching me, but I don't look back. Knowing we were going to be alone and actually *being* alone are apparently two very different things. Adding in the confusing bodily reactions to his mere presence, I'm a big ball of freaking out. I order enough food to feed an army, and I'm just hanging up when long, tan fingers wrap around my elbow.

"Got a second?"

Those dang tingles come back, radiating from where his rough hand encircles my arm. Brandon looks down as if surprised to find it there and takes a step back, releasing his grip. The warm sensation lingers.

"Sure," I say.

Pushing himself onto the granite counter in front of me, Brandon rests his hands on my shoulders. "Thanks for doing this for Baylee. It means a lot. To both of us."

Ignoring the shiver teasing my spine, I look into his sincere expression and nod. "It's really no problem. This is important to Kaitie, too."

We stare at each other, and a tension-filled silence falls between us. I refuse to let my eyes drift down to his full lips. Or let myself wonder if he's thinking about our kiss as much as I am.

Or if he wants to do it again.

Nope, definitely not thinking about the kiss.

"Brandon, about last night—"

"Listen, last night was—"

We both stop, and I laugh nervously. "Go ahead." Biting my lip, I cast a glance toward the doorway. The last thing this conversation needs is a couple seventh-grade eavesdroppers.

"Okay." Brandon swallows and rubs his palms on the front of his jeans. "I just wanted to make sure... I mean, we're cool, right? Things kinda got sketchy last night, but I don't want any weirdness between us."

Oh.

Not what I expected, but infinitely better than hearing that kissing me was like making out with his sister. And this works perfectly with my plan anyway. Brandon and I are just friends. Awesome. Good to know we're on the same page.

"No," I tell him. "Yeah. We're cool. Zero weirdness."

I force a smile to prove my point, and we stare at each other some more. With absolutely zero weirdness.

The seconds drag on in silence.

"Well, that's good," he says, visibly drawing a breath. "I'm glad."

"Me, too."

Thankfully, the doorbell rings, saving us from any further non-weird comments. Baylee races down the steps, Kaitie on her heels, and squeals erupt from the family room. Brandon laughs and shakes his head. "There's my cue."

For a second it looks like he wants to say more, but he turns on his heel and jogs up the stairs. And I go and greet eight giggling girls.

Head in the game, Reed.

BRANDON
BRANDON'S ROOM, 8:45 p.m.

I crack my knuckles and look at the sketch I've been working on since my forced seclusion a few hours ago. We agreed my presence at the estrogen-fest downstairs would be weird and complicate things. I'm just not sure what it would complicate more: whatever it is that girls do at these things or my friendship with Aly.

Sketching is a trick a counselor suggested after Dad got sick and I became the man of the house at thirteen. I do it to deal with feelings I can't or won't talk about. If I were in a self-analytical mood, I'd find it interesting I took out the pad tonight, but something tells me that kind of thinking can only lead to more problems.

No surprise after the past week, this sketch is of Aly. Two different Alys to be exact, a sort of before-and-after morphing into one girl. The first Aly doesn't have on any makeup, her hair is in a messy ponytail, and she has on track pants and her ratty *Block This!* T-shirt. The second Aly's hair falls around her shoulders, her eyes are smoky, and she's in cut-off shorts and a bikini top, her daily uniform on the camping trip.

Staring at one makes me feel happy and relaxed. The other confuses the hell out of me. She's the same girl with the same cute nose and sassy smile in both pictures, so the answer is obvious.

The damn makeover is the problem.

A mouthwatering scent wafts through the crack in my door, and my stomach grumbles. I glance behind me at the clock on the nightstand. For two hours I've sat here with nothing to do other than fixate on the girl messing with my head. I deserve some of those snacks I helped put out earlier. Getting up, I throw my pencil across the room and follow my nose to the kitchen.

At the entrance, I stop outside the door. I'm starved, but the girls are huddled around the butcher-block island, and curiosity has me waiting. Aly turns from the oven and lays a tray of piping hot cookies on the counter. I'm so hungry I could eat the damn tray.

"Girls, it's imperative you learn this now." She levels them with a mock-serious expression, and her rapt audience leans in. "Boys are gonna come, and boys are gonna go. Unfortunately, some friends may even do the same. But dessert, y'all, will *never* let you down."

I smother a laugh as Aly's signature smile breaks across her face. She grabs a spatula, pries off a gooey chocolate chip cookie, and plops it on a plate. My stomach grumbles again, and I step forward to snag one. Then I hear:

"Boys suck!"

And I jump back. What the hell? But no one is even looking in my direction. Apparently, the statement was in regards to the suckiness of boys in general, not me in particular, but going in there now would be like stepping on a live grenade. Not happening, grumbling stomach be damned.

"But not Brandon, right, Aly?" I halt mid-backtrack as Baylee's friend Britney leans her cheek on her hand. "I hear y'all are dating now. He's so *hot*."

Baylee pretends to gag, and Kaitie scrunches her nose. Aly laughs, and, curious how she'll respond, I press against the door jamb, still out of sight. This I *have* to hear.

"My older sister said he's a heartbreaker," another girl interrupts. I think her name's Ashley. "She says Brandon changes women like he changes underwear." She gives the group a smug smile before turning to Baylee. Her smile withers. "No offense, Bayls. Or-or you, Aly."

My sister looks to the ground, fidgeting with her sleeve, and my hands clench at my sides. I have reasons for hooking up, but it's none of this girl's business. And my sister doesn't need to be hearing shit about me from her own friends. I want to go in there and say that very thing, but the look in Aly's eyes stops me.

Her gaze sharpens before the hint of a smile tilts her lips. Resting her elbows on the island, she leans in like she's about to confide a secret. "Brandon *is* pretty hot, huh?"

My eyebrows shoot up. That's not what I expected her to say.

"And you're right, Ashley, he does date a lot of girls. But he *never* leads them on." Aly directs this at Baylee, and a grateful smile tugs my mouth. I should've known she had my back. Then a sort of faraway look crosses her face as she breaks off a piece of cookie and licks the chocolate from her fingers, staring at the bare wall over their heads. "It's not as if the boy can help that he's easy to fall in love with."

The grateful smile freezes on my face as cold hits me square in the back.

Shit.

Freshman year, I knew Aly wanted more, but I thought she was over that by now. I hope she is because my feelings are still the same. During Dad's illness, Aly was my rock. She came with her parents to the hospital with a never-ending supply of mindless games and homemade cookies. The night he died, she shot hoops with me for hours without saying a word. Our families were close so I'd always known her, but those months bonded us. She was the one bright spot to emerge from that hell.

After months of watching Mom cry in that hospital room and a year seeing her battle being a widow, I learned what love really does—it leads to misery. Friendships last. Relationships end. Three years ago, I refused to screw up the one good thing I had going. And I still won't. My friendship with Aly is way too important to mess with.

Aly shakes her head and focuses on the girls again with a smile. "Not that *I'm* in love with him or anything." She rolls her eyes like that would be absurd, and my lungs inflate again. I lean against the doorframe in relief. "I'm just saying that, despite the number of girls he's dated or his reputation, Brandon's one of the good ones."

That almost makes me laugh out loud, but I choke it back before I give myself away. One of the good ones. That expression exists for guys like Drew. But for someone who *changes women like he changes underwear*? Not so much.

At this point, the girls can keep their cookies. I've heard enough. I turn with the intent of hightailing it out of there, and the hardwood creaks under my foot.

"Hey, no boys allowed!"

Heaving a sigh, I walk in palms up and say, "Just grabbing a snack."

Aly's cheeks glow pink as she nibbles the corner of her lip. Fidgeting with her ring and staring at the ground, I know she's worried I heard what she said. It's wrong to tease her, to flirt and push the issue with preteen witnesses, but I can't help myself.

"These smell good," I say, coming to a stop in front of her. Placing a hand on the counter near her waist, I reach around for the tray with the other and whisper, "They smell like *you*."

I probably shouldn't have said that.

A soft puff of air hits my neck as Aly gasps. The warm cookie I'm trying to snag sticks to the pan so I twist it, but the action only brings me flush against her. Breath hisses between my teeth as I shift my hand to her hip. The heat from her body seeps through the thin material of her shirt, and I fist the soft cotton.

Looking down, I see the pink of Aly's cheeks has turned a vibrant crimson. Slowly, she lifts her gaze to mine, and her eyes crinkle. *So damn beautiful.*

Giggles from the audience kill the mood—thank God—and I unclench the thin material of her shirt. I swallow hard and grab a handful of her special double chocolate chip cookies, this time prepared to stay locked away until morning.

♥ ♥ ♥

"It's 2:00 a.m. and I'm bored outta my mind."

Talking to myself is not a good sign. Since leaving Aly in the kitchen, I've spent hours going through our yearbook, determined to find Aly another guy to set her sights on. Anyone other than Justin. The problem is that the rest of the clowns at our school aren't good enough either. So that leaves me with Plan B: getting her to realize she's not a *Casual* and calling an end to this charade.

How I expect to convince her of that is still a big fat blank.

Sprawled across my bed, tossing a baseball over my head, my eyes keep darting to the sketch I pinned to the wall. I broke my personal rule of never hanging my work where anyone can see it, but this one feels important. Like it somehow holds the answer to my problem.

I pitch the ball again, perhaps a little too forcefully, and it bangs against the ceiling. Starving isn't helping my mood. After those stolen cookies hours ago, I ventured back down only one other time, to grab a few slices of pizza, and ended up interrupting a spa treatment. Why girls like coating themselves in green goop, I'll never know. About an hour ago, after what felt like hours of non-stop pounding bass and preteen giddiness, things started quieting down.

The girls have to be asleep by now. *All* the girls.

If I sneak downstairs, grab a couple slices of pizza, and come right back, no one will ever notice. I slowly crack open my door and listen.

Silence.

Carefully, I make my way down the stairs and step over mounds of passed-out girls on the floor before padding into the kitchen. The pizza box on the counter calls my name. I flip the top, grab a slice, and look out the window.

The woven hammock strung between the two oak trees in the backyard is gently rocking back and forth. I lean closer and see a pair of bare legs push off the ground. Even with the dappled moonlight filtering through the leaves of the trees, I know it's Aly.

My eyes shift between the hammock swaying softly under her body and the sanctuary of my room. Where I *want* to go and where I *need* to go. Pizza box in hand, I hesitate and then turn and walk out into the cool night air.

I've never been good at doing what I should.

Aly doesn't see me coming. She's staring up at the stars in a simple tank top and shorts, her hair piled on her head in a messy ponytail. She's sexy as hell.

Damn.

"Hey," I say roughly.

She jumps. Hand to her heart, she looks at me and says, "Holy cannoli, Brandon, you scared the crap out of me!" She takes a deep breath and lets it out on a laugh. "If I wasn't before, I'm definitely awake now— Hey, is that pizza?"

I grin and hold out the box. She scoots over, patting the space next to her on the hammock. When I lower myself down, my weight causes her to sink against me. We're pressed together, shoulder to thigh. She leans over to grab a slice, and the tips of her breasts glide across my stomach. I clench my teeth, holding back a groan.

The slight breeze carries the sound of chirping crickets and distant cars. Wisps of hair blow around her face. I grab a slice and turn it around to gnaw into the stuffed crust. "Having fun?"

Aly pops a pepperoni into her mouth. "Yeah, the girls are sweet and totally think I know what I'm talking about. I feel like Yoda."

She grins and kicks her foot out to swing us. It only makes me more aware of how close her body is. Grabbing onto the distraction, I say, "Well, we *are* getting old and wise. We're gonna be seniors on Monday."

"I know. Can you believe it?" Aly slaps my chest excitedly. "Before you know it, we're gonna be at A&M."

"That's the plan," I say, handing her the last slice and tossing the box on the ground. "But let's get through this year first. Fast-forward too much and you'll miss that road trip you've been planning forever."

For as long as I've known her, and that's been a while, graduation for Aly has meant a nationwide road trip. She has a huge map of the United States tacked on the back of her door with all the places she's read about and wants to visit highlighted in a rainbow of colors. The thing's practically covered. I have an open invitation to join her, but there's no way I could swing that. Who'd cut the grass, take out the trash, and cook when Mom works?

I wouldn't know what to do, leaving my responsibilities behind for an entire summer.

Aly grins and kicks her foot again. A mosquito crawls across my bicep. I brush it off, and my fingers graze her smooth arm. Without thinking, I skate my fingers down to her wrist and lift her hand, noticing how tiny it is inside my own. How soft it feels against my rough skin.

I look up into her wide eyes.

Aly exhales a shaky breath. She glances at our joined hands and slowly slips hers away. "I-It's late," she whispers. "I better go inside."

That's what she says, but she doesn't move. She stays lying next to me, temptation snapping between us, and I'm glad. I don't *want* her to move. I want a replay of the other night. My heart pounds so loud I know she hears it. We're so close I feel her quickened breaths on my face, and I'm seconds away from taking her.

She places her hand on my chest...and pushes to her feet.

Big blue eyes gaze down at me. Aly worries her lip between her teeth, and everything in me clenches, wanting to mimic that very gesture. The sound of the crickets grows louder in the heavy silence until she finally says, "Good night, Brandon."

Her voice is soft, unsure, and if I tried, I know I could convince her to stay. But that would be wrong. Our friendship is too important. "Night."

Aly's gaze lowers to my mouth and the skin burns, feeling her phantom lips on mine. She steps back, turns, and walks back to the house.

The back door closes with a decided *click,* and I throw myself against the hammock, the force of it rocking me back and forth.

What in the hell are we doing?

I look at the endless sky, fighting the urge to run after her. I search for constellations, one of the few things Dad taught me before he got sick, but I'm not thinking about astronomy. As my eyes trace the lines of the Big Dipper, I imagine I'm tracing the lines of Aly's body. I replay the last few moments she was out here with me and fill in the gaps of what could have happened had she stayed.

MONDAY, AUGUST 16TH
6 weeks and 5 days until Homecoming ♥

ALY
FAIRFIELD ACADEMY, 7:22 a.m.

Don't throw up, Aly. Do NOT throw up.

That's my new mantra as I stand like an idiot outside the main door to Fairfield Academy. I feel Brandon's concerned gaze drill into the top of my head. When we got here this morning, I didn't even have to tell him I needed a moment to gather myself before going inside; he just knew.

"You ready?" he asks, tightening his hand around the handle.

I'd like to say no, but that will get me nothing. I devised Operation Sex Appeal and Project Pretend Hookup, and now I need to *own* it. The camping trip was a success. This will be, too.

Lifting my head, I throw on a brave smile and say, "Let's do this."

Lips that I've spent *way* too much time thinking about lately tighten into a thin line, but Brandon nods and opens the door. I step through and embrace the chaos. Mobs of people are huddled against the lockers. The polished floor beneath my feet reflects the multicolored fliers plastering the newly painted walls, and a glorious mix of antiseptic, perfume, and aftershave stings my nose.

It *looks* like and *smells* like every other first day back to school. But it *feels* like anything but.

And just like that, the brief moment of confidence vanishes. I yank on my hem. Our school has uniforms, but yesterday I mistakenly let Kara *adjust* it. I pull the waistband as low as it can go and rub my eyes with both hands, trying to psych myself back up. They return covered with makeup. I close my eyes, with no other option but to laugh in self-loathing. Any second now, my classmates are going to turn around, take one look at me, and know that I'm a fake. That I'm just pretending. They'll see through my trendy, Kara-approved disguise and clown-like makeup and laugh me right out of the building.

Brandon slides his thumbs under my eyes, then takes my left hand and laces our fingers together. A sense of calm envelops me. I look into his eyes, grinning as he sends me a wink. That one flirty gesture eases the mounting tension in my shoulders more than any words he could have said. With a subtle nod, I roll my shoulders back and turn to face the hallway.

Here we go.

Brandon gives my hand a reassuring squeeze, then gently tugs me through the crowd, ignoring the people staring like we're a walking celebrity sighting.

"I hear Evans's English course load is crazy," he says, acting as if today is any other day. He maneuvers us around a group of gawking girls, adding, "I'm depending on you to have my back for essays."

The girl in the center openly sneers at me, a look of pure venom on her face. I swallow. "Deal," I reply, striving to match his relaxed tone. And failing miserably. "But only if you have *my* back in calculus."

A couple lockers down, two guys lean against the wall. One focuses on my chest while the other makes some kind of creepy, puckered kissy face. My breathing spikes. I glance at the girls' bathroom across the hall, and the urge to bolt for a stall is fierce.

Shouldn't getting what I want feel better than this?

"Aly?"

Brandon's voice snaps me back to our conversation. "Calculus. Right. Tell me again why I have to take it?"

He watches me as a crowd of girls heads into the bathroom, and I can see in his eyes that he knows what a head case I'm being. But he plays along anyway. "Because you're brilliant and tested out of algebra freshman year?"

Freshman year. Apparently, it was a year of life-altering events.

Aside from when I stupidly confessed my feelings for Brandon, the day I let Mom convince me to take the placement test would be my do-over. I ended up passing it by the skin of my teeth, but it locked me into the honors track for math. For English, history, and even science, I deserve that placement, but math and I have never gotten along. Thankfully, Brandon's a mathematical genius. He's saved my butt more times than I can count, and my only shot of surviving this year is through total dependency on him again.

He stops in front of my locker, two over from his own. He wraps his arms around me and squeezes tight, advising in my ear, "Don't let them see ya sweat."

Nodding, I turn away, pretending I don't hear the whispers. I swirl the dial of my cold metal locker and it springs open, and I try to stay busy reattaching pictures and unloading and reloading notebooks until the homeroom bell rings. When it does, I nearly sink to the floor in relief.

"Ready?"

"Ready to get out of this hallway, that's for freaking sure," I tell him, taking a breath as people scurry left and right. And to think, I only have eight more hours of this.

Brandon takes my shaky hand and steers me down the winding hallway leading to our class. On the stairwell, his hand slides to the small of my back.

He's not really touching you, I chide myself. *Remember it's all for show.*

But the heat from his fingers seeps through my uniform polo and my nervous system sends zings of electricity pulsing down my legs.

Concern over incredulous classmates fades as my entire body zeroes in on his touch.

Still doesn't mean anything.

I miss a step, and his arm wraps around my waist to steady me. Warm breath tickles my ear.

Doesn't mean anything either. Brandon is just being chivalrous. And he's leaning in close so I can hear him.

Wait, he's talking.

"Sorry, but I totally missed what you were saying," I confess as we enter the classroom.

Brandon's eyebrows draw together. He motions toward two empty seats in the back, and I follow him down the crowded aisle, laser stares pinging the back of my head. Tossing his bag on the floor, he sits on the edge of a desk and crosses his arms. "You okay?"

The muscles of his arms bulge against the cotton of his shirt.

Just peachy. My body's betraying me, and my head's complete mush, but otherwise I'm fantastic.

I force my gaze away and slide into my seat. "I'm fine. Caffeine hasn't kicked in yet, I guess."

He frowns like he doesn't believe me. Lacing his hands behind his neck, he studies the ground and asks, "But you'd tell me if something was wrong, right?" He lifts his eyes, and his face twists in concern. I *hate* that my crazy hormones make him look like that.

"Of course," I promise. "I tell you everything."

Well, practically.

The bell rings and the rest of the class files in. Brandon taps his fingers on my desk as Lauren Hays's voice rings out over the P.A. system. "Morning, my fellow Hokies! Your favorite class president here, welcoming you to another new year filled with change, excitement, and discovery..."

So far, I'd say she has it about right.

WEDNESDAY, AUGUST 18TH

6 weeks and 3 days until Homecoming ♥

⌒⌒⤳

ALY

BRANDON'S TRUCK, 5:30 p.m.

⌒⤳⌒

Today's agenda: Getting back to normal.

I glance over at Brandon drumming on the steering wheel and pretend to sit in comfortable silence. In truth, I'm completely weirded out. Awkwardness has surrounded us all week, transforming every glance and thrilling touch into an exhausting game of "is it real or is it pretend?" At our first rec team practice, I couldn't tell what the girls found more interesting: our skill drills or watching sparks fly between their coaches. But today, I'm a girl on a mission.

We *will* get back to normal again. I *will* get my priorities straight, my focus back on Justin and Homecoming, and the fantasies about my best friend out of my head. Or at least two out of three.

"Thanks again for waiting," I tell him, shifting in my seat. Only a week into school, and calculus is already kicking my ass. Brandon waited around until my practice ended so he could tutor me. Just another reason why this boy rocks so hard—and why I need my head fixed. "Calculus is the bane of my existence."

"You'll get the hang of it," he says, pulling into my driveway. "All you need is the right tutor." He gives an exaggerated wag of his eyebrows, but my eyes sink to his lips. I bet there's a lot of things he could tutor me in.

The *creak* of his door and him hopping down clue me in to how well I'm doing so far with my mission. Does he know what I was thinking? My stomach flips as I answer my own question. Of course he knows. I have the sophistication of an infant. Brandon's face, however, is completely expressionless as he helps me down, giving nothing away. He follows me silently up the walk and into my spacious kitchen.

Mom grins from her station at the stove. Wiping her hands on a towel, she sets a large tray of brownies on the granite counter. "Thought y'all could use a snack."

I inhale the scent of cocoa and break off a piece. As the sugar hits my bloodstream, I take in my surroundings.

The low rumble of the dishwasher. Mom chopping vegetables at the island. The metallic sound of her spoon hitting the simmering pot on the stove. This is *exactly* what we need. A safe, parent-filled environment with the perfect amount of chaos to ensure there is zero chance of a charged moment. My shoulders relax, and I lean against the back of my barstool.

Kaitie flies into the room, wide-eyed and breathless. "Mom! We're gonna be late!"

Mom looks up from stirring and squints at the digital clock on the microwave. "Oh, you're right."

She puts the cover on the pot and turns the temperature to low, and my gaze darts to the calendar hanging on the fridge, filled with reminders of appointments, events, and holidays. Written in red on Wednesday: *Kaitie's Youth Group: 6:00.*

There goes our parental supervision.

Mom grabs her keys off the Texas Star hook hanging near the back door. Lifting several covered trays of food, she cranes her neck to tell us, "We'll be back in a couple hours. Dinner's ready, and I made more than enough, so, Brandon, dig on in."

The door closes, the garage door rumbles open, and with that, we are alone.

Enter weirdness.

The sound of the dishwasher magnifies. Somewhere the house settles, and I swear I hear the second hand of a clock ticking—but all our clocks are digital. We silently take out our books, flipping to tonight's assignment. The formulas and graphs look even more confusing than normal. My right hand itches to creep over and claim his, so I shake it.

"Cramp," I explain.

He nods. My foot bounces against the wooden leg of the stool, and as I scratch my head, I glance at the clock.

We've been alone for three minutes.

In my peripheral vision, I see Brandon shift in his seat and crack his knuckles. He turns his head, and our eyes meet.

"Is this weird?" I ask after a tension-filled pause.

He hesitates, then nods. "Why is that, you think?"

"I don't know," I admit—or, actually, lie. I can't answer for him, but I know part of the weirdness is because of my crazy reactions to his presence lately. "I'm getting scared, though. What if we're not able to go back to being friends like before once this 'experiment' ends?" I let my hand close around his. "Besides Gabi and Kara, you're my best friend."

Brandon slides a section of my hair behind my ear. "Aly, we'll always be friends. Don't ever worry about that." His voice is so confident, so sure, that I can't help but want to believe it. "It's that damn kiss that messed everything up."

My spine straightens in shock. Ever since the sleepover, Brandon's avoided or changed the subject every time I've brought up our kiss—further proof that he regrets it.

His lips press into a frown. "We just need to pretend it never happened."

Inside, I wince. I can't let him see that it hurts—after all, he's only confirming what I already knew—but the truth hits like a spiked ball to the face. Forcing a smile, I ask, "Can it be that easy?"

"Sure." Brandon nods once, as if making up his mind about something. "Stand up."

Confused, I let him pull me up. He takes a deep, cleansing breath and widens his eyes, suggesting I do the same. I feel like I'm in yoga. Then he says, "Now we're gonna shake the memory out, like an Etch A Sketch. Remember those?"

"Uh, yeah?"

Brandon starts shaking his head violently back and forth, just like you would an Etch A Sketch, and I can't help but laugh. He stops and grins. "Don't just stand there. Try it."

With reluctance, I shake my head and even add a few jumps in for good measure. Surprisingly, it's kind of fun. He does it some more, too, and after a minute, we share a smile.

A nice, silly, comfortable, platonic smile. A *normal* smile.

"Friends?" Brandon asks.

I nod. "You know it."

"See? Everything's fine," he says, tweaking my nose. "We're still us, and nothing will ever change that."

He exhales in relief and stretches his arms above his head. The hunter-green polo lifts, a strip of his stomach creeps into view, and I swallow my tongue.

Yeah, I'm not sure that worked as well as he hoped.

FRIDAY, AUGUST 20TH
6 weeks and 1 day until Homecoming ♥

BRANDON
LONESTAR THEATRES, 7:20 p.m.

It's dinnertime, which means Aly is grumpy. The movies are slammed on weekend nights, and she rarely has time to grab anything to eat after practice. As I walk up, Gabi lifts her head behind the ticket counter, and I wave the McDonald's bag in the air. She motions me through the door with a smirk, one that becomes an actual smile when I hand over a chicken sandwich. Say all you want about guys, but I've learned the way to a *girl's* heart is through her stomach. Especially when French fries or chocolate are involved.

The lobby is crowded. Following the salty smell of popcorn, I pass no fewer than three wailing babies and a half-dozen kids screaming for candy. By the time I hop over the swinging door to the refreshment counter, my ears feel like they're bleeding. Out of the seven lines of customers, Aly's is the longest, so I reach into the bag for a greasy bribe and hand it over to her coworker Barbara.

"For me?" she asks, batting her fake eyelashes as she takes the cheeseburger. "Boy, if you were fifty years older—or I was fifty years younger—I'd rock your world." She gives me a quick once-over as she chuckles at her own joke. "I'm guessing your motives aren't completely selfless, but lucky for you, I'm easily bought."

She waits for Aly to hand a couple their change and hip-checks her. "I'll take it from here." Aly's nose crinkles in confusion, and Barbara nods her head in my direction. Aly grins. "Go enjoy your break with Stud Puppy, sweet girl. Believe it or not, I was young once myself."

Aly pecks her wrinkled cheek before eagerly keying her code into the machine. "Thanks, Barb. I'll be back in thirty!" Her shoes squeak on the sticky floor as she rushes over and envelops me in a quick hug. "My hero."

The sweet scent of her hair fills my head, and I quickly lean back, masking my discomfort with a smile. "Outside?"

"God, yes." She holds her palms over her ears and makes a pained face. "Quiet, *please*."

We walk across the lobby, under the overhead screen playing an endless loop of previews, and through the door, plopping down on the metal bench farthest from the ticket counter.

Aly looks at the bag between us and shimmies her shoulders. "What'd ya bring me?"

"Quarter Pounder with Cheese, hold the pickle, French fries, and a Coke, no ice. What else?" I've had her order down for years.

She squeals with delight and dives in. Around a mouthful of fries, she asks, "So what brought you to our humble establishment tonight? Severe boredom or just desperate for my company?" She smiles as she asks so I know she's joking, but honestly, she's not that far off.

I take a bite of my Big Mac and hold up a finger, chewing as I contemplate how to answer. I have a proposition, but I've been debating all day whether or not to suggest it. On one hand, it'll be an excuse to hang out with my best friend again. On the other, it could complicate things even more. I swallow and ask, "What are you doing tomorrow night?"

"After my shift here, nothing," she says, wiping her hands on a napkin. "Definitely no hot dates lined up or anything," she adds with a teasing jab to my ribs.

I smile back, but it's forced. The burger in my mouth tastes like cardboard. I tell myself it's a gut reaction. That I'd feel the same way thinking about a guy asking out *any* girl I'm hooking up with—but that's a lie. I wouldn't give a shit with any other girl. But Aly's not just any girl.

Ignoring that train of thought, I say, "Good, you do now. You get off of work at seven, right?"

She tilts her head and squints. "We're going out? Like, on a real official date?"

"A *pretend* official date," I clarify.

Just the thought of a real date with Aly gives me hives. A real date could lead to real dating. Aly is a *Commitment,* whether she wants to believe it or not, which means she'll want a real relationship. One beyond our easy, dependable friendship. Those kinds of relationships end. I see it every day in the halls at school, and I saw it in my dad's hospital room. I don't want that for us.

"But Saturday night *is* date night, and since it's not like either of us can ask out anyone else, I figured we might as well have some fun during this experiment." I give her the smile that normally gets me what I want and hope she can't see my uncertainty. "Don't you think?"

"A pretend official date," she muses.

She bites into her cheeseburger and quietly chews. The silence only amps my nerves. Maybe I shouldn't have suggested it, but after the tension of the past week and my inability to get anywhere in my own plan, I decided we both need a night of fun.

"A date with Heartthrob Taylor, huh?" Aly laughs and twists to give me a full body appraisal. "I finally get to see what all the hoopla's about. Does this mean I'll learn your moves, too?"

"I can't give out all my trade secrets," I tell her with a grin. "But you'll have a good time."

"Count me in."

We inhale the rest of our food before Aly's break is over, falling into our usual conversations about nothing and everything. Things have been better since yesterday's Etch A Sketch exorcism, and sitting outside now, it's almost as if nothing has changed between us. I certainly don't stare at her mouth as she chews on her French fries or when she sips Coke out of her lipstick-stained straw.

Or sniff her hair again when we hug goodbye.

Walking back to my truck, I hear her call my name.

"What should I wear tomorrow night?"

A conundrum. What I'd like to see Aly in and what type of outfit is best for our friendship are two completely different things. "Whatever you'd wear on a usual date would be fine," I reply, walking backward.

She nods, looking deep in thought, and I turn back around, unsure of which outfit I hope she'll choose.

SATURDAY, AUGUST 21ST

6 weeks until Homecoming ♥

BRANDON

ALY'S HOUSE, 7:30 p.m.

I ring the doorbell and step back to gaze up at Aly's window. She's tied back her yellow curtains, and I can see her running around inside, probably trying to find a purse or matching shoes in her disaster of a room. I kick the red brick and ponder the night ahead.

As I see it, the night can end in one of two ways: our comfortable friendship will return after a night of fun and goofing around or being with Aly on a date—even a pretend one—will make kissing her again all too tempting.

I close my eyes and beg the universe for the first outcome.

From the other side of the door, I hear the rhythmic thump of shoes hitting the ceramic tile. I straighten in preparation to greet Aly, but when the door opens, I feel my smile freeze on my face. I take in her white lace halter top and the short denim skirt showing off her tan legs and swallow.

I hadn't been sure which outfit I wanted her to choose, and now... Well, I'm still not sure which would've been better for our friendship, but I'm damn sure enjoying the view.

"You look amazing."

A blush creeps up her neck. She bites her lip and fidgets with the neckline of her top. "Um, thanks."

I clear my throat and remember why I'm here. *Playful and fun.* I hold out my elbow and say, "Your chariot awaits, m'lady."

She grins and hesitantly slips her hand into the crook of my arm. The feel of her soft skin instantly has me imagining other soft things: her hair, her cheeks, her *lips.* I screw my eyes shut, replace the thought with baseball stats, and glance down. "I see you've banished the heels for the night."

Aly nods vehemently. "They are the devil. From now on, it's either ballet flats or sneakers on these bad boys." She stops to wiggle a black, flat-footed shoe.

I breathe a sigh of relief at her playful tone. This is good. We stop at the passenger door, and as I help her into the cab, my fingers graze her bare lower back. Her blue eyes meet mine and then dart away. I cough and close her door, muttering a string of curses as I round the bumper and slam the door on my side.

Aly smiles nervously. "So where you taking me?"

By the grace of God, I choke down the response I'd like to give—*back to my room*—and force a nice, lighthearted, friendly smile as I back out of her long driveway. "All will be revealed in time."

"The thrill of suspense, huh?" She leans back, obviously getting more comfortable with the situation. "I am intrigued, Mr. Taylor."

"Good," I say, waving at the security guard in front of her neighborhood. "You should be."

I tune the radio to the country station she loves but I rarely allow, and she rolls down the window, letting the warm breeze fill the cab of the truck. Hair blowing in the wind, she laughs and sings loudly over the sound of cars zooming by. Happy to see her singing in front of me, I join in, doing my best to murder the tune, which only makes her laugh harder and sing louder.

When we pull into The Station, our final destination, I'm nervous. If this were a real date, I would've taken her to the stereotypical "dinner and a movie" or even to a party. But all that seemed too boring. This place seems tailor-made for Aly—video games, pool tables, shuffleboard, and, of course, food.

"Interesting choice," she says, eyeing the building normally frequented by older couples or game heads. Her face is in profile, but as I search her expression, I note her trademark grin is glaringly absent.

"You don't like it."

I knew I should've stuck with the same old routine.

This is why Aly deserves someone better than Justin. Guys like him and me aren't cut out for this shit. "Aly, look, we can go somewhere else. I just thought—"

"No! Are you kidding me?" She twists around to face me with an incredulous look on her face. "This is awesome. I was actually a little nervous about being on a 'pretend official date' with Brandon Taylor, but this'll be fun!"

She pushes open her door, and I jump out my side, relieved I didn't screw the night up before it even started. When I arrive at her door to help her down, Aly beams at me with such a playful smile that I make it my mission to keep it there.

Offering my elbow again, I ask in a fake British accent, "Well then, shall I escort you in, miss?"

That beautiful smile grows as she lifts her nose in the air and replies, "Yes. Please do so."

Laughing, we walk across the crowded parking lot and into the brightly lit building. The techno symphony of bells and beeps from video games, the crack and clash of pool balls colliding, and a cacophony of voices and laughter assault us.

"Pick your preference: eat first or play?" I ask, leaning in so she can hear me over the noise.

"Hmm. Tough choice." She taps her lips with a pointed finger, but my gaze does *not* linger on her soft, glossy mouth. "While food is always a good option, I think I wanna play. Ready to have your butt handed to you in shuffleboard?"

I laugh at the smug look on her face, and any hint of sexual tension dissipates. *Thank God.* "Honey, Wii doesn't count." We're both athletes so we're naturally competitive—and sore losers. But Aly's delight in decimating me in virtual shuffleboard a few weeks ago is annoyingly adorable. "Besides, that night was pure luck, sister."

She rolls her eyes, holds her fingers up in the shape of a W, and mouths, "Whatever."

"You just watch," I say, leading her to the billiards section. "I got my A game tonight."

A guy about our age sits behind a cracked wood counter looking bored. He has eyebrow and lip piercings and a purple tint to his heavily gelled hair. Aly's mood is infectious, so I decide to have a little fun.

"Good evening, chap," I say, continuing the British ruse. The dude fingers his lip ring and eyes me curiously. "We'd be delighted to play a rousing game of shuffleboard, wouldn't we, darling?" I turn to Aly with a playful smile.

She snorts and then, straightening her shoulders, collects herself. "Yes, that sounds like a spiffing idea. Let us do that."

The guy widens his eyes like he thinks we're crazy before turning to grab the colored weights. I chuckle and reach for my wallet to start a tab. I don't care if the whole place thinks I'm nuts as long as Aly is laughing again.

We make our way to the empty shuffleboard table in the back, and Aly calls over her shoulder, "Cheers!" Turning back with a grin, she smacks my *bum* and plucks one of the blue weights out of the case. "Ladies first."

"Oh, bloody hell," I tease. "All right, do your worst."

With the feel of her hand lingering on my *arse*, sending ripples of awareness to other areas as well, I step to the side and motion her forward. She sets the weight on the table and leans over to line up her shot, her face a mask of determination. She gives the weight several practice pushes, and I take a step back to give her room.

Her movements cause her skirt to rise, exposing the smooth skin of her upper thigh. I swallow and avert my eyes as her weight skids across the table.

"Pure luck, my butt," she crows. I look back and see it stopped right on the edge. A perfect slide—if I don't bump it off.

"Beginner's luck perhaps," I reply, picking up a red weight. I push it across and not only do I miss her weight by a mile, mine crashes off the edge into a pile of sand. Aly snickers.

"Oh, sod off," I say with a grin.

Unfortunately, it doesn't get better from there. We play three games, and despite my best efforts, Aly wins them all.

"Obviously, the problem is I am unaware of my own strength," I say in response to Aly's third victory.

She giggles and her eyes twinkle. "Whatever you say, *love*."

I fold my arms across my chest, but can't help but smile. "Are you ready to eat now, or shall we continue the royal arse-kicking?"

The minx laughs again. "Food, please," she says melodramatically, allowing her body to go limp against the side of the table. "I'm positively famished."

I shake my head and walk to the other side to gather the weights. While I stack them in the box, Aly strolls ahead, past the rows of coin-operated pool tables and older guys leering around their cues. She doesn't seem to notice the attention, but I do. She stops in front of a flashing video game and peers down with a smile. I dig in my pocket and drop a stack of quarters in front of her.

"Might as well keep the winning streak alive," I say. She looks up, the red and blue lights from the machine lighting up her wide eyes, and I lift the box of weights. "I have to bring these back, but let's see how that beginner's luck holds up against a bunch of zombies."

Aly laughs. "Challenge accepted."

She plops the quarters in the machine, and pre-recorded screams echo behind me. I stroll up to the counter, nodding at the purple-haired guy kicked back on a stool, fingers flying over his cell phone.

His eyes shift to the box of weights when I set them on the counter, then back down again to his hands.

"Do you mind?" I ask, drumming my debit card on the counter. "I'm kinda on a date here."

The guy sighs and pockets his phone, then takes his sweet-ass time ringing me up. By the time I walk back to where I left Aly, I expect to find her knee-deep in zombie bodies.

Instead, I find another body.

A polo-shirt-wearing guy's body, leaning over her with his arms caging her on either side of the machine.

Polo-Boy's head looms over hers, his mouth entirely too close. He lifts his hand and skims it down Aly's arm. She lurches and glances over, widening her eyes at me in a silent plea.

Long strides cover the distance between us, the world tinted red. I grab the fabric of the guy's shirt and force him around. "Get your hands off her."

Polo-Boy looks me over. "Just keeping the girl company." He stands up tall and, despite being several inches shorter than me, sneers dismissively. "You shouldn't leave pretty little things like this alone. You never know who might come around to steal her."

Just keep talking, asshole.

My hands clench at my sides. Deep breaths rack my chest. The guy lifts his chin and laughs, and my entire body tenses as I rear back, ready to strike.

A soft hand grabs my fist. "Brandon, leave it alone." I drag my gaze away from his and glance down into Aly's frightened eyes. "Please, let's just go eat." She steps between us and lowers her voice. "Don't let this jerk ruin our pretend date, okay?"

Pretend.

More than the gentle pleading in her voice, the seemingly innocuous word strips me of all fight. I blink and stare down at my hand. *What the hell am I doing?*

All around us, people are watching, hoping for a show. Polo-Boy is smiling, acting like it's just another Saturday night. Like he does this all the time. But I don't.

I mean, sure, I've gotten into a few fights in my life, but never at a place like this. Never with a complete stranger. And *never* over a girl.

Aly laces her arm around mine and tugs gently. I nod, slowly and wordlessly, and walk away.

Behind us, Polo-Boy snickers.

"What an asshat," Aly mutters. "Thank you for that."

I give her a tight-lipped smile. She shoots me sideways glances as we walk to the dim restaurant section lit up by twinkle lights. I nod at a waitress in a fluorescent teal shirt, and she asks, "Two?"

"Yes, please," Aly answers, a little too loudly.

The girl grabs a couple sets of rolled utensils and old, peeling menus and leads us to a back booth. We pass a middle-aged couple and a family of four, but other than that, the restaurant is empty. I drop onto a vinyl bench seat that smells strongly of bacon.

"I don't know why," Aly says, sliding in across from me, "but I'm craving a bacon cheeseburger." Her smile is so bright it's like she swallowed a light bulb. Obviously, my caveman behavior freaked her the hell out—not exactly the feeling I was going for tonight.

I give her the chuckle she's clearly looking for, wishing I could explain what happened back there.

Wishing I understood it myself. Instead, my gaze drops to the graffiti'd tabletop.

Names proclaiming forever love have been carved into the thick wood. I glance back at Aly absently playing with her hair, and my stomach convulses, almost as if Polo-Boy had snuck back and landed a sucker punch to my gut.

The waitress brings us two waters, saying she'll be right back for our order, and I snatch my glass, gulping it in three long swallows. Crunching on the ice, I curse myself for not noticing the signs. I've never let myself fall for a girl before, but I've had more than enough experience watching Drew.

This is bad.

Aly closes her menu and beams at me. "I've decided. Bacon cheeseburger it is. What do you want?"

What do I want? To go back in time and stop your stupid makeover. To stop the urge to put Polo-Boy's head through a wall. To stop fantasizing about scooping you up, dragging you back to my truck, and kissing you until you can't see straight.

"Chicken wings," I tell her.

The waitress appears again, miraculously with another water, and takes our order. It can't come quick enough. My empty stomach churns, and my wired body thrums on the cracked vinyl seat. All the tension and awkwardness of the previous week is back and then some.

I force a smile for Aly and continue chomping on a mouthful of ice, shattering it into tiny pieces. Working my jaw back and forth, I will myself to get over it. To act like nothing has changed. As far as Aly is concerned, it hasn't. She doesn't know how badly I screwed things up tonight.

And she never will.

ALY
BRANDON'S TRUCK, 11:15 p.m.

Brandon speeds down McAllister Drive, the glowing neon lights from the passing fast food restaurants casting an eerie glow on his intent expression. He grew quiet during dinner and hasn't spoken more than a handful of words in a row since, but tonight has still been one of the best nights of my life. Certainly, the best date. There's no denying it anymore; my crush is back full force.

And that's a problem.

Three years ago, Brandon told me he doesn't do relationships. He's proven that every day since with the countless girls he has dated. A night of fun and defending my honor isn't going to change that, as much as I may wish otherwise. He dates *Casuals*, and while that is exactly what I'm trying to become, I can't casually hook up with Brandon. He means too much. *It* would mean too much. And there would be no going back when it ends.

It's not as if my feelings even matter. The only reason we went out tonight is because of my plan to get Justin's attention. And it's working. My confusion between fact and fiction kept me preoccupied this past week, but I haven't missed the glances he's been casting in my direction. Operation Sex Appeal is trucking along right on schedule, and I didn't even have to annihilate Lauren Hays...as if I had any clue how to do that anyway. They called it quits all on their own. I don't know if it's because Justin wised up or if a week is the norm for a *Casual* hookup, but he's a free agent again. If I lose focus now, it will be as if the last two weeks were for nothing. Especially since the boy who has me discombobulated doesn't want me anyway.

I've gotten over a crush on Brandon in the past. I can do it again.

The crush-in-question glances at me before turning back to the road. We drive down the quiet, tree-lined street of my neighborhood in silence. I don't know what to say to fix this. I don't even know what happened or if it's all just in my head. One minute everything seemed great—we were joking and laughing—and the next it was like he threw a wall up between us.

His truck rumbles into my driveway, and without hesitation, Brandon hops out. He comes around to my side, opening and leaving his hand on the door.

The tension between us practically crackles.

"Want to come in?" I ask. "I'm sure I can hustle up some brownies or something. Maybe we can have a rematch on Wii?"

I realize him staying will mess with the whole "getting over the crush thing again," but I don't want him to leave. I want the joking and laughter back. I want the flirtation.

Brandon scuffs the toe of his boot on the ground. "Nah, it's getting late. Long day, you know?"

"Sure, yeah," I say, unbuckling my seatbelt. "Absolutely." It *has* been a long day. Practice, our first rec match, and then work for us both. But if he wanted, I'd easily find the energy to hang out.

Especially if hanging out involved *making* out.

Whisking away that notion, as if that would ever happen again, I scoot to the edge of the seat. But I hesitate to move any further. With Brandon standing right in front of me, we are at eye-level. Kiss-level. That whisked-away notion comes right back as the memory of our dared kiss plays in my mind. The taste of the forbidden fruit. But he makes no move to lean in.

"Well, thanks again for tonight. I had a wonderful time."

Brandon nods. "Me, too."

I take his hand as he helps me down, and a zing runs up my arm. His other hand steadies me once my feet touch the ground, and a glutton for punishment, I lift my head, waiting for him to inch toward me, to pull me closer. My teeth bite into my lower lip as I search his face for any clue about how he is feeling.

He simply stares back, a trace of a smile on his full lips.

"Goodnight, Aly." His low, silky voice sends a shiver down my spine. "I'll call you later."

I mumble a goodbye, barely hiding my sigh of disappointment. He closes the passenger door, and I begin the slow trek up the red-brick path leading to my front door. I let myself in, knowing he won't drive away until I do, and watch him back away through the white wisp of my curtain. Then I sink against the hardwood.

I'm in so much trouble.

Friday, August 27th

5 weeks and 1 day until Homecoming ♥

BRANDON
BRANDON'S TRUCK, 7:15 p.m.

I punch the steering wheel in frustration. "Get your shit together!"

A movement makes my head turn mid-rant, and the soccer mom in the car beside me smiles in amusement. I lift my hand in an awkward half-wave, the red light changes to green, and I push my foot against the accelerator, taking my frustration out on the floorboard of my truck.

Tonight is Fairfield's back-to-school dance. Normally, I don't give a shit about school dances, but Aly wants to go. So here I am, running late, and the closer I get to her house, the more pissed off I become. Not about the dance, but about the fact that going with her tonight is only gonna screw things up more. Turning onto her street, I resume the speech I've been giving myself for the last ten minutes.

"Man up. Get your shit together. Figure out how in the hell you're gonna hold her without attacking her on the dance floor. And do it quick."

The last week has been the longest ever. Pretending we're hooking up is exhausting. It's even more draining pretending to be the same old Brandon and Aly when we're alone. That Etch A Sketch exorcism didn't do shit. And thanks to my brilliant idea for a pretend date, I've spent the last week denying I'm falling for my best friend.

Pulling to a stop in front of Aly's house, I take a deep breath. With a flick of my wrist, I cut the engine and listen to the silence. I've sat in this exact spot more times than I can count. In many ways, Aly's house is like my sanctuary. A place I go when my own home feels like a graveyard. I glance up at the bedroom window of the girl who knows me better than anyone, the only person I let see me cry after Dad died. I won't let this experiment take that or her away from me.

Tonight, I'm going to prove that Aly and I can go back to our normal, easy friendship.

Throwing open my door, I trudge up her sidewalk, plant my feet outside her front door, and ring the bell.

"Coming!"

I step back and see Aly stick her head out her second-story window.

"No problem," I call back up. "Take your time."

More time to get my head on straight.

Aly disappears behind a film of yellow curtain, and I turn to look out at the quiet neighborhood. Up and down the street, the lights blink on, filling the air with a low hum that matches the thrumming of my nerves. Across the street, old Mr. Lawson sits at his usual perch under a gigantic American flag, drinking beer and mumbling to himself. Two little girls ride their bikes around the cul-de-sac, smiling and waving. Just a normal, run-of-the-mill Friday night. Except not.

I thrust my hands into my pockets, jiggling the loose change from my Taco Bell run earlier tonight, and grab my pack of Trident. I toss a stick into my mouth and chew furiously. Supposedly, the smell of peppermint can calm your nerves.

I grab a second stick and shove it in, too.

With the clacking sound of Aly's shoes approaching the door behind me, I remind myself again about tonight's mission. All I need is focus. I take another deep breath for good measure and rock back on my heels, ready to greet my best friend. She opens the door, wearing a black dress molded to her skin, and I let the air out in one big huff.

Shit.

ALY

FAIRFIELD ACADEMY SCHOOL GYM, 7:30 p.m.

My stomach thumps along with the bass pounding from inside. I'm standing in line next to Brandon, waiting for him to flash our school IDs (no way was an ID fitting in this getup), frustratingly aware of the distance between us. In *every* sense of the word. If anyone glances in our direction, I'm sure we appear far from the happily hooking up couple we've been selling, but what they're not seeing are the explosive sparks snapping just under the surface.

A couple falls in line behind us, and I feel my date shift. Brandon lowers his head and gives me a small smile—the same odd one he's worn since picking me up tonight—and holds out his hand. I swipe mine across my skirt and take it, hoping he misses the shiver when we touch.

It's game time.

Yeah, it's safe to say my crush has intensified. In fact, I think it's progressed from simple crush to severe liking. Possibly even falling. And that scares me to death. The last thing our friendship needs is for Brandon to figure out how I feel and then get weird around me. Or weird*er*. But then, every once in a while, he gets this look in his eyes that makes me think I'm not the only one feeling the change. That maybe, just maybe, the line between fact and fiction is blurring for him, too.

We inch forward in line, and I spy the photo display set up in the corner. Tonight's theme is "A Year to Remember." A backdrop shows two silhouettes dancing in each other's arms, the girl's head thrown back in laughter. I shift my attention back to Brandon. Can tonight be the night that breaks the curse?

My Wall of Shame was the original inspiration for Operation Sex Appeal. At first, this mission was about feeling lovable, datable. Possibly even landing a boyfriend. In the beginning, I didn't even know about *Casuals* or *Commitments,* and Justin Carter only became a goal when I decided to experience how the other half lives.

Based on our embarrassing past, I didn't consider Brandon an option before. He is, after all, the guy who kickstarted the curse. But even though he's technically another just-a-friend date, for all intents and purposes, he's also the current man in my life. He's supposed to be my fake *hookup*, but the longer this experiment lasts, the more he feels like my pretend *boyfriend*—only with less and less emphasis on the "pretend." Maybe Homecoming doesn't need to be my endgame after all. Maybe tonight, I found a way to meet both my goals.

Brandon and I may *finally* be on the same page.

Trying very hard not to overthink it, and praying that he doesn't either, I lace our fingers together, wrap my other hand around his elbow, and lean my head against Brandon's arm.

Immediately, he tenses. "Aly..."

"Next!"

I step out of the embrace and flash the junior behind the ticket counter a smile. Then, pretending I don't see the corners of Brandon's mouth curve down as he distractedly fishes our IDs from his pocket, I turn to take in my first post-makeover dance.

The metallic doors that usually separate the large gym from the only slightly smaller cafeteria are open, creating one massive partying space. The gym holds the DJ and dance floor, and the cafeteria hosts the refreshments and guys left behind while their dates dance. A sea of green and white decorations covers the rows of tables holding discarded purses, and at the long table on the edge, right near the dance floor, I find our friends.

Seeing them comingled is still crazy to me. Gabi, Kara, and I have considered ourselves floaters, not really identifying with any particular group and sitting freely with almost all. But like the rest of the student body, we've always followed the Unwritten Law of Fairfield Academy: *Thou must not sitteth in the row of tables along the edge unless one is a member of the Beautiful People.*

Gabi coined the term, but everyone knows the law. Those tables are reserved for the most popular jocks and queen bees. Naturally, Brandon and his crew sit there, along with Lauren and the rest of the dance team. You'd expect that to include Gabi, but she never goes along with anyone's expectations. Up until the camping trip, our home base was somewhere in the middle. Occasionally, I'd wave to Brandon or send a text to be funny, but I *never* sat with him. He invited me, but I knew I didn't belong. Lauren would've made sure everyone else knew it, too.

But the Unwritten Law has one amendment: *Anyone dating a member of the Beautiful People receives an automatic pass to sit with the elite,* which means for the past two weeks, I've gotten a pass. Of course, I've dragged Gabi with me. Kara tagged along, too, being accepted without complaint and proving what I guessed since the beginning—if not for me, she'd be one of them.

Now, I watch my new circle own the table. Kara digs furiously through her purse, with a lovestruck Daniel on one side and Gabi on the other, pretending to ignore the equally smitten boy beside her. Carlos waves his hands as he animatedly tells a story to Justin, who I note appears to be dateless, and then I spy Drew.

Satisfied we are, in fact, students at Fairfield Academy, the junior waves us in, and I lean in so Brandon can hear me over the music. "Did you know Sarah was coming this weekend?"

He looks over to where Drew holds Sarah snugly in his arms, chin tucked on the crown of her head, having never looked happier. "No, I didn't," he murmurs, seeming as transfixed by the couple as I am. "I haven't talked to Drew much this week."

That surprises me, but I don't dig deeper because Sarah suddenly leaps out of Drew's lap, barreling toward us. "Aly!"

I freeze in place as the overzealous dynamo throws her arms around me, even though we barely know each other. Like the rest of the group, Sarah and I have traveled in similar circles for years, but we never quite made it to the jumping-up-and-down-while-hugging stage of friendship.

Baffled, I pat the girl's back. "Sarah!" At my failed attempt to mimic her former-cheerleader squeal, I wince and hear a telltale *click*.

Gabi smirks from behind her beloved Canon EOS Rebel. "About time you two arrived." She glances at Brandon and then wiggles her eyebrows suggestively. "As lovesick as Drew and Sarah are, at least they know to save the making out for *after* the dance."

A weird look crosses Brandon's face as I disentangle myself from Sarah's arms, and I wonder if anyone notices. "That's only because we've been together for a year," Sarah says, plopping right back on Drew's lap. "Besides, they have years of catching up to do."

Awkwardness descends, made even more obvious by the fact that Brandon can't look at me. He takes a seat, head down, and though the guys appear oblivious, all three girls look back at me with various shades of concern. *Great.* Kara stands, giving my elbow a tug. "Come with me to the bathroom?"

Gabi hops up. "I'm coming, too."

I tell Brandon I'll be right back, pretending I don't notice the relief that seems to cross his face as I follow my friends into the crowded bathroom/locker room. Girls are everywhere, misting hairspray, reapplying deodorant and makeup, gossiping, and crying. We squeeze ourselves into an unoccupied crack of space in front of the end sink, and Kara takes out her tangerine lip gloss, pumping the wand before meeting my eyes in the mirror.

"So what's Brandon's deal?" she asks, coating a shiny lip. "He seems like he's in some type of mood. Is there trouble in paradise?"

Hard to have trouble in paradise when you're not in paradise, I think, rolling my eyes like Brandon's moods are no big deal. "I don't know. Can guys get PMS?"

"More like MBHS," Gabi replies. "Male Butt-Hole Syndrome. It's an epidemic."

Kara snorts as she scrunches her hair in the mirror, and I itch to ask my friends for advice, to get their help in deciphering Brandon's confusing guy-speak. But I can't. They both believe we're dating for real, and it's way too late to fess up now. I'm on my own with this one.

"That may not be a technical term, but Gabi's right," Kara says. "Guys are strange creatures. Don't let it get you down." She takes a final appraisal of herself and then says, "Well, as long as you're okay, you girls ready to jet?"

Gabi nods and peels herself off the wall. They both look at me. The truth is, I'm not ready to go back out there yet, but I do need a moment alone. "You know what, I'll be right behind y'all. I just need to use the bathroom."

Gabi tilts her head, eyeing me skeptically. "You want me to stay with?"

"Nah, go ahead." I paste on a sunny smile. "I'll be right there."

"Okay," she says. "But if you're not out in ten, I'm sending out a search party."

I laugh because that's what she was going for and keep the smile up as my friends walk out of the bathroom. Then, once they're gone, I sink down onto a bench, put my head in my hands, and close my eyes.

Why does this have to be so confusing? I have my own conflicting feelings to deal with—making myself over into someone better, hoping guys will finally notice me, stressing about becoming a *Casual*. Isn't that enough without stressing about Brandon, too?

Or how he feels about *me*?

I grab fistfuls of hair and squeeze, yanking near the roots. Then my thoughts catch up with me and I freeze.

Could that be it?

Could the reason Brandon has been acting so crazy lately be because he's just as confused about me? Maybe even waiting for an opening to see if I feel the same?

The thought sends a giddy buzz through my limbs, and the mounting tension of the past two weeks fades away. It's likely I'm getting my hopes up all over again, just as I did that first dance our freshman year. But there's a chance that this time is different.

It's definitely possible.

"Aw, did Brandon grow tired of you already?"

Even with my head down, I recognize Lauren's voice. The confident, entitled tone is often imitated but rarely duplicated. From what I hear, it's hereditary. Feeling cornered and alone—*why did I send Kara and Gabi away again?*—I keep my eyes on the cracked tile floor.

Lauren laughs. "Tell me—how does it feel knowing the only way you were able to get him was to change everything about yourself? Your clothes, your hair... Hell, you actually look like a girl."

At that, I lift my head. The crowd around us quiets. Peyton, a sweet, quiet senior, meets my eye across the locker room and gives a sympathetic smile.

"It's pretty sad that after three years you had to resort to all that." Touching her heart, Lauren sighs. She turns to address her audience and raises her voice an octave, clearly enjoying the attention. "Well, at least she knows what he's interested in. No delusions he wants Aly for her *mind*."

The crowd—everyone other than Peyton—snickers, and Lauren turns to leave.

And I just sit there.

The truth of her words replays over and over like a repeating track on my iPod, leaving me unable to come up with any semblance of an intelligible comeback.

Of course Brandon doesn't want me. Have I not learned anything since freshman year?

For a minute there, I actually let myself believe that our fake relationship could be something real. That the last few weeks of pretend meant as much to him as they did to me. But as Lauren just pointed out, if Brandon *is* confused about his feelings, it has absolutely nothing to do with me.

He's just infatuated with Forever 21.

♥ ♥ ♥

Out in the gym, Kara and Sarah are shaking it on the dance floor, with Daniel and Drew rocking from side to side behind them. Gabi is back at the table of abandoned purses, hands laced behind her head, black combat boots propped up on the chair opposite her.

"You're on purse patrol?" I ask, sneaking a glance at Brandon. He and Carlos are talking baseball. Again.

"You know it." Gabi wiggles a bag of salt-and-pepper potato chips at me, and I shake my head. "Dancing's too much school spirit."

That sort of statement coming out of the mouth of a *dance team* member never fails to make me laugh. Even when the world's turned upside-down, I can count on Gabi to keep it real.

"Well, I'm going out there." This earns me a wide-eyed look of shock from my rebel friend, and I turn to Brandon, already knowing how it will play out. "Any chance you feel like shaking it?"

"Um, I think I'll just hang here with Carlos." He leans back in his chair and gives me a tight smile. "But you go have fun."

Yep, he doesn't even want to dance with me. I'm an idiot.

Hurt, disappointment, and embarrassment slam into my ribs, almost stealing my breath. Humiliated, and not wanting anyone else to see it, I zigzag through the crowded dance floor to my friends, clenching my jaw to keep from crying.

Just as I reach them, a familiar voice rumbles near my ear. "I like this one."

I spin around, surprised to find Justin standing behind me. He jabs a thumb at the DJ, and I nod, attempting a smile. "Yeah, me too."

Eyebrows lifted in question, Justin takes a step closer and starts dancing. With only a slight hesitation, I do, too. We're part of a group, after all, and it's not as if Brandon's wasting energy caring about what I'm doing...even if the rest of our friends seem confused. The six of us stay together for the next two songs, mostly the girls sticking close and dancing in a circle while the guys bounce around the perimeter. But eventually, couples pair off.

To my right, Kara and Daniel grind on each other like they're in a Rihanna video. To my left, Drew and Sarah sway slowly despite the upbeat tempo. That leaves me with Justin. Grinning, he dances closer, and for a moment, I feel guilty. As if dancing with him is a betrayal.

I can't read Brandon's expression from across the room, but the very fact that he's sitting there reminds me this *thing* between us isn't real. He's not worried that I'm dancing with another guy. Brandon knows Justin was the original target for this mission, and with the weird way he's been acting, he probably hopes *I* remember it, too.

I squeeze my eyes shut against all the drama I've created. Who knew a little game of pretend could result in such a disaster? Opening my eyes again, I vow for the rest of the night to stop worrying about the stupid makeover and have fun. Or a really close facsimile.

Fake it 'til you make it, right?

Swinging my hair around, I move my hips to the rhythm of Beyoncé.

"You got moves, girl," Justin says, leaning in close so I can hear him.

The smell of mint and soap tickles my nose. "Thanks."

I lean back and look at him. *Really* look at him. Before the makeover, Justin would've never said anything like that to me. He certainly wouldn't be smiling at me the way he is now. The player rep he's so carefully built is definitely there, but there's more, too. A genuineness in his brown eyes that surprises me. He holds my gaze for an extended moment before glancing down and then away.

Operation Sex Appeal is working. Right now, on this dance floor, I should be happy. But as Lauren's words replay in my mind, they zap every ounce of joy from this moment.

Justin leans forward again and says, "You know, you look great tonight. Brandon's a lucky guy."

A half laugh, half cry escapes my throat. Tears spring to my eyes, and I blink them away. "You look good, too."

And he does. He's wearing dark-wash jeans and a form-fitting black tee. Simple and sexy as always, and he's dancing with *me*.

Snap out of it!

The song ends, and the DJ changes vibes, choosing to put on Adele's slow and sultry version of "Make You Feel My Love." Pathetically, I look to the cafeteria, but Brandon isn't there.

"Wanna dance?"

I turn back and see Justin holding out his hand. "Um, sure. I guess."

He wraps his arms around me, and those brown eyes stare intently into my own. I look away, and we move to the music. Justin's pulse beats against my cheek.

"Mind if I cut in?"

Brandon's voice sends my heart into my throat. My head pops up, but he's not looking at me. His eyes are locked on Justin, and his lips are pressed so tight they're almost white.

"Hey, she's your woman, isn't she?" Justin backs away with his palms up, looking as if he's fighting a smile. "Just keeping her company, man." Transferring his gaze to me, the smile softens. "Thanks for the dance, Aly."

I nod, but I don't reply because suddenly Brandon is pulling me close. His hold isn't as tight as Justin's, but I feel safe and secure in his arms. He doesn't dance quite as well as Justin either. Brandon's movements are stiff and even a touch clumsy. But having him hold me, breathing in the intoxicating cologne I bought him, letting myself pretend it's real for just a moment is all I need. I lay my head against his chest and close my eyes.

The song is about things a person would do for the one they love. Listening to the lyrics, dancing with Brandon, knowing that I'm most likely falling for him...it's intense. Especially since I have no clue what he's thinking or feeling. Are the lyrics messing with his head, too?

He clears his throat, and I look up.

Brandon doesn't look swoony or contemplative. He looks *pissed.* "Looks like you two were having fun."

My head jerks at the gruff accusation. The feel of his arms around my waist and the tingle radiating from the hands splayed on my back are forgotten as I ask, "Are you angry with me?"

"No." A muscle ticks in his jaw. "Why should I be?"

The tightness in his eyes and tension in his shoulders call bullshit, but I have no idea why he's mad. Nothing he's done in the past week has made any sense at all. But then, neither have I. "On your word?"

Brandon shuts his eyes. For a tense moment, I wonder if he'll be honest with me. If he's so angry or upset that he'll actually lie. But then he says, "No. Not on my word." He groans in obvious frustration, and pinpricks of apprehension stab the back of my neck. "I don't know what the hell's wrong with me." When he opens his eyes again, the soft green is dull with exhaustion. "Wanna go get some air?"

I swallow heavily. *No, not really.* When in the history of the world have those words ever led to a happy ending? Never. But since I don't really have a choice, I do what I have to do.

With Adele's voice singing about a highway of regret, I follow him through the gym door. Out on the dimly lit breezeway, Brandon slumps onto a wooden bench, his elbows on his knees and his head buried in his hands. I lower myself beside him, waiting for whatever bomb he's about to drop.

Laughing darkly, he looks straight ahead into the black night, avoiding meeting my eyes. "This pretend thing isn't working out too well, is it?"

He's breaking up with me.

The ridiculousness of that thought hits me like a cold wave, and I squeeze my eyes against the onslaught. You can't break up what was never together. But my heart didn't get that memo.

Instantly, my nose burns, and my head feels as though it's caving in. I blink rapidly, fighting to keep the tears from escaping, and swallow to relieve the pressure.

I can't let Brandon see how upset I am.

"I guess you're right," I answer, my shaky voice betraying me anyway.

He says nothing to that, so we sit in silence—me trying not to have a panic attack, him staring at the brick wall, still refusing to look at me. The warmth of his body practically scorches my left side, but it's as if he's a million miles away. As if seventeen years of knowing each other and the last three as best friends never existed. We're simply two strangers sharing a bench.

And that hurts worst of all.

"I'm sorry for everything," I say in a low voice. He turns his head in acknowledgement and looks at me. His eyes are so sad it crushes me. "I had no clue things would get so messed up. All I wanted was for guys to look at me differently. To finally *see* me."

Brandon gives me a small smile that doesn't meet his eyes. "And it worked." Raking his hand through his disheveled hair, he adds, "At least it gave me an excuse to hang out more with my best friend," clearly trying to make me feel better.

It doesn't.

Hearing him call me that used to make me happy. Now it's like a knife to the heart. How could I be so stupid to believe a guy like him would ever fall for me? That he'd feel anything close to what I have the past few weeks?

Brandon doesn't do relationships. I knew that.

Approaching footsteps have us falling silent again as two shadowed figures turn the corner. When the soft light falls over them, I see it's Adam and Chelsea. Walking, holding hands. Him giving her the same smile he once gave me. It's as if the universe is a vindictive bitch, holding a flashing neon sign: *See, Aly? You're never going to be good enough.*

He glances at Brandon and then back at me, forehead wrinkling in concern. It only makes it worse. I give a subtle nod to show everything is fine, but I don't bother with a smile. Adam knows me well enough to see through that.

I wait for the happy couple to disappear into the shadows. "You're right, Brandon. The past few of weeks *have* been fun." I pause a moment to gather courage, then say, "But we should probably end this pretend whatever-we-are thing before we ruin our friendship."

An inner-voice mocks me. *Are you sure you haven't done that already?*

Brandon opens his mouth and hesitates, and stupid hope builds—only to be demolished when he closes it again. He shakes his head and then looks over with what can only be relief in his eyes. "You're right."

Great, that's what I was going for.

The last bit of hope takes every ounce of air in my lungs with it. If I don't give in to the emotions roiling inside soon, my chest is going to explode. But I will myself to contain it just a little longer. After everything that's happened, I can't break down in front of Brandon. I *can't.*

He stands and shoves his hands into his pockets. "Want me to bring you home?"

"Nah." I force a smile, knowing damn well he can see through it, too. "I'll get a ride in the Death Mobile."

He nods and kicks the bench in front of him. "See you at the game tomorrow?"

"Yeah." I rock on the bench, every muscle clenching to hold it together. *Please go. Please, please just go.* "I'll be there."

We hold each other's gaze a moment more, and then he walks away. I watch his back, counting his steps until he disappears down the stairs and into the parking lot. Then, and only then, do I let go of the emotions wreaking havoc on my insides.

♥ ♥ ♥

Twenty minutes later, Gabi finds me curled on the bench.

"Hey, girl, I've been looking for—" She stops, takes in my blubbering face, red eyes, and runny nose, and says, "I'll be right back with Kara!"

Gabi has never been good with emotional stuff. I drag my fingertips beneath my eyes and grimace at the thick coat of black I wipe off. The double doors open, and Gabi reappears, only this time with the entire freaking cavalry in tow. Kara and Sarah fall around me, each grabbing a hand, as their respective dates huddle near the wall, looking completely out of their element. The door opens a third time, and Carlos and Justin join the party.

Fantastic.

I don't have to say much—the fact that I'm bawling like a baby and Brandon is nowhere in sight makes the situation quite obvious.

Still, Carlos asks, "Where's Brandon?" Gabi shoots him a death glare and slaps his arm. "What the hell, woman?"

Ignoring him, she pushes my feet off the bench, tugs me up, and then slides in on one side as Kara takes the other. Wrapping me in a three-way hug, Gabi declares, "Men are idiots."

I sniff and look at the crowd standing around awkwardly, more than half of which are guys. Drew lifts his chin in consolation.

Kill me now.

Sarah kneels down, leaning her head against my lap. "Are you okay? Gabi's right, boys are stupid." She glances back at her boyfriend and clarifies, "Not you, honey. Brandon. What is his deal? He ignores the obvious for years, finally wises up, and then—" She turns to me and asks, "Wait, what did he do exactly?"

Kara hands me a ball of wadded-up toilet paper, and I drag it across my eyes. "Nothing. We broke up. It was mutual."

The looks on their faces confirm that nobody is buying the pre-canned line.

Sarah pats my hand. "Aly, don't worry. Everything is going to be okay. You'll see."

Gabi rolls her eyes, and I struggle not to do the same. Sarah means well, but being consoled by someone completely in love? It doesn't help. And Drew tugging on his ear, mumbling condolences, *really* doesn't help. Without a doubt, Brandon is going to hear all about my sob-fest now. Drew's a sweetheart, but keeping his mouth shut isn't one of his strengths.

I hear the gym doors open yet again, and I just *know* who it's going to be. In case I hadn't gotten the message, the universe thought she'd stick it to me one more time. And that comes in the form of Lauren.

From the expression on her face, I can tell she didn't know we were there. For once, she doesn't look plastic or haughty. The confidence I've grown to expect from her and all the other *Casuals* is noticeably absent, replaced with slumped shoulders and a downcast gaze. For about a nanosecond, I see a girl who appears just as lost and sad as I do. Exhaustion radiates from her being.

But then, registering her audience, the old Lauren returns. Shoulders snapping back, she lifts her chin as her sharp eyes take in my balled tissue and emergency response crew. Smirk in place, she tosses me a haughty, "Have a great night," and continues strolling past. But after everything that has happened tonight, it lacks the usual sting.

Gabi pulls Kara to the side, and they start whispering heatedly. I hear the phrase "payback's a bitch," and not knowing if they are talking about Lauren or Brandon only makes me cry more. This isn't anyone's fault but mine. Carlos shuffles his feet and scratches his arm, reaching out to pat my head like a dog every thirty seconds. Justin taps his foot against the brick wall, eyeing me behind an unreadable mask. Daniel pockets his phone and then takes it back out, obviously lost as to what to do.

The old saying "misery loves company" is a complete load of crap.

I grab Kara's arm. "Guys, I just wanna go home, get in my jammies, throw a blanket over my head, and wallow. Can we please get outta here before the entire dance comes pouring out to get the gossip firsthand?"

There's no doubt in my mind Lauren is working her phone, spreading it as we speak.

Kara's eyes widen, coming to the same conclusion. "Daniel, we gotta go." Grabbing my arm, she pushes me forward. She totally gets self-preservation.

Daniel, obviously happy to have a task to do, yanks his keys from his pocket and tromps ahead. I turn to offer the group a halfhearted wave filled with balled-up toilet paper, then follow him, arm in arm with Kara, to the parking lot.

When they drop me off ten minutes later, the house is dark. I let myself in quietly, my shoulders slumping in relief. My parents are great at the whole listening without judgment thing, but I really can't handle going through the whole ordeal again. I grab a Coke from the fridge and a container of Double Stuf Oreos from the pantry and creep up the stairs to my room.

Setting my heartbreak cure on the nightstand, I throw myself onto the bed and stare at the painted ceiling-scape Gabi created. The bright yellow sun and fluffy clouds that greet me each morning normally make me smile.

Not tonight. They're too damn joyful.

I grab my silky, yellow, *cheerful* pillow and chuck it at the ceiling, grunting with the effort.

Now that felt good.

Leaning my chin back, I stare at the Wall of Shame and laugh in disgust. I didn't even get a just-a-friend picture from tonight's dance to add to the wall. Somehow, that's even more pathetic.

I shake my head and survey the photos, remembering each dance, each guy. Each time I wasn't enough. Then I eye the calendar mounted over my desk.

The countdown to Homecoming is on; it's time I got back to business. My priorities slipped the last few weeks, but from now on, my eyes are set firmly on the prize. This is about being confident and *Casual*. And getting Justin to ask me to Homecoming.

He is supposed to be the end goal, not Brandon. Now I remember why.

I kick my shoes across the room and fold myself into bed. I have an early practice in the morning, followed by our rec team's second volleyball match. As tempting as it is to ditch both, I can't let down my team, and I won't disappoint Kaitie or Baylee. Brandon either. Everything that happened tonight was my fault, not his. Tomorrow, I'm just going to have to put my head down, plow through on autopilot, and endeavor to get through the match without making things between us worse.

If that's even possible.

SATURDAY, AUGUST 28TH

5 weeks until Homecoming ♥

BRANDON

FAIRWOOD CITY PLAYGROUND, GYMNASIUM, 12:45 p.m.

I glance at the gym's closed metal doors and unfold last night's sketch from my pocket. In it, Aly sits on the bench I left her on last night. Her hair is up in the messy ponytail of pre-makeover days, but she's wearing last week's lace halter top. Tears pool in her usually sparkling blue, makeup-free eyes. My stomach hurts.

I've gone through some horrible shit in my life. I've watched my dad battle a sickness and lose. I've watched my mom work to utter exhaustion to try to support us and my sister cry over forgetting the sound of our dad's voice. But walking away from Aly, both my longtime friend and the girl I've seen the last three weeks, was honestly one of the hardest things I've ever had to do.

Being on the dumped end of a break-up fucking sucks. Hell, it sucks being in a break-up period. My normal hookups just sort of fade, both parties growing bored and moving on to greener pastures.

That's the joy of *Casuals*. No drama, no pain, no tears.

No fear.

And fear is exactly what I feel as my gaze darts back and forth between the sketch and the gym doors, every cell in my body on red alert for Aly's appearance. A screech on the linoleum makes me jump. I look up, but it's only Baylee doing warm-up drills. I glance again at the clock and tap impatiently on the bench.

Last night couldn't have gone worse. All my preparation and self-lectures flew out the window the second Justin put his hands on her. I should have just danced with her to begin with, instead of hanging back with Carlos, trying to gain control over my impulse to scoop her up and drag her back to my truck. Unfortunately, watching her toss her hair around and sway her hips on the dance floor only turned me on more. And when Justin moved in for the kill, I couldn't take it.

Our conversation on the breezeway was humiliating, but after I pounded the heavy bag in my garage for an hour, I decided she was right. We needed to end our fake relationship and get back to reality—our friendship, minus the PDA—before we lose everything.

I just pray it's not too late.

At eight-fifty on the dot, the doors finally open.

I quickly pocket the sketch, stand up, and shove my hands into my deep pockets.

The army-green coach's polo hangs loosely on her small frame, almost baggy like her old clothes. With her hair up in a ponytail and worn-out khakis, she looks like the Aly I've known for years, except for one small difference. She won't look at me.

Eyes down, she stalks across the floor, plops her water bottle on the bench, and drops her bag.

I clear my throat. "Morning."

Aly glances up, but her eyes reach no higher than my chest. "Hey."

Seconds tick by in silence. She pulls at her ponytail and bounces on her toes, never once meeting my eyes. I take a step to close the distance between us, and she scampers to the opposite side of the gym, where she pulls Baylee and Kaitie into a conversation.

Obviously, the last place in the world she wants to be is next to me on the sidelines.

Which, the more I think about it and the longer I watch her avoid any and all eye contact, is complete crap. I may not be well-versed in the area, but isn't holding a grudge and being pissed supposed to be the right of the *dumpee*?

Aly remains on the other end of the gym until the rest of the team shows up ten minutes later. When she does eventually make her way back to our bench, she sits beside me and wrings her hands in her lap. I stare at those hands, aching to fill the silence between us, to make things right, but no words come.

She just needs time. That's all. I'll give her some space, let these feelings fade, and we'll be back to normal again. Everything's fine.

The down ref nods, signaling the match is about to begin. Aly stands to lead the girls in warm-up stretches, and I call over our setter to talk strategy. My gaze continues bouncing back to Aly, hoping she'll look at me, smile at me, prove this nightmare isn't happening. The whistle blows, the girls file onto the court, and Aly finally glances up.

Her sad eyes devastate me as she says, "Let's do this thing."

♥ ♥ ♥

The buzzer echoes across the crowded gymnasium. A final look at the scoreboard confirms we smoked Oak Cove 25-2. Aly jumps up, and the parents erupt in applause. After shaking hands with the other team, our girls storm the bench, the sound of their sneakers squeaking across the court like nails on a chalkboard.

Baylee jumps on my back, kisses my cheek, and screams, "Way to go, bro!"

She hops down and whirls around to Aly. She grabs her hands, spins her in a circle, and deposits her in front of me before chanting, "Woot! Fairfield kicked some *A-S-S*! Fairfield kicked some *A-S-S*!" and leading the others in what can only be described as a variation of the Funky Chicken.

I shake my head and smile despite the hurt clawing my chest. Baylee's enthusiasm is nothing if not contagious. I sneak a glance at Aly, and the hole in my chest closes a fraction. A radiant smile lights her face as she watches Kaitie dance around with the rest of the team.

She's so beautiful.

Our eyes meet. Flipping her hair, she smiles uncomfortably and says, "Congratulations, Coach."

I cross my arms and nod. "Right back at ya, Coach."

We are a breath away from touching, almost as close as we were when I held her on the dance floor.

Determined to salvage what is left of our friendship, I lean down and pull her into a hug. It's awkward as hell, but we have to start somewhere.

When I pull away, her eyes are red.

Baylee and Kaitie rush over. "Aly, you and Kaitie are coming to the house for lunch, right?"

Aly glances at me and shakes her head. "Sorry, we can't. We need to get home."

"No, we don't." Kaitie puts her hands on her hips. "Mom's catering and Dad's golfing. I wanna go to Baylee's."

Aly pinches her lips and then, with a tight smile, lowers her voice. "Kaitie, I need to go home. I have an English paper to write, and then I have to go to work."

Kaitie opens her mouth to argue, and the fiercest expression I've ever seen Aly wear crosses her face. Her eyes flare, almost in desperation, and the cords in her throat stand out against the skin. The effect is so startling Kaitie shuts her mouth and Baylee and I exchange a look.

Aly grabs her bag off the floor and flings it on her back. "Great job today, Bayls. Brandon, I-I'll see you later." She grabs Kaitie's arm and tugs her out of the building.

Baylee watches them leave. "Just a wild guess here, but I'm gonna say you two are fighting."

Aly's vanilla scent still clings to the air. I drag my hand across my face and close my eyes.

Are we fighting? Hell if I know. We argue on a daily basis, but always about stupid crap that doesn't mean anything. But this feels different. And that's what scares me.

MONDAY, AUGUST 30TH
4 weeks and 5 days until Homecoming ♥

ALY
FAIRFIELD ACADEMY, 3:05 p.m.

News of the breakup went viral before Kara's car even left the parking lot, and by Saturday afternoon, it was splashed all over Facebook, Twitter, and text messages across the county. When my own phone buzzed with the news, I suddenly found myself sympathizing with the jilted Hollywood starlets who read about their heartbreak in the tabloids.

The thought of going back to school without Brandon as my safety net had me edgy all weekend, and the reality is even worse. Walking the halls alone, I feel every stare, hear every whisper. Girls regard me with a mixture of pity and triumph, and guys wink and leer as I pass. I'm back on the market again, and their reaction is what I said I wanted when I devised Operation Sex Appeal. Getting attention, being noticed—I thought it would be fun.

This is decidedly *not*.

What's worse is the ache in my chest every time I see Brandon.

By the time the final bell rings, the only thing I want to do is dive headfirst into a tub of Ben &

Jerry's. But first, I have to make it through an hour with Lauren. As I wait for the senior class board meeting to start, I bury myself in my well-loved copy of *Jane Eyre* and attempt to look busy.

A shadow falls across the page.

"Hey, Aly." Brandon's restrained voice is void of all the humor and playfulness our usual exchanges hold.

I can't bring myself to look past his scuffed-up Chuck Taylors. "What's up?"

"Nothing I guess." He shuffles his feet. "See you at practice later?"

My shoulders slump. I'd totally forgotten about our weekly practice.

Will this day never end?

"Yep," I say, flipping a page I didn't actually read. "I'll be there."

"Cool." Pause. "All right, then. See ya."

My eyes follow his stride down the aisle and through the door. I sigh. "See ya."

I lay my head down on the smooth desktop. *It takes a special kind of stupid to mess things up this badly.*

"Now, now, Aly, don't be sad." I turn on my ear and find Lauren smiling wickedly from her perch on top of a desk two aisles over, surrounded by minions. "Many girls better than you have been dumped by Brandon Taylor."

Clearly, the hint of the human being I glimpsed after the dance has disappeared. Pasting the best impression of a smile I can manage on my face, I say, "Thanks for your concern, Lauren, but I'm fine."

"Sure you are, sweetheart," Lauren continues. The rest of the board members lean forward, blatantly eavesdropping for their latest Facebook-blast, and she snickers. "But are you sure you don't wanna take a personal day? It's not like you're really needed here or anything. Everyone knows Vice President is just a placeholder position."

You can handle this. Just stay calm.

In a tight, overly sweet voice, I say, "I don't need a personal day, Lauren, because the breakup was mutual."

She smirks and rolls her eyes at the gathered crowd. "Sure it was." Spinning on the desk to face our class secretary, she says in an exaggerated whisper, says, "I don't know what Brandon saw in her to begin with."

Blood rushes to my cheeks. Obviously, Lauren is not going to get bored with this game any time soon. This is the second time in four days she's attacked me publicly. And keeping quiet at the dance has haunted me all weekend.

Say something. Anything. What would a Casual *do?*

Clearing my throat, I sit up tall, saying, "More than he saw in you apparently."

Every tap, every creak, every whisper silences.

Holy crap, did that really just come out of my mouth?

Lauren's horrified face tells me it did. Suddenly, I can no longer feel the seat beneath me. All sensation below my waist is gone. There's a roaring in my ears, and I clamp my teeth shut.

I attempt not to cower as Lauren huffs. She rolls her tongue in the pocket of her cheek, eyeing me up, then swivels to her hungry followers—eager to lap up every morsel of her hate to spew in future gossip—and starts whispering. The evil look she casts in my direction tells me she's getting the last word. As if I didn't already know.

I bounce in my seat, eager to keep the ball rolling. To prove I'm a *Casual* who can stand toe-to-toe with the best and hand it right back. But I've got nothing. Every comeback I think of sounds juvenile.

What are you whispering about, huh?

If you have something interesting to say, why don't you share with the rest of us?

Lauren, you're nothing but a mean, mean, not-nice girl.

Yeah, that would do it. I shake my head in disgust.

Ms. Evans, the senior advisor, emerges from her office and effectively shuts Lauren up. At least for the moment. I straighten my shoulders and grab my pencil, ready to bury myself in whatever project Ms. Evans has for us, no matter how idiotic.

"The dance Friday night was a huge success," she says, riffling through a large stack of papers on her desk. The heady smell of newly photocopied pages permeates the air. "Lauren, you did a fabulous job managing the committees. You clearly inherited your father's business sense. He must be so proud."

At the praise of her corporate big-shot father, Lauren's plastic smile falters briefly before returning to its former radiance. "Thank you, Ms. Evans. I learned everything I know about delegation from him."

"Excellent. Now, our next event is Spirit Day. It's our job to plan the main event. The junior class, as you may remember, is in charge of the Homecoming Dance the following week. Let's see, I have the theme they chose somewhere..." She shuffles her papers, spreading them around her desk before locating what she is looking for. "Here it is: 'Starlight Fairytale.'"

I keep myself from gagging, but the rest of the class erupts in groans. Could they be any more cliché? It's not that the one we picked last year, "Under the Sea," was that poetic, but choosing a non-lame, school-wide event to tie into that cheese-fest of a theme is gonna be a challenge.

Spirit Day is normally a joke, consisting of class team-building exercises and skits before whatever random event the senior class comes up with. In the past three years, I have suffered through jitterbug lessons to coincide with the "At the Hop" theme, luau lessons for the "Polynesian Sunset" theme, and swimming lessons to go with the "Under the Sea" theme. The previous senior classes were very big on lessons.

Lauren speaks up, her voice oozing superiority. "Ballroom lessons. It's perfect."

How original.

Ms. Evans nods. "That's a good option. It certainly goes with the fairytale ball aspect of the theme. I'll write that on the board. Anyone else? Any other suggestions?"

The classroom becomes eerily silent. None of Lauren's friends would dare come up with their own idea, but as everyone just witnessed, Lauren and I are not friends. This is my chance to stick it to her and, for once in the school's history, get a stinking fresh idea.

I rub my forehead and stare a hole into my desktop.

Fairytales. Cinderella. Stargazing. Telescopes. Prince Charming. Stars.

Do I know any star names? Isn't there one named Beetlejuice—or is that Michael Keaton? I'm much more knowledgeable about Hollywood stars.

Ian Somerhalder, Ryan Gosling, Kanye West, Taylor Swift...

Wait, that's it!

"Ms. Evans?" The rest of the class turns toward me, and I sink lower in my chair. "W-what about a talent show? I know it's a stretch on the word 'starlight,' but actors and musicians are considered stars, aren't they?"

Expressions of shock and astonishment meet the suggestion. Then the room explodes in conversation and I can't tell if it's due to the brilliance of my idea or its sheer stupidity. My bouncing foot rattles the desk in front of me, and I gnaw off the rubber eraser on my pencil.

Ms. Evans's voice rings over the noise. "What a unique and interesting idea, Alyssa. Does anyone else have an idea to contribute?" She scans the silent room and then writes "talent show" under "ballroom lessons." "Why don't we take a vote? All in favor of Aly's idea to have a talent show as the Spirit Day event this year, please raise your hands."

One by one, hands shoot up. With each one, so does my confidence. Even Lauren's lapdog, our class secretary, hesitantly votes for my suggestion.

Lauren surveys the room with a mild grimace, then nods with the enthusiasm of a dental patient. "I agree. Aly's idea is wonderful. It's exactly what we should do."

Sure it is.

I barely hold in my snort as victory shoots through me. I did it. I actually did it.

"Splendid. And what an example of graciousness, Ms. Hays." Ms. Evans turns her back to circle "talent show" with a bright purple marker, and Lauren nails me with a lethal glare.

And there goes my momentary surge of confidence.

While I did want to steal Lauren's thunder in theory, the reality is not as exhilarating as I hoped. If I'm reading her stare correctly, the verbal bashing earlier was mere child's play.

And only the beginning.

I decide to take what glory I can from that small victory and leave before I have my ass handed to me. Grabbing my backpack, I dart to the podium.

"Mrs. Evans, I completely forgot that I need to pick up my sister before volleyball practice." I gesture toward the giant wall clock over the door. "I have to run. Is that okay?"

"I'd say you earned the right to leave a little early," she says with a smile. "We can handle it from here. I'll fill you in on anything we decide tomorrow in homeroom."

"Thanks." Feeling the heat of Lauren's stare, I hurry through the door, pausing only to turn and close it behind me. Lauren waves and smiles sweetly.

Message received: *Game on.*

THURSDAY, SEPTEMBER 2ND
4 weeks and 2 days until Homecoming ♥

BRANDON
TEXAS SPRINGS CARWASH, 4:30 p.m.

I ram my phone back in my pocket and reread the same page in *Hamlet* for the thirteenth time. I still don't see how this is supposed to be English. I have no clue what these people are saying. Chomping on a Twix, I chug my Dr Pepper in the off-chance a sugar rush is the missing ingredient in my story comprehension, then I pick the play back up and try again.

Didn't think so.

This is the exact situation where I'd normally call Aly. My fingers itch to do it now, to hear her perky voice and have *her* explain this crap to me, just as she's done with countless other assignments. Hell, I just want to call Aly. But that's not an option. She needs space, and I'm going to give it to her. For now. Everything will go back to normal in a few days.

It has to.

Every day, our falling out becomes more obvious in the things I can't share with her, talk to her about, or get her opinion on. And with assignments like Shakespeare thrown at me, it's hard to miss how much we fill each other's gaps. I speak math, and she speaks whatever version of English *this* is supposed to be. Together, we pull each other along just enough to stay in the honors track. But apart? My chances don't look so hot.

The ding overhead signals a car is waiting, and I gladly dog-ear my page. Stepping from behind the register at the front desk, I walk outside, ready to greet the latest customer. Even the blast of heat smacking me in the face can't tempt me back to Shakespeare.

But the metallic-blue BMW idling out front sure can.

My steps slow as I watch Lauren fluff her hair and smack her lips at her rearview mirror. Just what I don't need today.

Before I can backtrack and grab one of the guys to help her, the driver-side door opens. She steps out in her skimpy dance uniform, and I grudgingly walk over.

"Lauren."

Smiling, she places her cold hand on my arm. "My car's *really* dirty, Brandon. I think I'm gonna need your special treatment."

Ignoring the innuendo, I brush her hand away and grab the clipboard off the wooden peg. A minute passes with nothing but the sound of my pencil scratching on the work-order form and cars speeding on the highway. Lauren's come in enough times that I can fill out her information in my sleep.

When I hand her the torn-off copy, her fingers ensnare my wrist. "Sorry about Aly." Her voice begs to differ, a fact she confirms when she says, "Actually, I'm not. She isn't good enough for you."

I inhale deeply and glance at the security camera. As much as Lauren deserves it, Earl will kick my ass for throttling a customer. Instead, I keep my eyes on the page and shake off her hand. "Your car will be ready shortly. Wait inside and I'll tell you when it's done."

Sidestepping her huff of disappointment, I slide behind the wheel, throw back the cramped driver's seat, and fire the ignition. Twangy country music—the kind Aly always listens to—pours out of the speakers, and I punch the button to change the channel. I drive to the red canopy around back where the vacuums are and yank the parking brake. Throwing open the door, I haul out the slick front floor mats and bang them against the wooden fence bordering the rear of the lot. As I bend down to grab the second set from the rear, Drew walks out the employee door.

"I see the viper's here," he calls, jerking his head toward the building where Lauren waits.

"Yep," I snap, bashing the second set against the canopy poles. "Aren't I lucky?"

Drew crouches beside the trunk of the car, keeping a safe distance from the flogging. With eyebrows drawn, he says, "I guess she figures she's got a shot now that you and Aly aren't together anymore."

I stuff the mats through the automatic mat cleaner. "Well, she's wrong."

He stands and strolls over, grabbing the hose to vacuum the driver side. "You know, I get why some guys go for her over-the-top routine," he says, raising his voice over the hum. "But personally, it completely turns me off. I'm not into that shit anymore."

I look down and kick the machine in front of me.
Yeah, me neither.

Drew hangs the vacuum back up and leans across the hood. "Listen, dude, I don't know what happened with Aly, but something is obviously eating at you. You know if you want to talk, I'm here."

I don't answer. Instead, I wrench the mats out of the machine and hurl them to the ground. The hum of the vacuum kicks on and I pick up the hose to do the passenger side. Drew grabs it out of my hand.

"I got this." He pushes my shoulder toward the employee door. "Go take a break."

Adrenaline is tearing through my veins, and I don't even know why. The last thing I need to do is sit around the break room, but seeing Lauren and being around Drew's too-perceptive stare is just pissing me off more.

I lift my chin. "Thanks, man."

Drew nods and begins suctioning the sunflower seeds wedged in the crevices of her car. I jog to the employee break room, arms and legs shaking, heart pounding. Inside the cool room, I sink onto the duct-taped sofa and kick my feet up on the makeshift table. With fingers itching to draw, I close my eyes and pray for numbness to take over.

Twenty minutes later, Drew finds me with my eyes squeezed tight and my head in my hands, still waiting.

FRIDAY, SEPTEMBER 3RD

4 weeks and 1 day until Homecoming ♥

ALY

LONESTAR THEATRES, 8:15 p.m.

Gabi looks up from flipping through a copy of *US Weekly* as I back into the employee break room, buttery popcorn and Coke in hand. I'm exhausted and staring at three more long hours. I fall into an empty seat at the stained utility table, and Gabi frowns, stealing a handful of my dinner.

"You need to have a party."

"Huh?" I take a ginormous sip of my caffeinated drink, waiting for the buzz to hit my veins. "Exactly what part of my dragging ass screams 'celebration' to you?"

"None of it," she admits. "Which is my point. You, my girl, need a pick-me-up."

What I *need* is to snap out of my Brandon-fog. According to the countdown calendar, I have one month left to somehow solidify myself in the *Casual* group and get Justin to ask me to Homecoming. Writing horrifically bad poetry and crying into my pillow is no longer a luxury I can afford.

"A party, huh?"

I'm not convinced a ton of strangers trashing my house will do what Gabi hopes, but it *will* serve another purpose. My parents are out of town for the weekend, my sister is spending the next two nights at Baylee's, and I have the house to myself. What better way to prove I'm a *Casual* than throwing a party when the 'rents are away?

As if sensing possible victory, Gabi nods. "Yep, and if you give me your key when I clock out at four tomorrow, I'll have everything ready when you get home. All you'll have to do is take a shower, get gorgeous, and enjoy." She scarfs another mouthful of popcorn and leans back in her folding chair, waiting for my assent.

It takes about five seconds. "Okay, I'm in," I say. "But you better help me hide the valuables."

We pass the bag of popcorn back and forth between us, each working the contacts on our phones to spread the word. I hesitate over Brandon's name before sending a quick text and then turning off my phone. If he replies, I'll spend way too long overanalyzing every word, and I have to get back to work. When nothing remains of my dinner but a smear of neon-yellow liquid on the table, I head back out before the eight-forty-five rush trickles in.

I key my code into the register and squat down to inventory the candy. A few minutes later, a pair of jean-clad, muscular legs appears opposite the glass case. When I pop up, I am eye-to-chest with Justin.

After fouling things up so badly with Brandon, I didn't think it was possible to feel any more depressed. Apparently, I was wrong. Staring at Justin, all the mistakes I've made the last month rush back. If I had just stayed focused on my mission—getting *his* attention—Brandon and I wouldn't be in such a mess right now.

But as the expression goes, the past is the past. I can only go forward. Regain focus. There are still four weeks to turn Operation Sex Appeal from a complete and utter failure into a victorious mission of triumph.

And that starts tonight.

"Hey, here to see a movie?" Wincing at my impressive observation skills, I say, "Err, what I meant was, what movie are you here to see?"

Justin flashes a lopsided grin and points at the little boy standing next to him. "I'm taking Chase to see the new cartoon that just came out."

"*Trolls*?"

Chase jumps up and slaps his hands on the counter. "Yeah, *Trolls*!"

Justin laughs. "Obviously, my man here is excited. And since no movie would be complete without snacks, we thought we'd come see the expert."

I smile at his brother eagerly eyeing the options. "Chase, buddy, what's your favorite kind of candy?"

"M&Ms," he says decidedly. "And Reese's Pieces. And Raisinets. And—"

"Ah, a chocolate lover, huh?" I interrupt. If he's anything like me, he could go on forever. "A kindred spirit. Tell ya what—why don't you narrow it down to two of your absolute favorites, and I'll see what I can do to get your brother to buy them?"

"Two?!" he asks, beaming up at me, all thick lashes and wide brown eyes.

I nod with a smile, but when I look back at his older brother, my throat constricts again.

"Two, huh?" Justin arches his eyebrow and places his elbows on the counter. He leans in and whispers, "So what are you going to do to convince me?"

Holy cannoli. All of the blood in my body pools in my cheeks, and I swallow hard. What on earth possessed me to suggest I had any power over this boy? Justin is a force to reckon with, and I'm a dork of epic proportions. Seeing Chase so excited was impossible to resist, but faced with the older Carter brother, looking surprisingly eager for me to pay up, I'm clueless.

"Um, offer my employee discount?"

Mortified, I close my eyes and groan.

Truly, Aly, your flirting skills are unmatched.

Hidden behind a veil of darkness, I laugh sarcastically. "Are you convinced or what?"

"I guess," he says, his voice warm and amused. "But your negotiation skills could use some work." My eyes snap open, and he grins. "I'm teasing. Anything the boy wants, he can have." He reaches down and ruffles Chase's hair. "Big brother's treat."

"Yes!" Chase does a fist pump, looking utterly adorable, and then turns to me with an expression implying the topic is of grave importance. "I've decided. I'd like Reese's Pieces and Raisinets, please."

Grateful to be back on an even playing field—talking to a six-year-old—I reply, "Both very fine choices, young man." I grab the candy and, without meeting Justin's eyes, ask, "Anything else?"

"A large Coke," Justin answers, resuming his position against the counter. I fill the cup with sticky soda, trying to slow my breathing, and he continues. "As for anything else, guess only you can answer that."

Even *I* can't misinterpret that line. My heart pounds in my ears, and a giddy smile threatens to erupt as I pass Justin his drink with trembling hands. He wraps his hands around mine, removes the drink with his left, and caresses my empty hand with his right. Slowly, I meet his eyes, and his mouth kicks up in the lopsided grin that sets girls' stomachs fluttering.

"I'm glad I saw you tonight, Aly."

"Yeah, you, too," I say breathlessly, mentally shaking myself for being the world's worst flirt. "It's, uh, really sweet of you to spend your Friday night with your little brother."

His lopsided grin morphs into a slow and sexy smile, and I instinctively bite my lower lip. "Aly, I'm not a complete asshat."

Justin laughs as he says it, so I know he's joking, but I still feel like crap. It's not that I thought he was bad; I just knew he earned his reputation for a reason. But apparently, Mr. Big, Bad Player Man has an unexpected sweet side, too. We stand there for a moment—him smiling, me gaping—before Chase grabs his arm. "We're gonna miss the movie!"

I snap out of the trance and giggle. "Sorry, bud, but don't worry. You have plenty of time. The previews haven't even started yet."

Justin lets go of my hand and takes out his wallet. Pulling out a twenty-dollar bill, he says, "I'll see you tomorrow night." At my perplexed look, he laughs. "Your house? The party?" He holds up his cell phone, proving just how fast word spreads. Technology is a scary beast.

"Right, of course." I hand him his change, praying I'll stop being such a freak by then. "I'm glad you can come."

They head toward theater number five, where *Trolls* doesn't start for another twenty minutes, and Barbara sidles up to me.

"T-r-o-u-b-l-e," she mutters, handing me a stack of large cups.

"What?" I ask, snapping my gaze away from Justin's retreating backside.

She points in his direction and shakes a long, weathered finger. "That boy is what. I know trouble, and that was it."

My smile returns, and I say, "You know, Barb, you're right. Justin is nothing but trouble."

And a perfect distraction.

SATURDAY, SEPTEMBER 4TH
4 weeks until Homecoming ♥

BRANDON
LONESTAR THEATRES, 5:25 p.m.

"You missed a hell of a night, man. Only one fight went to a judge's decision." I climb out of Justin's Jeep Wrangler and shake my head. "It was a nonstop, brutal ass-kicking."

Drew and Carlos hop out the back and meet us in the crowded parking lot. Last night I hosted our annual fight night: beer, chicken wings, and UFC pay-per-view. Since freshman year, the tradition has gone on without fail. But this year Justin bailed.

"Something came up last minute."

Or someone. Whenever Justin is vague with the details, I know a girl is involved.

"But next one's on me," he says, slapping my shoulder. "Fight, wings, I'll even class things up with some Crown, all right?"

"Yeah, whatever." I nod in acknowledgment, trying to shake off my shitty mood. It's been a long-ass day. Our team won their match this morning, but standing on the sideline with Aly was awkward as hell. Her practice ran late so we didn't get a chance to talk beforehand, and she ran out after like her car was on fire. Mom was stressed about bills, work was violently hot, and Justin was being straight-up weird. When Earl called it a day at the carwash, I knew I couldn't just sit around waiting for Aly's party tonight. I needed to see her again. Right now, a smile to show that we're okay would mean everything.

We get our tickets, and the four of us enter the lobby. Immediately my eyes find Aly. She's across the room handing an elderly couple their change, and as they walk away, her gaze shifts in our direction. Time seems to stop. But then her adorable face lights up in a smile and a tiny dimple pops in her right cheek.

It's the first time in over a week she's looked at me like that. My neck muscles relax, and I let go of tension I hadn't realized I'd been holding.

Things are getting back to normal.

We cross the room, and I crack my knuckles, racking my brain for something to say. As I do, Justin edges in front of me.

Aly shakes her head and that smile widens. "Can I help you?"

His hands on the glass case, Justin peers down at the candy choices with a stupid frown. "I don't know. Got anything good here?"

She giggles. "You oughta know. You're starting to become one of our regulars."

I look between them and ask the ever-brilliant, "Huh?"

Justin looks up as if he forgot I was there. *Right.* Aly gnaws on her lip. "Justin was here last night," she explains. "He brought his little brother Chase to see *Trolls.*"

"Is that right?" I ask, smiling tightly.

The concept of "family time" isn't in Justin's vocabulary. Since I've known him, the only things he's done with his parents were when he absolutely had to. As for Chase, Justin's a decent brother, but he acts in his own interests. He had motives for the impromptu sibling bonding.

I knew he bailed on us for a girl. I just hadn't expected that girl to be Aly.

Justin won't look me in the eyes. Behind me, I can feel Drew going Dr. Phil on me in his touchy-feely head. I don't need to talk about my feelings. I know what they are. Pissed. Confused. Hurt for no reason. And, more than anything, fucking *jealous*.

The same fire that had me stalking across the gym floor last Friday scorches my veins as Justin and Aly gawk at each other. My mind flashes to Polo-Boy and my desire to put the guy's head through the wall. I eye the glass case in front of Justin and tighten my fists.

I know I shouldn't be surprised. This is what Aly wanted all along. But Justin doesn't deserve her.

The lovebirds continue with their banter, and like a glutton for punishment, I stand there.

"I'll have a small Coke," he says, leaning against the counter.

"You know, for only a quarter more you can get the medium."

I've heard Aly's sales pitch hundreds of times, but it never sounded so flirty before.

"Sold." Justin grins as he digs in his back pocket for his wallet. "I see those negotiation skills are improving."

Drew puts his hand on my arm. "Carlos and I will meet you inside." Annoyed at the pity in his eyes, I brush his hand away. He takes a step back and nods at Aly. "See you at the party."

Left as the third wheel, I decide I may as well eat. "Give me a—"

"Small popcorn, extra butter, medium Dr. Pepper, extra ice, lots of napkins." As she rattles off my order, her flirty smile shifts into a sad one. She fills the cup with ice and says, "I called Kaitie on my break, and she was still bouncing off the walls over our win."

I want to be witty. I want to be flirty and knock Justin down a peg. Hell, I'd settle for being boring and comfortable—but nothing comes out. For the first time in our friendship, I am completely without words.

Aly gets the rest of my order together, pulling a bag of popcorn from the cabinet and scurrying to the butter station. Justin stands beside me, slurping on his Coke.

After collecting my change, I take out my phone and make a production out of checking the time. "Movie's gonna start, so we should get going." I grasp Justin's shoulder and push. "Coming?"

"Right behind you, man," he says, shaking me off.

Justin drums on the counter, waiting for me to leave, but I plant my feet.

I can stand here all day.

His eyes dart from me to Aly, who watches us both in confusion. Finally, he gives her a tight-lipped smile. "See you tonight, Aly."

♥ ♥ ♥

Justin's Jeep is parked in my driveway. We've been sitting here in silence for going on three minutes. Three minutes doesn't seem like much—a commercial break, the average length of a song—but sitting for that long, waiting for Justin to man up about making a move on Aly, feels like an eternity.

Wanting to speed things along so I can get the hell out of here, I throw off my seatbelt and put my hand on the door handle.

"Hey, Brandon, can we talk for a second?"

I sigh and lean back in the seat.

Justin fingers the Mardi Gras garter belt hanging on his rearview mirror. "Why did you break up with Aly?"

"You know why," I answer, narrowing my eyes. If he knows something about our deal, he better spill it. "We decided we were better off as friends."

He nods, as if that was what he expected. "So you don't have feelings for her then?"

I shift in my seat and drag my hand over my face, trying to decide how best to answer. But I shouldn't have bothered.

"Because I want to ask her out," he admits. "But if you have a problem with that, I won't."

I squeeze the back of my neck to keep myself from saying what I'd like to. Because the truth is, Aly isn't mine anymore. She damn sure isn't my fake girlfriend, and lately it doesn't even feel like she's my friend. She made it clear she thinks being with Justin and getting her heart broken is what she needs to do. She'll have to learn the hard way.

"Do whatever you want, Justin. I don't care who Aly dates."

Drew would've called me on my B.S. immediately, but Justin grins. "Thanks, man."

With a nod, I throw open the door.

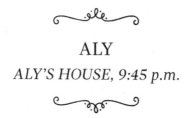

ALY

ALY'S HOUSE, 9:45 p.m.

The party is raging. A steady stream of partygoers started arriving a half hour ago with no end in sight. People are everywhere. They're in the kitchen, attacking what's left of the party spread. They're crowded on sofas, clustered on counters, and standing in groups around the pool. Even more are dancing in the halls.

Music pounds the walls of my living room, almost eclipsing the sound of the couple getting hot and heavy on the loveseat next to where I'm standing—not hiding, exactly—in the back corner.

A plastic cup floats before my eyes a second before a whiff of spicy aftershave tickles my nose. "Hiding out, huh?"

I sigh at the familiar voice behind me. Accepting the cup, I toss the liquid back and let the bitter taste of beer douse my parched throat. "I'm not hiding, Adam. More like, observing from a distance."

He chuckles. "Ah, I see the distinction. Seriously, Aly, what are you doing tucked in the shadows next to the soft porn?" He tilts his head toward the couple getting it on next to me and wrinkles his nose. Despite the hurt that still lingers from our breakup, I laugh.

"I don't know," I say, deciding to confide a little. When we were together, Adam was a good friend. And an excellent listener. "It's just—I'm sure you've noticed the, ahem, improvements to my wardrobe since we dated last year?"

He smirks. "Now that you mention it."

I sweep my hand down my current outfit, the sleeveless-white-top-and-belt/skirt ensemble. "Kara's handiwork, if you couldn't tell."

Adam leans back to appraise the outfit. "Can I ask what was wrong with the old Aly?"

I bite back my first response: *Wouldn't you know?* Instead I ask, "The truth?" He nods, and I take a breath. "I got tired being that girl. You know, the one everyone thinks of as a friend and whose own boyfriend ends up feeling the same way." I shoot him a look, and Adam winces. "I guess I wanted to see how the other half lives for once. Be popular, have adventures, get noticed. Surge with confidence."

His kind eyes study my hunched shoulders plastered against the wall. "And how's that working?"

"It's not." I roll my eyes and release a breath. "I mean, sure, I'm not invisible anymore. I nearly flashed the entire senior class fifteen minutes ago in the belt of a skirt Kara insisted I wear. If that and feeling completely awkward and uncomfortable in your own living room while people size you up like a slab of beef counts, then yeah. I'm rocking this." I hang my head and pretend-sob. "Do I not look as though I'm surging with confidence?"

The soft smile on his face says *no* for him. "Listen, I know I'm the last person you want to hear this from—" Someone turns up the music, and Adam leans in. "—but there was nothing wrong with the old Aly."

My chest grows tight, and a knot twists in my stomach. Chelsea is dancing with a group of girls a few feet away. She looks back and smiles at us, clearly not worried or jealous that her boyfriend is talking with me. And why should she be? He chose *her.*

"I know I hurt you," he says. "And I hate myself for that. But I liked the girl I dated. I even fell for her a little." I look at him in shock, and Adam shrugs. "It didn't stop me from falling for Chelsea, but that had nothing to do with you. We just weren't meant to be."

I nod, my throat too thick to talk. He's right. After the last month with Brandon, I realize my relationship with Adam didn't even come close. And *that* had been pretend.

Adam nudges my shoulder. "If it helps any, what you're doing is working. Guys are definitely talking."

I smile halfheartedly as I take another sip of beer, my hungry eyes following the latest wave of people to arrive. Guys may be talking, but there's one who still sees me, will *always* see me, as the same old Aly.

Or, at least, the same Aly with a better wardrobe.

Brandon joins a group of guys huddled around the keg Kara got Daniel to bring in the kitchen, and Lauren follows in his wake. My stomach twists.

Did they come together?

Adam waves a hand in front of my face. "You okay there, Ace?"

Plastering a smile across my face, I nod. "I'm great." I drain my cup and set it down in the planter in the corner. "Adam, would you like to dance?"

BRANDON
ALY'S HOUSE, 10:00 p.m.

I brush off hands and walk past people trying to get my attention. I'm sure I look like a dick, but I'm a man on a mission. A masochistic one.

Justin was walking up Aly's driveway when I parked down the road, so I know he's in here somewhere. Whether he went straight to making his move or stopped to hit on a few girls along the way is the only question. I edge through a crowd cheering on some idiot with a beer bong and push my way into the living room. Bodies dance on top of each other and it's hard to pick anyone out, but I quickly find Aly.

She's in the middle of the floor dancing with Adam. He whispers something in her ear, and her eyes close as she laughs. A warmth hits my chest. Strands of hair stick to her flushed cheeks, and as she gathers her hair in a ponytail off her neck, I wonder how we'll ever get our friendship back if I can't stop wanting more every time I see her.

I finally find Justin on the outskirts of the room, eyes tracking Aly as fiercely as my own, waiting to make his move.

What will she say?

The questions have been driving me crazy all afternoon. Of course she'll say yes. That was the point of this whole thing. Will she call me to talk about it? As much as I want our friendship back on track, I don't think I can stomach that conversation.

The song ends and another begins. Justin stalks across the room. My jaw clenches as he clasps Adam on the shoulder, leaning in to speak with him. Adam nods, hugs Aly, and disappears into the crowd.

Aly's hands are behind her back, and she fidgets with the ring on her finger as she bounces on her toes. Justin lowers his head to whisper in her ear, and then they start dancing. Even from here, I can see her blue eyes sparkle.

She looks happy. Like a jackass, it makes my gut tighten because I'm not the one putting that look in her eyes.

As much as I'd love to, I know I can't go break them up. But I also need to know what happens. I look for a place to sit so I'm not just standing around gawking like a loser, then head for the sofa. A tortilla chip crunches under my heel, crumbling into Aly's carpet, and I park my ass on the arm of the large sectional sofa.

"Hey there, handsome."

I look down and see Lauren on the sofa beside me, straightening her back to display her cleavage to better advantage. The smile on her face says she knows exactly what she is doing. I turn back to the dance floor, and she yells over the music, "Wanna dance?"

"Nah, I'm just chilling," I say, squinting in an attempt to read Aly's lips.

"Cool." Lauren inches closer on the sofa. "It's warm in here, isn't it?"

"Not really." Did Aly just say yes? To what?

"Maybe a drink would cool me down." She bumps my knee with her empty cup, and I glance down. Actually, that may help.

"Sure," I tell her, taking the hint and the cup. "I'll be right back."

I take the long way around the room, creeping closer toward Aly and Justin, but the music makes it impossible to eavesdrop. He's probably asking her out right now, and there's nothing I can do about it. I failed. Failed to redirect her from Justin, failed to convince her she's a *Commitment*, and failed to keep our friendship from falling apart.

I grab the vodka and two-liter of Sprite off the kitchen counter and bring them to the island, my eyes never straying from the disaster unfolding on the dance floor. As I pour the drink into an empty cup, Justin speaks in Aly's ear again. She glances up and meets my gaze.

ALY
ALY'S HOUSE, 10:14 p.m.

"I hope it's not too soon," Justin screams into my ear, "but I'd like to take you out some time."

Wrenching my eyes away from Brandon's, I focus on the guy in front of me.

Did Justin Carter just ask me out?

"Seriously?" I ask, my voice breaking in disbelief.

He nods slowly, looking almost worried. "Friday night?"

My feet stop moving. I lose the connection between my mouth and brain. Someone bumps me from behind, but I continue staring in confusion. When the left side of his mouth kicks up in a lopsided grin, I realize he's waiting for an answer.

"Y-yeah," I stammer. "That would be great."

"Good." He pulls me closer and adjusts his steps to the slower beat now playing on the stereo. He lifts my chin to look into my eyes. "I really like you, Aly."

Holy cannoli.

I lay my head on Justin's chest and breathe in his minty scent. Across the room, Kara points a finger between us, and when I nod, answering her unspoken question, she does a happy dance.

"Gabi! Picture!" Kara's voice travels over the music as she flags down Gabi like an air-traffic controller to where Justin and I stand.

Gabi pushes people out of her way, not-accidently bumping into Lauren's lap in the process. Lauren sneers, and Gabi leans in to tell her something, ending with a pointed finger right at my waist, which is wearing Justin's arm like a belt.

Lauren's eyes narrow and she turns her head away—but not before mouthing the word *slut*.

Heat floods my cheeks. I scan the crowd, wondering if anyone saw. Couples dance around us obliviously, and Justin tightens his hold around me. "Ready for your close-up?"

I look up in confusion, and he turns our bodies for Gabi to snap a picture. He mugs for the camera and then taps Gabi on the shoulder. "Give me a copy of that, will ya?"

She lowers her chin and peers up at him, like she's waiting for the punchline or looking for his angle. "Sure. No problem." Then she looks at me as if to say, *Is he for real?*

Dazed, I lift a shoulder in response, then lean back into the hard muscles of Justin's chest, sure that I've stepped into some type of alternative universe... until I see Brandon hand Lauren a drink.

I blink, not really wanting to watch but unable to look away. He sits on the armrest next to her, and Lauren presses her chest against his thigh. She smiles up at him, and he nods before lifting his head. His eyes lock on mine as if he'd felt the weight of my gaze, and he totally catches me staring.

Swallowing past the lump in my throat, I drag my eyes away.

There's no denying it. Heartthrob Taylor is back in business.

And I have a mission to complete.

Monday, September 6th
3 weeks and 5 days until Homecoming ♥

BRANDON
FAIRFIELD ACADEMY, 1:15 p.m.

Drew chugs his water bottle and towels off the weight bench before switching places with me. Burning off energy in the athletic department during unstructured period is a benefit of being on the baseball team, but one I normally don't use until the season gets closer.

Today I'm willing to make an exception.

I take a deep breath and lift the bar while Drew stands behind me to spot. I press the weight in rhythm with my breathing, trying to block out the image of Justin and Aly.

They are everywhere.

My day started with a run-in at the lockers, where no amount of banging my books around could drown out their banter. Then I made my escape to English, only to have them follow. Evans assigned seats the first day, which means Aly still sits beside me and I had a front-row ticket to witness Justin plop his ass on her desktop and pretend some more that he's extended-hookup material. Of course, once the bell rang and Justin fled for his own class, Aly and I sat in silence.

The hits just kept on coming as the day went on. There were run-ins with the happy couple in the hallways between classes and again at the lockers, but the last straw came at lunch. Trying to stomach my tacos while Justin sat with his arm around Aly, whispering in her ear, was impossible.

Worse was the nagging feeling it should've been me next to her.

"You want to talk about it?" Drew asks, easing the burden of the weight as I nudge it back onto the rack.

I close my eyes, panting. "About what?"

Drew throws his towel over my head, and I sit up slowly, drained from exertion.

"The reason you're killing yourself," he says. "Whatever has you maxing out on a weight you couldn't lift a week ago. The thing causing that vein to pop out of your forehead."

I stand and grab my bottle of water. "Don't know what you're talking about." I guzzle the liquid and pitch the empty bottle into the recycle bin near the door. "Just working out."

Inside the locker room, I snatch a clean towel and head to the showers. Drew follows.

"You don't have to tell me shit," he says, stepping into the neighboring stall. "But I'm not going anywhere, if you change your mind."

I twist the knob, and the water pressure hesitates in spurts before pounding the tile. The hot water jabs at my chest like hundreds of tiny knives, and I close my eyes to duck my head under the torrent. I don't want to talk about Justin and Aly. I want to pretend it isn't happening because watching them together has made me realize the friendship I had with her is over. Maybe we'll be friends again eventually, but we'll never go back to the way things were. Too much has changed.

I finish showering and wrap the towel around my waist, heading back to my gym locker. Drew stands with his back turned, pulling on his green Fairfield Academy polo shirt.

I straddle the metal bench and sit down. "Sorry for being a dick."

Drew nods in acknowledgement and closes his locker. "You should talk to her," he says, tossing his comb into his bag.

"That's the last thing I should do." I stand and twist the combination until my locker springs open. I pull on a pair of boxers and toss my towel into the wire basket against the wall. "I just need to get over it. Keep busy. Hook up with someone else."

"You really think that's better than talking to her?" Drew asks incredulously.

I zip my khaki pants. "Yeah, I do," I lie. "Aly's got a lot on her plate right now. She's convinced she needs to be someone she's not, and she refuses to hear anything I have to say about it." I step into my unlaced sneakers. "The girl is stubborn as hell."

Drew sucks in his lips, repressing a smile. "Gee, that must be annoying."

"You're not funny, dude." I hike my leg up on the bench to tie my shoe, and Drew walks around the other side.

"You're really gonna let this go." He leans against the cool steel wall behind him and crosses his arms. "You're gonna give up and go bag another *Casual*, aren't you?"

Grabbing my bag, I shove my locker shut. "I'm not giving up anything. I never wanted a relationship. That's your deal." He shakes his head like I'm in denial, pissing me off. "Getting back to fun and easy is exactly what I need."

Friday, September 10th
3 weeks and 1 day until Homecoming ♥

ALY
THE ZONE, 7:20 p.m.

A fast-flying ball slamming into the cage in front of us sends me crashing into Justin's chest. Apparently, dating for *Casuals* includes a heart rate check.

"You get ten points for originality," I say, breathless, craning my neck to look at him. "But your plan has one tragic flaw. I suck at baseball."

Justin squeezes my shoulders. "You happen to have your own personal batting tutor this evening," he says, leaning down to place his mouth against my ear. "And I'm prepared to offer extensive hands-on instruction."

His lips brush the side of my neck, and my stomach jolts. Spinning around, I take a step backward and press my back against the metal cage.

A week going out with Justin Carter and that touch highlights the extent of our lip action. It hasn't been for lack of trying on his part; I'm just a skittish freak. When he tried kissing me at the party last weekend and I pulled away, I think we both chalked it up to nerves. But after pulling away again tonight, I can't help but wonder what the hell is wrong with me. The perky blonde currently eyeballing Justin from the counter would have *zero* problems making out with him.

"Aren't I the lucky pupil?" I ask, going for blasé, but a nervous laugh leaks out. "Then by all means, lead me to the classroom, professor."

He eyes me curiously but takes my hand, lacing his fingers with mine. Walking beside him, I cast a sidelong glance and berate myself for acting so crazy. Justin Carter is holding my hand. This is what I wanted. I spent weeks trying to make this very thing happen.

Get your head in the freaking game, girl!

We stop in front of a cage halfway hidden behind a trophy case, and Justin pulls open the gate.

"Typically these places have rules about one person at a time in these things," he says, ushering me inside and pointing to a sign that states that very thing. "But the owner is one of Fairfield's biggest boosters, so he won't give us any problems."

He sets down the bat and a helmet and leads me to the sidewall for the grand tour. "Now, we don't have to worry about tokens because we paid for thirty minutes, but this button right here is important. It sends a signal to the pitching machine on the other end. See that yellow light over there? That means the machine is ready to go. When you hit this button, the red light turns on, and balls start flying about every twenty to thirty seconds. When the light goes off, your turn is over and we switch."

I eye the machine ready to spew projectiles at my face, and swallow.

"You want to go first?"

"Sure," I say with fake bravado, totally suppressing a traumatic flashback from P.E. "Bring it on."

He holds out a helmet covered in scratches and gouges, with yellow foam cushioning hanging loose on the inside. It looks like it survived a crime scene. With only a slight shiver, I reach out to grab it—but he doesn't let go. Instead, he gently pulls me forward, and that slight shiver gives way to a mega one.

Justin runs the back of his hand across my cheek, and when I stiffen, he sighs. "Aly, you need to relax. I'm not gonna bite. Well," he clarifies with a wicked grin. "Not unless you want me to."

My pulse thumps madly in my ears and I try to smile back, but my mouth doesn't cooperate. "I guess I'm just nervous," I admit, forcing my body to relax. It's weird being this close to him, alone.

Justin tucks a strand of hair behind my ear. "But why? You know me. We've been friends for years."

"No, we haven't," I say, surprised when a flash of hurt crosses his face. Not knowing where else to put my hands, I place them on his chest. "Justin, we've hung around the same circles for years, and we're friends with the same people, but you and I have hardly ever talked. You've barely even looked at me in the three years I've known you." I tell myself to shut up, that this is *so* not first date or *Casual*-like conversation, but I can't seem to stop the monologue from spilling out. Lauren's words from the dance keep haunting me. "Why now?" I ask. "Is it because of the new clothes? The hair and makeup? Or is it because I went out with Brandon?"

As soon as the questions leave my mouth, I regret them. Now I look like a head case on top of a motor mouth, and really, I'm not sure I want to know his answer. But surprisingly, Justin doesn't look annoyed or impatient with me ruining the mood yet again. He looks earnest.

"It has nothing to do with your clothes," he says, his full lips hinting at a smile. "Or Brandon. Not exactly. It's you. Aly, you changed this summer. He just managed to notice it first."

I shake my head. "You mean my wardrobe changed," I stupidly persist, glancing down at my current outfit, plucked straight from a store mannequin. If I hadn't shown up like this at the campground, there's no way Justin would've looked twice.

"No, *you* did." Gently placing his hands on either side of my neck, Justin tilts my chin up so he can look into my eyes. His warm brown eyes seem determined. "There's a sexy confidence about you now that was missing before."

I almost laugh aloud. *Confidence? What have you been smoking?*

When I scrunch my nose, he grins. "It's true. I've been watching you the past few weeks. Singing at karaoke night, kicking everyone's ass at the beach volleyball competition, prancing around the campground and the hallways at school... Something's changed in you. It's like you flipped a switch, and this new confident, sexy girl came out."

As he speaks, I close my eyes and let the movie memories play. Scared out of my mind on the makeshift stage. Spiking the ball and Brandon throwing me up in the air in victory. Holding his hand in the halls.

Justin's right. I did change. The version of me who did karaoke and strutted around the campground had a brighter smile, a bounce to her step, and, strangely enough, a certain confidence. It had nothing to do with what clothes I wore or how I did my hair and *everything* to do with the guy I was with—and the girl I let myself be when I was with him.

Even in the midst of monumental discomfort and overwhelming confusion, Brandon helped me feel comfortable with who I was on the inside. He believed in me, and that faith gave me the confidence to step out and try some crazy things. At least, crazy for me.

I guess I *have* been pretty badass.

I open my eyes, and Justin smiles. But now all I can think about is Brandon. How he made me feel those weeks we said we were pretending and the look in his eyes when we decided to stop. And I think about our kiss on the beach.

I *really* think about that kiss. Brandon kisses like the boys I read about in books. The boys who can make time stop and worlds change. "Cute and funny" friends don't get kissed like that, and it sucks that the only reason I *did* was because of a dare. But there is heat in Justin's stare. Heat that has nothing to do with a dare. It may only be there thanks to Operation Sex Appeal, but wasn't that the point of the makeover?

Justin runs his thumb across my lips, his eyes seeming to ask permission as he lowers his head. He waits, his mouth nearly touching mine, giving me full control. He won't kiss me if I'm still unsure. That understanding and lack of pressure, along with sensing his desire, makes my decision clear. Here, in front of me, is a great guy who wants me. A guy who, unlike Brandon, sees me as sexy and datable.

My heart feels like it's about to beat right out of my chest. I lick my lips and swallow, then close my eyes and erase the distance between us. A puff of air hits my mouth as he exhales in shock, but then, he takes over.

Kissing Justin is an experience. He's bold and aggressive. He coaxes my lips apart and draws the bottom one into his mouth, sucking as he spears his hands through my hair. He tugs the ends with just an edge of bite, and it's more than obvious the boy has skills. But guilt is a twisted knot in my gut. And it's growing.

I squeeze my eyes shut, wishing the feelings away. Brandon has never—*will* never—think of me as anything more than a friend. The back-to-school dance proved that.

Why do I insist on torturing myself?

Ashamed and confused, I pull away and feel a rumble in Justin's chest.

"You're right." He leans his forehead against mine, and pants of minty breath hit my face. His lips are red and swollen, and they turn up in a mischievous smile. "We're in a semi-secluded corner back here, but we're still technically in public. And the things I want to do to you are not meant for children's eyes."

He chuckles low in his throat, no doubt waiting for me to lob a line right back. I will my mouth to smile, to react in some way...but I can't.

I'm not here.

I'm back on the beach with Brandon. I'm on our pretend date playing shuffleboard. I'm dancing in his arms, coaching with him on the sidelines, and playing basketball with him in my backyard.

The truth doesn't hit me like the shock to the system I would expect. More like a wave of calm serenity. The feeling of truth.

I'm in love with Brandon.

And I'm royally screwed.

My friendship with Brandon is truly over. I confessed my feelings to him once before, and it's amazing we were able to move past the embarrassment. That kind of miracle won't happen twice. The only thing I can do now, what I *have* to do, is attempt to salvage this date.

Struggling to breathe, sadness and regret crushing my lungs, I try and compose my features. Losing it in the middle of The Zone won't do me any good. I stoop to pick up the bat and remind myself why I'm here and what and *who* I gave up to make it happen. I may not be able to toss back witty, sexy banter like most *Casuals*, or make out with my date and not see my ex-best-friend/fake hookup's face, but for the love of everything holy, I can be an effing athlete.

I shove the helmet on my head. "I believe you promised to tutor me?"

Justin grins and rubs his hands together, clueless to the hurricane of emotions roiling through my body. "Yes, ma'am." He turns me around and places his hands on my hips, giving a thorough instruction in how to plant my feet and twist to swing. I exhale, fighting to shake the depression and recapture the feeling I had when Justin caught my eye across the bonfire. Everything I did the past month was to lead me to this moment and what comes next.

I can do this.

Justin moves to the sidewall, and I center myself. His hand hovers over the button. "You know, you look pretty hot with that helmet on."

I can't help but giggle. The thing reeks of sweat and body odor, and I feel like Darth Vader. "You're digging the battered helmet head, huh?"

"I'm digging you, yeah." His voice is low and sexy, and I know he means it. My smile fades. "Now, imagine the ball as your worst enemy's head," he instructs. "I'm giving you permission to whack the crap out of it."

My worst enemy? That's easy. At this moment, it's me.

His finger depresses the button, and the first ball flies. But it's not my face that comes screaming toward me—it's Lauren's. The rubber ball and aluminum bat smack against each other, resulting in a deadened *ping.*

At first, I'm in shock.

I actually *hit* it!

Then adrenaline takes over and I shout, "Holy crap, what a rush!"

I do a victory shimmy, and Justin laughs, calling, "Check you out, girl!"

The pride in his voice is unmistakable, and as the second ball flies out of the machine, a familiar desire to bring my game to the next level, to impress my coach, surges through me. My grip tightens in preparation.

This time, though, when the ball whacks against the bat, there are no happy endorphins. A sharp sting of electricity zings up my arm to the not-so-aptly named funny bone, and I howl.

"Mudderbrudderfribbadiber," I curse, dropping the bat. I shake my arm and begin hopping around like a demented flying squirrel. *Holy crap, this hurts!*

"Aly, you can't drop the bat! Another ball's—"

Too late. By the time I register the *thoomp* from the pitching machine, the ball is flying at my head. But I don't duck like a normal person would do. No, my volleyball training rears its stupid head and I swat the dang thing down with my bare hand.

"AHHHH!"

Now the demented flying squirrel has had squirrel babies as I tuck my throbbing hand under my armpit, cradle my other elbow into my rib cage, and continue to leap and mutter obscenities in pain. Justin tugs me against the wall, away from any more mishaps, and pries my hand out to examine it.

When I notice him biting off a smile, I wrench my hand back.

"You're laughing at me," I accuse through clenched teeth.

He schools his features. "Aly, I'm sorry, but you should've seen yourself." He pauses to cough, an obvious attempt to subdue further laughter at my expense, and says, "You looked like you were performing some type of tribal war dance or something."

Sulking, I nurse my injuries as balls continue to fly past our faces. Then my vivid imagination takes over, conjuring up a possible vision of my "performance," and a graceful snort escapes. Justin looks up in relief.

"It still hurts," I tell him, "and you should've done a better job hiding your pleasure in my pain—"

"I didn't—"

"T-t-t. Shh, I'm speaking," I say with a begrudging grin. "*But* I can see where it may have been a little comical to witness. Although, I assure you, there was nothing funny in the actual experience."

"I'd think not." He straightens my arm and lightly runs his finger along the growing red welt across my palm.

"Please tell me that burnt-rubber smell is not my hand." I sniff the air, looking for another possible source, and Justin rolls his eyes.

"That smell is the hot rubber from the wheels on the pitching machine, you goofball," he says with a shake of his head.

At the front of the cage, the red light turns off and the yellow light clicks on, indicating the end of the turn. Justin stands, dusts the back of his jeans, and grabs his bat. I begin pulling myself up, and he leans down again.

"What are you *doing*?" I ask as he carries me across the threshold of the cage as if it's our honeymoon.

"You're injured," he says, breathing easily as he walks past the trophy case. "I'm taking care of you."

"My legs aren't injured, you idiot." I cast an embarrassed glance around, taking in the amused onlookers, and bury my head in the crook of his neck.

"We've gotta pick better pet names than 'goofball' and 'idiot' if this relationship is going to work," he says, ignoring my struggling attempts to climb out of his arms.

Relationship?

A sinking feeling creeps into my stomach, and the silly, lighthearted feeling I'd grasped so tenuously slips away.

He nods at the portly gentleman holding the front door open. "Thank you."

We arrive at the Jeep, but instead of putting me down as he jiggles the keys out of his pocket, he simply leans back and shifts the additional weight to his chest. He then opens the passenger door, carefully sets me down, and proceeds to buckle me in.

"I'm not completely helpless, you know," I tell him, thrown by his surprising tender side. Where's the legendary player I bargained for?

"I'm nothing if not thorough." He meets my eyes and gently presses a kiss against the raw flesh of my palm. When he attempts to mimic the gesture on my lips, I keep my mouth pressed tight and make an awkward smacking sound.

Justin leans back and gazes into my eyes. I'm sure he's never had a *Casual* do *that* on a date before. At least I'm memorable. "Sorry, I'm just not feeling well."

"I understand." He gives me a small, tight-lipped smile, then closes my door, and I throw my head against the doorjamb.

Three weeks. Homecoming is in three weeks. Ever since Brandon told me about the *Casuals* and *Commitments*, my goal has been to get Justin interested and then ask me to the dance. It's finally within my grasp, and I'm screwing it all up.

Brandon was only supposed to be an assist—not the target. If I give everything up now just because I realized I'm in love with a boy who will *never* love me back, not only will I be an idiot, but I'll be an idiot who threw our friendship away for nothing. There's no way we can come back from the damage I've done. The only thing I can do is stick to the game plan and somehow find a way to get over Brandon.

Tonight, Justin proved he can be more than just a goal in a crazy scheme. Buried deep down inside his player exterior is actually a surprisingly great guy who can maybe even make a good boyfriend. Maybe it's been him all along that I'm meant to be with, the guy to break my curse and prove that I'm a *Casual*.

My brain has everything figured out. Now I just need my heart to get with the program.

SUNDAY, SEPTEMBER 12TH

2 weeks and 6 days until Homecoming ♥

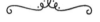

BRANDON

BRANDON'S HOUSE, 11:30 a.m.

Eminem blares out of the speakers, urging me on as I pound the heavy bag, sending it swinging on its chains. I draw a ragged breath and deliver a right cross, slamming the bag into the wall of the garage. The metal shelf shakes, and I reach out to save a box of Christmas decorations from smashing onto the concrete floor. I put them on the ground, then turn back to land a roundhouse.

My workouts have certainly improved the past two weeks.

I ran out here as soon as church ended, desperate for an outlet. We sat with Aly's family again, but she wouldn't even look at me. When the service ended, I heard our moms whispering about some *date* and looking at me in concern. Fuck that.

My cell phone vibrates on the toolbox, shaking the nuts and bolts together with a metallic clink. I lean over to read the display, hope burning out the exhaustion in my chest. But it's Lauren.

I press ignore, sending her to voicemail. Then I turn back and plow into the bag again. I go until my chest burns with the need for oxygen, and then I go a little more.

Justin fell for the game, just like Aly expected. And he wasted no time in making his play, my history with her and our friendship be damned.

If he hurts her...

My vibrating phone sets off another round of metallic clinking. Sweat pours off me and I peel off my shirt, using it to sop up the mixture of sweat, dirt, and dust clinging to my body. I throw off my gloves, chugging my water bottle with a shaking hand as I silence the buzz. This time, I know it's not Aly. What I don't know is if it ever will be her again.

Holding the phone, I consider texting Aly myself, getting it out in the open and fighting for our friendship. But I can't. My head's too messed up, jealous about her date with Justin and terrified that I'm not just falling for her, but that I've already fallen. Aly can't know those things. They don't change anything.

The house alarm's *beep beep* breaks into my inner-tirade, and Mom leans against the laundry room door. Frowning, she turns off the music. "My walls were shaking so hard I thought they discovered another fault line in Texas." She reaches back inside for a towel and throws it at me. "Want to talk about anything?"

I shake my head. "Nah, I'm okay," I tell her, breathing heavy. "Thanks, though."

Her pinched eyes say she's still worried, and she walks over and kisses the top of my head. "Well, if you're not gonna talk, then go take a shower. You stink."

Swatting her thigh with the towel, I laugh. "Glad to see you putting the Parenting with Self-Esteem training to use."

"Boy, if I thought you had a self-esteem problem, we'd be having a whole other conversation." She steps back inside the laundry room and says, "Now, hurry up, we're going out for lunch. I'm in the mood for something spicy."

The door closes and my phone goes off again. I read Lauren's X-rated text, and, realizing what I have to do, I reply.

ALY

ALY'S HOUSE, 1:45 p.m.

"*And* then what happened?" Gabi asks, digging a spoon into the pint of Chunky Monkey between us. We're in the middle of my queen-size bed rehashing my date. Between practice, our rec game, and then a slammed day at work, I was too wiped to give any details yesterday, so my friends took matters into their own hands, showing up with calorie-laden goodness.

"Justin took me to his house, made an icepack for my hand, and cooked us omelets for dinner." I lick my spoon as I replay the night in my mind. "He's completely different than I expected."

Kara opens her bag of veggies, picks out a celery stick, and takes a healthy, tasteless bite. "Did you get to meet his stinking rich parents?"

"No, they weren't home." Their eyes widen, and I shake my head. "Nothing happened. I'm telling y'all, he's not as bad as people say."

What I don't tell them is that when I wasn't trying to distract him from making out in the empty house, I got him to talk about *why* it was empty. Looking around his enormous living room, it didn't just look like no one was home; it looked like no one even lived there. After gentle prodding, Justin admitted his dad pretty much lives out of a suitcase, traveling for work, and his stepmom is more concerned with spa treatments and social events than playing homemaker. From the way he describes it, I gather any scrap of maternal instinct she does possess goes straight to his stepbrother Chase.

Seeing Justin in his house, getting a look behind the curtain, added another layer to the mystery. I can't imagine what it would be like growing up without my parents constantly in my life, wanting to know every detail and planning ridiculous family-bonding nights.

"If nothing happened," Kara says with a look implying she doesn't believe that at all, "what did you do all night?"

"I didn't say nothing happened. I said nothing *much* happened." It's not my place to spread Justin's dirty family laundry, and it's not as if we only talked. I wrinkle my nose at their eager expressions. "We kissed."

Gabi folds her pillow in half and shoves it under her chin. "Why do I get the feeling it wasn't all stardust and moonbeams?"

I sigh. "I don't know. Justin's great. But something just felt...off." I bite my lip and twist the silky fabric of my throw pillow, waging an inner battle over how much I can tell my friends. The weight of dishonesty is oppressive, but if I come clean now, they'll hate me.

I've already lost Brandon. I can't lose Gabi and Kara, too.

But I also can't ignore the clawing in my throat and chest anymore. I desperately need to talk to my friends, to hear them say these feelings for Brandon will go away. That the pieces of my heart will one day glue back together and someday we can even be friends again. That one day I will actually be able to breathe when I think about him. Or talk over the lump in my throat when his name comes up, or I imagine him with some other girl.

The decorative ruffle on the pillow rips, and I stare at the jagged fabric in my hands. The least I can do is be honest about how I feel. Sitting up, I tuck my legs under me and admit, "I need help."

Their eyes widen at the tears in my eyes. Gabi and Kara lean forward simultaneously in support, and guilt tears through me, making me feel even smaller, even weaker. How amazing would it feel to be completely honest, to let them know how badly I messed everything up and how much I lost?

"When Justin kissed me," I say, preemptively wincing at what I'm about to reveal, "I couldn't stop thinking about Brandon."

Kara blinks. "Yikes. Sucks to be Justin."

Gabi reaches over and smacks the back of her head. "Way to go, Ms. Sensitivity. We're supposed to be supporting *Aly* right now."

"No, she's right." I groan and fall back against the bed, digging my hands into my eyes. "That about sums it up. What is wrong with me?"

"Nothing," Gabi assures me, wiggling my foot. "You're just confused."

"No, I completely suck as a human being," I mumble, reaching for the pint of ice cream. "Who goes out with the hottest guy in school and freaking fantasizes about being with someone else?"

"Um, not to be obtuse again, but Brandon's pretty hot, too," Kara cuts in.

Gabi shoots her a glare. "Aly, I'm sure—"

"*And* it's not like the person I'm fantasizing about is wasting any time pining for me," I continue, digging a heart-shaped trench through the center with my spoon. "I doubt my face floats in Brandon's mind when he's off sucking face with his flavor of the week."

Gabi pries my hand away from the carton. "Have you even seen him with anyone lately? I don't recall a single girl draped on his arm since before y'all hooked up. Maybe he *is* thinking about you. "

Kara sprawls beside me and runs her fingers through my hair. "Are you really this upset just because you thought about Brandon? I mean, everyone fantasizes and plays the *what-if* game, Aly. It's perfectly normal behavior."

"But that's not fair to Justin," I say wearily. "He's been so sweet and understanding. He deserves better than to have me thinking of some other dude whenever he kisses me."

"What about the other, non-kissing stuff?" Gabi asks. "Does that feel off, too?"

I lift a shoulder. "He makes me laugh. And he definitely has the 411 on what girls like to hear. He's almost too smooth to be honest." I pause. "But, even though he opened up about some family stuff, we don't really talk or have a lot in common."

Not like Brandon and me.

"Talking's overrated." Kara looks up from braiding my hair and points at me with narrowed eyes. "And I'm still not buying that's what made you all leaky-eyed. Spill it."

I shift under the scrutiny and throw Gabi a look, but she joins in with her own intent stare. I huff and sink further into the pillows. "Well, it's not just that I thought about him during our date. I kinda realized something huge after Justin kissed me."

Gabi nods, a smug smile creeping onto her face, and Kara's fingers stop braiding.

"I'm in love with Brandon."

"Well, duh."

"Excuse me?" I ask.

Gabi rolls her eyes. "I said duh. As in, 'no duh.' An expression meant to convey the sentiment of *Where the hell have you been?* and *Are you seriously just figuring this out?*"

I look at Kara, who shrugs in response. "Wait, I knew y'all thought we were hot for each other, but there's a huge difference between *that* and me being in love with the guy."

"Well, yeah," Kara admits. "But once you got together, the love part was pretty obvious."

I gape at them incredulously. "And no one thought they should clue me in?"

"Sweetie, don't even." Gabi pushes up on her elbows. "Every time we've brought up our thoughts on the Brandon situation, you've bitten our heads off. Besides, we thought you knew. Like Kara said, it was pretty obvious."

Awesome. If it was so obvious, then Brandon must know, too. No wonder he wanted out.

Kara scoots up and grabs my hand. "So what are you going to do?"

I sigh and lay my head on her bony shoulder. "What can I do? Brandon broke up with me. This earth-shattering news doesn't change that. But it's probably not fair to keep dating Justin, right? When I'm in love with someone else?"

Gabi digs out a heaping spoon of ice cream and hands it to me. "Not to fall bias to gender stereotypes, but I honestly don't think Justin will care if you use him. I doubt he's out looking for a serious relationship here. You've seen the girls he usually dates."

I lick my spoon and think about Lauren.

"And there's nothing wrong with just having fun sometimes." Kara bumps my shoulder. "Live a little. Flirt, loosen up, have an adventure. Do something completely *un*-Aly-like for once."

I almost laugh aloud. Kara just described the exact type of girl I have been trying to become. A *Casual*.

"Kara, you're right. I probably *should* just shut up and enjoy it." I take a deep breath. "But I'm starting to think maybe I'm just not built that way."

As soon as the words leave my mouth, I know it's the most honest thing I've said in a long time.

MONDAY, SEPTEMBER 13TH
2 weeks and 5 days until Homecoming ♥

ALY

FAIRFIELD ACADEMY, 12:00 p.m.

The cafeteria hierarchy established itself the first day of ninth grade. It's wrong on so many levels, just like the guys' chauvinistic ranking system, but it exists. And for the last three years, it's been comfortable. Lunch used to be the one period I could count on in the school day *not* to cause anxiety. That was before I started dating Justin.

As I slide my bright orange tray along the stainless steel rails in the kitchen, inhaling the aroma of greasy pizza and fries, I think about the mess I've made. My first two weeks eating with the Beautiful People were fine. Even though Brandon and I were just pretending, sitting beside him felt right. As though I belonged, even though I didn't.

But sitting next to Justin—*whom I'm legitimately dating*—while staring across the table at Brandon—*whom I actually love*—is nothing short of awkward.

Justin reaches across me for my tray and kisses me on the cheek.

"Please curb the PDA until I have something in my stomach," Gabi grumbles behind us. "I'd rather not dry heave today."

He smiles and nods for me to walk ahead of him. "You're funny, Gabi. How did I not know that?"

She shrugs. "Could it be you were too busy sucking face with a bunch of skanks to notice the brilliant females around you?"

I shoot her a murderous look, but Justin just flings his head back and laughs.

If I survive the next forty minutes, it'll be a miracle.

Grabbing my plastic carton of milk, I wait as Justin pays. Posters for the upcoming dance and talent show decorate the path to our table. As I sit down, feeling the squish of dropped French fries under my ballet flats, I realize Justin hasn't mentioned Homecoming yet. And time is ticking.

"Anyone thinking about entering the talent show?" I ask the table at large, hoping I can steer the conversation to include the dance the following weekend.

Gabi dusts crumbs off her seat and plops down next to me. "Y'all know the whole thing was Aly's idea." She nudges me with an elbow, then folds her huge slice of pizza and shoves it into her mouth.

"Not the *whole* thing," I clarify. "It was Lauren's idea to make the talent show a fundraiser and move it later in the day."

After I bowed out early from the board meeting, the group took my talent show idea one step further. Lauren suggested changing it into a competition with an entrance fee to raise money for our school's philanthropy, a local elementary school. She also proposed moving it a few hours later and selling refreshments, thus raising even more.

Although I'll never admit it to her face, the girl took my idea to a whole other level.

"I might toss my hat in the ring," Carlos says, leaning over Justin to get my attention. "Wanna team up? You can sing while I play the guitar."

The blood drains from my face, and I shake my head back and forth. "Uh, no. I don't think that would be a good idea."

"Come on, you rocked at karaoke." Carlos scrapes his chair back to look at me. "You'd be helping a brother out. No one wants to listen to an idiot play guitar by himself for three minutes. And you heard me sing, Aly. I need ya."

A tray drops on the table across from me. "Are you begging for a date again, Carlos?"

I look over to see Brandon watching me before he turns to Carlos with an exaggerated sigh. "Man, I told you there are better ways of getting a girl to go out with you."

Nine days.

It's been nine long days since that day at the movie theatre. The day of my party. The last day we spoke.

And it's been three days since I discovered I'm in love with him.

Yesterday, church was almost painful. Our hands brushing when we sat and when we stood, but never once looking at each other. I *couldn't* look at him. If I had, he'd have known everything I'm feeling—if he doesn't already. But now, I can't stop.

There's a tightness in his eyes that I'm not used to seeing, a rigidness in his shoulders normally not there. But he's still gorgeous. Same model lips, same soft green eyes. And my heart reacts just the same as ever—by banging around in my chest like it wants to jump out and say hello.

"You're not funny, dude," Carlos replies, although the humor in his voice says otherwise. "I was trying to get Aly to do the talent show with me."

Brandon meets my stare, and it's like an electric shock to my system. My tummy spasms as he studies my face, which I assume shows terror more than heartache because he shakes his head and says, "Sorry. My client only sings at events preapproved by her management. You'll have to find another partner."

I mouth a silent *thank-you,* hoping he doesn't see the tears welling in my eyes. Brandon to the rescue again. No matter what's going on between us, he never fails to save me.

The loud, chaotic cafeteria seems to fade as I stare into his calm, familiar face, and I make a decision. It hurts to be in love and know that I can never have him, but I refuse to lose Brandon completely. Friendship is infinitely better than nothing at all.

Justin scoots closer and puts his hand on my knee. "Your client?"

Brandon punctures his carton of chocolate milk with a straw. "I discovered her talent," he says with a forced smile. "That makes me her manager."

The guys enter some sort of silent eye war, and Gabi clears her throat quietly, shooting me a sideways smirk. Ignoring her, I pick up my lunch.

"Mmm. Gotta love pizza day," I say around a big, cheesy bite.

Justin takes the hint and Brandon does, too, and in the silence that falls, my yummy noises are amplified. Both guys chuckle at my exuberance, and for a brief while, things are okay. Not great, but not horrid either. That is, until a feminine voice says, "Thanks for saving my seat."

Brandon visibly tenses as Lauren takes the open seat beside him, sending him a secret smile. She rests her hand on his arm like it belongs there, and jealousy twists in my stomach.

Are they together now?

She wrinkles her nose as she examines his plate. "Do you *always* eat only one thing at a time?"

The way she asks implies a hidden meaning, as does the look she cuts in my direction, but I ignore both. "You've unearthed his dirty little secret," I say, balling up my rough brown napkin. "I can't tell you how many times I've dared the boy to mix it up a little. To try taking a bite of pizza and then, heaven forbid, a bite of corn, but it's like he physically cannot bring himself to do it."

I smirk at Brandon, daring him into our usual pattern of friendly teasing, and he folds his arms on the table with a smirk of his own. "Oh yeah? What about you, Ms. No-Ice-in-Drinks-and-Must-Lather-Myself-with-Cookie-Smelling-Lotion-Every-Day-So-My-Skin-Doesn't-Prematurely-Wrinkle?"

Lauren's lip curls up in obvious annoyance, but relief pours through my soul. Goofing off with Brandon, teasing, shared history, and inside jokes. This feels like home.

Gabi snorts and twists in her chair to point at me. "He got you there."

I grin. "Yeah, so I have my own odd quirks. But to love me is to love my quirks and all."

Justin slides his arm around the back of my chair. "I knew you came with a few quirks, goofball." His smile seems forced as he ducks his head to kiss my shoulder. "And personally, I love the cookie-smelling lotion."

"Goofball?" Brandon asks.

Justin's forced smile grows wider. "My pet name for Aly," he explains. "She calls me idiot." He lifts a hand to run it through my hair. "They have a certain ring to them, don't you think?"

Brandon makes a disgusted noise, and when his green eyes meet mine, they're void of any trace of our delicate truce and previous humor. Two steps forward, five steps back.

No longer hungry, I push away my tray.

FRIDAY, SEPTEMBER 17TH
2 weeks and 1 day until Homecoming ♥

ALY
ALY'S HOUSE, 9:25 p.m.

My eyes are on Justin instead of the big screen mounted on the media room wall. The glow from the romantic comedy on the television illuminates the slight dimple in his cheek, and as he laughs, I wonder again how I got here.

The movie is almost over, and I couldn't tell you a single thing about it. Most girls on a date with Justin Carter would claim that for an entirely different reason. But nope, no making out for us. Claiming exhaustion from work and practice, I excused my way out of it. And the fact that I felt the need to do so confirmed that I can't do this anymore.

Who is this girl I've become? Whoever she is, I don't like her very much.

My so-called relationship with Brandon wasn't real, but it felt like it was. Real enough to prove that I want a *real* relationship. Brandon was right. I can't do meaningless hookups—my emotions get way too involved.

Justin snakes his hand behind my back and pulls me down to lie next to him on the cool leather sofa.

He kisses the tip of my nose and grins. "I need an Aly-fix."

He cups the base of my neck and tries to tilt my head back.

I place my hand on his wrist. *This is it.* "Justin?"

"Mmhmm," he answers, tracing lazy patterns across my cheek with the tip of his finger.

My eyes flutter closed, and for a moment, I consider not saying anything. Going on with the ruse and hoping that my feelings will someday change. But that wouldn't be fair.

I wrench my eyes back open. "There's something I want to talk to you about."

He presses a quick kiss to my cheek and pushes himself up on his elbow. "Okay, but me first." He looks excited, which instantly has my tummy cramping. This can't be good. Brushing my hair behind my shoulder, he takes a deep breath and says, "Would you go to Homecoming with me?"

My jaw unhinges. "Huh?"

Justin puts his fingers under my chin and closes my mouth. "It's stupid, I know. You're my girlfriend, so obviously we'll go together, but I wanted to ask officially."

"Girlfriend?" I ask incredulously, my eyes darting between his eyes and lips.

The world starts spinning double-time.

He looks down, and a shy smile creeps up his face. In that moment, he looks young and vulnerable, and nothing like the heartbreaker of Fairfield Academy.

"If you want," he says softly. He draws a shaky breath and lifts his gaze back up to meet mine. "I'd like you to be. But it's been a while, so you have to promise to be gentle."

It is surreal. The last six weeks of chaos have built to this moment. The merging of my original goal—to be noticed by the male species and hopefully get a *non*-friend date to Homecoming—and the end goal—to prove I've changed, that people are seeing me differently, and that I could snag the interest of the biggest player, the male epitome of *Casual*.

The curse of the Wall of Shame will be broken if only I can just keep my mouth shut.

"Why have you been fighting with Brandon?"

Or not.

The question pops out unconsciously. I was prepared to break up with him or possibly even carry the charade on further like a spineless jellyfish, but I didn't expect those words to come out of my mouth. But I'm not going to take them back.

Justin doesn't flinch. He presses his lips together and absently strokes my arm. "You noticed, huh?"

After his territorial performance at lunch on Monday—all but peeing on me in front of the entire table—Brandon and Lauren started sitting at the other end. And whenever we've run into them in the halls, the tension has been electric.

Justin shoves a pillow under his head and scoots back so he can see me better. "I told you I used to watch the two of you together and I saw how much you changed," he says, reminding me of our conversation at the batting cages. "But at first, I have to admit, I didn't buy it."

You and everyone else, I think. What I say is, "Why not?"

He presses his lips in a thin line. "Aly, you're many things, but *Casual* isn't one of them."

I almost laugh. The guy I set out to win over—to prove I can change my image and become someone else—never even fell for it. There goes my Project Change My Status success.

"And Brandon's always been my wingman, so when he hooked up with you, a girl into relationships, it felt like he abandoned me for something we both said we never wanted." Justin squints at the cushion above my head as if he is still trying to make sense of Brandon's change. "Brandon ragged on Drew about being whipped harder than any of us, but then out of nowhere he showed up with you." His forced laugh is dark, but when he meets my eyes, the emotion in them strikes me. "Watching him, though, I started to think maybe you were the difference."

A tsunami of shame hits me. Justin's declaration of honesty contrasts so sharply with everything I've done since starting Operation Sex Appeal. And the worst part is that he left out a vital piece of information while drawing his angst-driven conclusion: the whole thing was a hoax. Not the makeover part, but definitely Brandon and me. Or, at least, we began that way. Justin is giving me *way* too much credit.

I open my mouth to explain, but he presses a finger against my lips. "If you haven't noticed, I don't do the talking thing. No one knows about my absent parents, and I never talk about feelings or any of that crap. But I feel like I can talk to you. At the batting cages, you said we've never really been friends, but to me, we were. And you were my only friend who was a girl. Watching you with him, I realized I wasn't angry. I was jealous. If anyone could make me want a commitment, too, it'd be you. And when Brandon dropped the ball and broke up with you at the dance, I saw it as my chance."

A half-laugh of amazement escapes my lips, and I blink a few times to clear away the crazy parallel universe I've somehow stepped in. "Justin, I don't know what to say. That is so sweet."

And completely undeserved.

Shaking my head, I twist my fingers into the soft cotton of his shirt, feeling the taut muscles of his chest flex beneath my touch. Before I confess, I need to understand. "But I'm not really sure what that has to do with the two of you fighting now."

Justin shakes his head and sighs as if I'm a child not comprehending something obvious. "The body wasn't even cold, Aly. He called it off, and I jumped in before he had a chance to change his mind. I saw what I wanted, and I took it. But that doesn't mean he can't try to win you back." He lowers his head and presses his forehead against mine. "I know I would."

Justin is officially perfect. He's a great guy, and he'd make an amazing boyfriend. I know I *should* be ecstatic, but what keeps flashing across my mind is that I'm lying here with the wrong boy. And I *really* don't want to hurt this one.

After an admission like that, Justin deserves so much better.

I squeeze my eyes shut and whisper, "I can't do this."

"Go to Homecoming?" The confusion is evident in his voice. "Okay... I thought girls were obsessed with that kind of thing, but we definitely don't have to. What do you want to do instead?"

I shake my head and throw it into his chest. From behind a wall of blackness, I force myself to be honest. "No, I don't mean Homecoming. I mean us. I can't do this."

Laughter from downstairs floats under the door, and his body goes still next to mine.

I lift my head and crack an eye open.

Shadows dance across his face from the flickering movie screen, revealing taut lips and a tense jaw, his emotions completely shuttered.

"What do you mean?" His words are slow and careful, and the abrupt change twists my stomach. But I know hurting him now is better than hurting him later. And that's exactly what I'm doing. Hurting him.

Without meaning to, I've been toying with Justin's feelings, using him to meet a stupid, self-imposed goal. What I did was selfish and unforgiveable, but now I *need* to try and make things right.

Calling on every ounce of courage in me, I press on, digging my nails into the fleshy palms of my hands. "I like you, Justin. A lot. More than I expected, which, considering I've been borderline obsessed with you since right before the camping trip, is saying something." I stop to take another breath and see his mouth soften a fraction. "Karaoke night? The change in clothes? I did those things to get your attention."

His eyebrows shoot up in surprise, and I offer a tiny smile. "I thought if I could get you to notice me, everything would fall into place. But, Justin, you need to know that as often as I imagined being with you, the reality blows every fantasy I've had out of the water."

Justin's body relaxes, reminding me that I have gotten off-track.

"*But*," I say, wincing when his face shuts down again. "It's not fair to you to keep going out. Not when my head is so messed up." I wet my lips, knowing I have to say this next part. For the first time in six weeks, it's time to be honest. But I dread the look on his face. Closing my eyes, I say, "Not when I'm in love with Brandon."

Admitting it aloud to Justin is almost as painful and embarrassing as confessing it to Brandon would be, and when I hear no other reaction other than a few shallow breaths, I get scared.

"Justin, I'm so, so sorry." Fearing what I'm doing, how I'm feeling, everything I'm giving up, I throw my arms around his neck and bury my head into his chest. "God, I don't know what I'm doing anymore. Was it wrong to say anything? It's like I'm watching us from a distance and I'm screaming at myself to shut up, that you're a great guy, but I just can't do it!"

The soft cotton of his shirt grows wet with my tears, and I cling to him, waiting for him to speak or do something. Knowing I deserve whatever he gives me.

Will he be hurt?

Of course he will.

Will he be angry with me? Yell?

All the possibilities are scary, but the nothingness is far worse.

After what feels like an eternity, Justin brushes my hair back and props a finger under my chin. He waits until I reluctantly open my eyes before exhaling a long, minty breath.

"It wasn't wrong to say anything." His voice is slightly guarded, but his eyes are understanding. "I think I would've liked to stay in the dark a little longer, but I appreciate your honesty." His voice cracks, somewhere between a sob and a laugh. "Shit. Relationships suck."

Anger would have been better.

If he were angry, at least I could've maybe defended myself. And later, while crying into my Oreos, I could hold onto it and tell myself things weren't that bad. That he wasn't as great as I thought he was.

But *this*?

This I can't handle.

My chest tightens, my stomach sinks, and I crumble. A sob hitches in my throat, and my ears buzz. I shake my head roughly, choking the words out. "No. No, they don't, Justin. Please don't—don't give up on relationships because of me. I used you, and I was wrong. You're amazing."

I press my face into his chest again, my shoulders shaking uncontrollably. After a few ragged breaths, I ask, "Is there any way you can forgive me?" I look up at him, suck in my lips, and drag my hand across my face. "Do you think we can ever be friends again someday?"

Justin heaves a heavy sigh and kisses the top of my head. "We're friends now, Aly."

He tightens his arms around me, and I give him a watery smile. He attempts a grin in return, and we stare at each other in silence.

I want to make things better, to lighten things up and somehow make it so that he doesn't leave this room hating me. But there is nothing I can do or say. I can't come back from this. I can't make it right.

At least not tonight.

Justin gives me a tight smile, then stands and shoves his hands into his pockets, looking uncomfortable. He walks to where he'd kicked off his shoes and slips them back on. Turning around, he puffs out his cheeks and snaps his fingers together. "I'm gonna go. I guess."

I meet him at the entryway of the media room and put my hand out, closing the door he'd just opened. I wrap my arms around him in one last hug. Holding him tight with my ear against his chest, I can hear and feel his uneven breathing, and my waterworks kick on again.

He kisses the top of my head and gently pushes me back. He slips through the door without a word, closing it firmly behind him, leaving me all alone.

Sinking against the door, I let the sobs overtake me.

SATURDAY, SEPTEMBER 18TH

2 weeks until Homecoming ♥

BRANDON
FAIRWOOD CITY PLAYGROUND,
GYMNASIUM, 12:20 p.m.

The metal doors bang shut. Aly treks across the squeaky floor, arms wrapped so tightly around herself you'd think it was January instead of summer in hot-as-hell Texas, and I watch from lowered lashes.

I flip the pages of the playbook, trying to appear busy as she plops down at the table beside me. Across the room, Baylee and Kaitie laugh, the sound highlighting just how silent the two of us are.

"Should be an easy win today," I say, grasping at straws. She hasn't even looked at me.

Aly nods stiffly, keeping her head down.

Huffing in frustration, I throw down the clipboard and squat in front of her. "How long are we—" I break off at the sight of her bloodshot eyes and immediately change direction. "What happened?"

She shrugs and looks away. "Allergies."

"Allergies, huh?"

She grabs the clipboard and starts writing like crazy, her white-knuckled grip on the pencil dangerously close to snapping it in two. Seeing happy-go-lucky Aly upset is bad enough, but having no idea why just shows how far we've drifted the last few weeks.

Aly lifts her eyes and, seeing I'm not going anywhere, sets the pencil down. "What do you want, Brandon?" She sounds exhausted, and her shoulders sag in defeat.

I crouch lower to search her red-rimmed eyes. "I want to know what's wrong. Are you sick? Hurt?" Aly looks away, and I grasp her chin, forcing her to meet my eyes. "Tell me what's going on."

She sighs. "I'm fine."

Jerking her jaw out of my grip, she picks the pencil back up, obviously assuming I'll let it go at that pathetic attempt. Her eyes dart to my chest, shoulders, and feet while she scribbles, her bouncing leg shaking the whole table.

Our entire friendship has been about honesty, calling each other on our bullshit. She calls me on mine all the time. Every day we spend not talking is torture, like my soul is inside-out and my nerves are being sliced by an electric can opener. I need to fix this. I need to find out why she's so upset, make it better, and get her back in my life.

"Really?" I ask, letting my frustration bleed into my voice. "On your *word*?"

Aly's head snaps up. It's the first time I've ever used the expression. I've never had to before because Aly's always confided in me willingly. Using it now, knowing she's holding back, hurts more than the silent treatment.

A range of emotions flickers across her face before she finally answers. "No, not on my word." She drops the damned pencil again and folds her arms on the plastic tabletop, laying her head down without breaking eye contact. "Justin and I broke up last night."

The thrill the words shoot through me is short-lived as I take notice of her pale, splotchy skin and puffy eyes. I was there when she broke up with Adam. She was a mess, consoling herself with endless chick flicks and mountains of chocolate, but she still never looked this bad. For her to be this upset over Justin, she must've fallen for him.

"I knew this would happen." Even as the words come out, I know I'm handling this wrong, but I can't seem to stop. Turns out, jealousy's a bitch. It makes my voice hard and cold as I say, "I warned you, didn't I? But you wouldn't listen. You were obsessed with that fucking *Wall of Shame,* and look what it got you."

A block of ice settles on my chest as soon as the words are out. The jealous, raging monster finally broke loose, verbally spewing hate on the one person who matters most. Aly's eyes fill with pain, and I know *I'm* the reason it's there. I vowed to protect her. Now I'm the one hurting her.

I really am a monster.

She bolts up, knocking the metal chair to the ground. "And you know everything, right, Brandon?" Her head falls back, and I watch in horror as tears spill onto her cheeks. It cripples me. "Who in the hell are *you* to lecture me? Have you *ever* put yourself out there and taken a chance?"

Her gorgeous blue eyes, full of tears, knock me on my ass. "No," I murmur with a shake of my head. She knows better than anyone that I haven't. "Aly, please, I'm sorry. I'm so sorry. I don't know—"

She laughs, a watery sound bubbling in her throat. "No, you don't know."

Too scared to open my mouth again and make it worse, but terrified of doing *nothing,* I stand and move to take a step forward. She throws her palms up to stop me. "I'm going home. Can you handle this alone?"

I nod, my heart thumping in my ears, my chest so tight my breaths are sawing in and out.

What the fuck just happened?

Aly storms to the double doors at the back of the gym, and I rake my fingers through my hair. Glaring sunlight carves a hole in the dim gym, and right before she steps out, Aly glances back, an unreadable expression replacing her anger.

Self-loathing consumes me.

If I had kept my mouth shut, none of this would have happened. Not our fake hookup. Not the kiss or pretend date. Not the fights or the distance between us.

And Justin would've never had a chance to hurt her.

My body shakes with the need to make him pay and the knowledge that I failed to keep it from happening. I check the clock on the scoreboard and square my shoulders. I won't fail her again.

In a little over two hours, the guys and I are meeting at Oakdale Park for a friendly game of football. Justin might think he can get away with treating girls like trash, but he's about to learn that, when it comes to Aly, all bets are off.

BRANDON
OAKDALE PARK, 2:58 p.m.

My truck rumbles as I park on the edge of the open lot and scan the huddled groups for Justin. By some miracle, our team won this afternoon's match, even with one coach gone and the other distracted as hell. We kept our season undefeated, but my mind has one, singular thought: Find Justin and make him pay.

Through my open window, I hear Carlos cackle. I shift my gaze, then find Justin stretching in the back right corner of the field. I kill the engine, toss my keys into the ashtray, and slam the door behind me.

No one notices me stalking across the grass until I'm almost on top of him. Carlos sees me first and says something that has Justin and Drew look up, confused. When Justin's weasel eyes meet mine, I spit on the ground, and he jumps up.

Carlos flies at me, pinning my arms behind my back. "Dude, what the fuck?"

"Stay out of this, Carlos," I warn. "This is between me and him."

Drew grits his teeth, muscles in his jaw popping as he struggles to push Justin in the opposite direction. Justin's hands claw his shoulder, trying to get around him. *Bring it on.* "Brandon, what the hell's your problem?"

"My problem, Drew, is this asshole thinking he can treat girls like shit," I say, blood roaring in my ears. "And thinking he can get away with doing it to Aly."

"You don't know shit about me and Aly!" Justin breaks free, and Drew grabs his shoulders again, twisting him back around. Justin curses and leans around to shout, "Or any other girl I've been with. Stay the fuck out of my business, Taylor."

"Oh, I don't know shit?" I ask, advancing steadily forward, dragging Carlos behind me. "I fucking know you played her. And that you brought your brother into it, making her think you're the sweet, misunderstood type." I draw a shallow, shaky breath and narrow my eyes. "And I know that you threw her away when you finished your twisted game."

Justin's nostrils flare. "You're fucking jealous. If anyone threw that girl away, it was *you*."

I growl, and Carlos pins my arms back tighter. "I saw her at the game. She was heartbroken." My voice breaks on the last word, and my fists clench tighter, aching to hurt him like he did her. "Because of you."

"Because of me?" Justin laughs darkly. "You're an asshole." He wrenches out of Drew's grip and pushes him away. "I don't need this shit."

He heads for the parking lot, and I'm about to yell after him when he spins back around.

"Believe it or not, I *do* care about Aly, so here's a little tip. The guy she's in love with? The guy she's so miserable about? Yeah, that would be you, dickhead."

He spits on the ground and takes off.

My arms fall forward as Carlos drops them. "He's my ride."

He races after Justin, and I slump to the grass, adrenaline slamming through my body.

Could it be true? Is Aly in love with *me*?

Exhilaration and disbelief mixes in my gut, and Drew crouches down and grabs my shoulders. "Dude, stop it! Stop blowing me off. Stop pretending this is about Justin. This is about *you*. And you not admitting what's fucking obvious to the rest of us is turning you into someone I don't know. The Brandon I know doesn't attack his friends." I sneer, thinking about the kind of *friend* Justin has been, and Drew shakes his head. "Even dicks like Justin."

My body shakes as I try and gain control of my breathing. As I come off the endorphin rush, a bit of sanity sinks in. "You're right." I close my eyes and throw my head back. "Dammit, I don't know what the hell just happened."

Drew huffs. "I do. What I wanna know is why. You gonna get real with me or what?" He relaxes his grip on my shoulders. "What's going on with Aly? Why did you call it off if it was gonna make you act like a lunatic?"

"I didn't," I say, dragging my hand down my face. "She did."

Drew's head jerks back. "Dude, I saw her after you left the dance. Believe me when I tell you, she thinks you dumped her."

"That's not possible." I kick out my legs, stretching out a cramp in my calf, and grab an unopened bottle of water. "Aly knows what went down. And I think I know when I've been dumped. Not that it's ever happened before."

He continues staring at me strangely, and Carlos jogs up. "Justin took off without me. Guess that means one of you gets the privilege of taking my ass home." He plops down and pounds my back. "Kid, you sure know how to break up a party." Using his shirt to wipe his face, he looks at me and then Drew. "So what'd I miss?"

Drew nods. "Brandon was just telling me Aly broke it off at the dance. Carlos, you were on the breezeway. How did you think it went down?"

"Like Aly had her heart ripped out and bitch-slapped." We both shoot him a look, and he shrugs. "I don't know. She looked upset, all right? Like a girl who'd been dumped. Definitely not the dumper."

I shake my head. "Not possible. She's obsessed with Justin, and breaking it off with me gave him an opening. Which he took," I say through gritted teeth. "She got what she wanted."

Drew grabs his own water and takes a long sip. Chucking the half-empty bottle on the ground, he pins me with a frustrated look. "Not to risk the wrath of Angry Brandon, but when have you ever known Justin to lie to make himself look *bad*? He just stood there in front of two other witnesses and told you he actually cared about a girl and that girl dropped him because she was in love with you." He looks at Carlos, who nods. "At least that's the impression I got."

Carlos clears his throat. "And, if I may inject an opinion, I believe Señor Cranky Pants feels the same way about her."

Drew snickers, and I reel again over the idea that Aly could be in love with me.

But I know it's not true.

"She's not in love with me," I say, lying down, exhausted, on the cool grass. "She might've told Justin that as an excuse, but it's not true."

"For argument's sake, let's say you're right. That still leaves you," Drew says, watching me intently. "Are *you* in love with *her*?"

I open my mouth to deny it, but I can't. It would be a lie. I know it and they know it. I'm not simply falling for Aly anymore—I'm in love with her. I've spent the last three weeks fighting it, afraid of falling in love and losing Aly. I've done both. I've lost the person I care about more than anyone in this world, and I'll do whatever it takes to get her back.

As if reading my thoughts, Drew says, "You need to tell Aly."

"No, what I *need* is to get our friendship back." Drew huffs, but I stand up, ignoring him. "Either telling Aly I love her will scare her off, or she'll want a relationship—and you know where I stand on those. Either way I'll lose her for real, and losing Aly would be like losing my dad all over again. I'd rather have her as a friend than nothing at all."

Drew squints up at me. "But what if it could be more?"

I shove my hands into my pockets and shake my head. "I don't believe in anything more."

ALY

ALY'S HOUSE, 3:20 p.m.

"*I* got the S.O.S.," Gabi calls, letting herself in the back door. "And I brought reinforcements."

Plopping a stack of DVDs and a carton of ice cream down on the kitchen counter, Gabi kicks off her shoes and tiptoes to the recliner where I lie curled in the fetal position.

"Oh, this needs the heavy artillery." She reaches in her back pocket for her cell phone and speed-dials Kara. "Hey, where you at? Good, turn around and grab a bag of Oreos, a cucumber, red nail polish, and one of those neon-green mud mask things. Yeah, it's worse than I thought." Disconnecting the call, she squeezes into the tiny crack between the armrest and my curled-up body. "Chica, what's going on?"

I sigh and lift my head to rest it on her shoulder. "You were right."

"I usually am."

Without looking up, I know she's smirking. Rolling my eyes, I continue. "You said Operation Sex Appeal was a stupid idea, and I should've listened. All that obsessing over Homecoming and where did it get me? Heartbroken and dateless, two freaking weeks before the dance."

Gabi rocks us quietly while she absorbs the information. "I take it you saw Justin last night."

"Saw him, stomped on his heart, broke up with him, and cried my eyes out."

"Hmm." I crane my neck and take in Gabi's scrunched-up mouth and forehead. She meets my eyes and shrugs. "I don't get it. Wasn't all this about Homecoming? And getting a guy? You had both, you rejected both, and you're miserable. What the hell, Aly?"

"I know!" Groaning, I tuck my knees tighter into my chest. "I just couldn't do it, Gab. You should've heard the stuff he was saying—he's amazing. He asked me to be his girlfriend and asked me to Homecoming..." I trail off, laughing at my wonderfully horrible situation before sighing and throwing myself against Gabi's side again.

"Wow. That sucks. I hate it when hot, popular guys do that stuff to me." Scowling at her sarcasm, I kick my foot against the coffee table, flinging our chair back. Gabi shakes her head. "I mean, asking you to be his girlfriend? Sounds like he deserved to be kicked to the curb. Girl power."

I uncross my arms to jab her in the side. "I'm sorry, I think your agenda's confused. Last night was self-loathing. Today is pity. And empathy, which seems to be in short supply everywhere I go." I sigh, shaking my head and remembering my conversation with Brandon. "Now kindly stick to the program or leave. I can berate myself quite thoroughly on my own."

Gabi chuckles, then wraps her arms around me and kisses the top of my head. "I'm sorry, you're right. Believe me, I pity you." I jab her again, and she laughs. "Okay, so Justin's out. Does that mean Operation Sex Appeal's out, too?"

Yes. No. Ugh!

Am I really thinking of calling the whole thing off two weeks before Homecoming? Granted, it's been a complete and utter disaster, but why give up now? *It's not like I have anything left to lose,* I think sarcastically, falling back into the self-loathing itinerary of last night.

I shake my head and frown. "No. A good soldier never gives up, right? Until I show up at that dance with a non-friend date on my arm, the mission must go on." Blinking my burning eyes, I exhale forcefully. "Change the subject. Please. Anything but Homecoming, Justin, Brandon, or sex appeal."

The back door opens with a *beep*, and Kara rushes in with an armload of grocery bags that have to be cutting off her circulation. She heaves them onto the kitchen table and huffs, fanning her bangs around her face. "Never fear, spa products are here."

Grinning, she kicks off her shoes and pads over to the recliner. Squeezing in on the other side of me, she pinches my face in one hand and studies it with puckered lips.

"Kara, if you're trying to kiss me, I should warn you. I'm nothing but a heartbreaker."

She rolls her eyes and pulls my face to plant a kiss on the bridge of my nose. "I'll take my chances. Besides, everyone knows I'm the heartbreaker. So which guy are we hating today, Brandon or Justin?"

I slump against her and reply, "Neither. If we must hate on anyone, it's me, but I'd rather we focus on distracting me from the self-loathing."

The grandfather clock in the hallway dings, and my stomach growls. I peel myself out of the leather recliner and reach back to help my friends up. "Time to feed the pathetic. What do y'all wanna do for lunch?"

Kara grins. "How about a gallon of ice cream, a row of Oreos, and a big glass of milk?"

I blink slowly, waiting to see if an alien life force has taken my health-aholic friend's place. Kara rolls her eyes at my slack-jawed wonderment and waves her hand. "I believe you've earned a day of junk food, and what kind of friend would I be to let you suffer alone?"

As miserable as I still am about Brandon and Justin, I can't help but smile.

She puts her hand on her hip. "Well, don't just stand there. Bring on the spoons!"

I hightail it to the kitchen before she can change her mind and am greeted by the chirping of Gabi's phone on the counter. Instinctually, I pick it up and see an incoming text from Carlos. While she's still in denial about her feelings, the two have definitely taken a turn for the closer since the camping trip. At least one good thing may've come out of this disaster.

"It's lover boy!" I call, laughing as Gabi snatches the phone out of my hand. She walks backward a few steps to read the message, and her jaw drops. "Must be something sexy."

Gabi shakes her head. "Brandon just attacked Justin at the park."

MONDAY, SEPTEMBER 20TH
1 week and 5 days until Homecoming ♥

BRANDON
FAIRFIELD ACADEMY, 12:00 p.m.

I push through the cafeteria doors with one singular focus: finding Aly. I gave her space on Saturday, figuring we could both use the time to calm down. When she didn't show at church yesterday, I took it as a sign to give her even more. But when she barely made it to homeroom before the bell rang, cheeks still red and puffy, I decided the time for space was over.

Unfortunately, this is the first block we've had together all morning.

I walk past the waiting underclassmen and nod at the guy standing behind her. I never throw my weight as a senior or the captain of the baseball team around, but today feels like a good day for an exception. The dude looks like a freshman and he quickly makes room, and after lifting my chin in thanks, I turn to Aly. Her nose is in a book, but she's so tense her shoulders are practically in her ears. She knows I'm here.

"Aly, I'm sorry." She doesn't react, and I glance back to see Short Man listening with interest. I raise two fingers in a mock-wave and continue anyway. "I was a jerk at the match. You needed me to listen, not give a lecture, and I swear I didn't mean any of it the way it sounded."

Those tense shoulders shudder with a breath, and Aly dog-ears her page. Turning sideways, she gives me an unreadable look. "It's fine."

The look in her eyes calls bullshit. Pulse pounding, I scramble to fix things somehow. "No, it's not. Aly, I was an ass, but you have to know I only said those things because I was upset. You deserve better than Justin—you *are* better than Justin. And seeing you in pain..." I swallow hard. "...it killed me. Seeing you hurt makes me crazy. I hate it. But I promise you—" I brush a strand of auburn hair behind her ear. "—I never meant to hurt you. I fucked up and I'm sorry."

A shimmer of warmth enters her eyes, and her pink lips part. She looks lost and vulnerable, and her voice lacks her usual cheerfulness as she says, "No permanent damage done."

I want to believe that's the truth.

I'd like to think an apology can fix everything. But I don't. Aly is back to staring ahead, and I can't come up with a single thing to talk about—other than me digging to see if what Justin told me is true, and doing that would do no good. It won't change things. It can't. But with that off the table, I have nothing. Our friendship has always been effortless, and now I'm grasping at straws. I rub the back of my neck.

Short Man bumps into me, and trays slam at the table next to our line. When I envisioned this conversation, it didn't happen in a crowded noisy line in the cafeteria, waiting for slop. Aly and I were alone, I apologized and she forgave me, our normal friendship came back, and all the messed-up, destructive love feelings flitted away.

Unrealistic, I know. But I never expected to be scared shitless.

"I heard you saw Justin this weekend."

My head snaps back. "Where did you hear that?"

"Carlos texted Gabi. Apparently texting is now allowed within the parameters of her no-high-school-boys policy." Aly gives me a searching look as we take a step forward in line. "Did Justin tell you anything?"

I hesitate, not sure what or how much to say. "He told me I had my facts mixed up. That you actually broke up with him."

She nods slowly. "Did he tell you why?"

A grandma in a hairnet scoops goopy pasta onto a tray in front of me, and I shake my head. Justin gave me a reason, but I still think he was playing me. "Not really. He said I should ask you."

Sidestepping in line, Aly shoves that stubborn lock of hair behind her ear and shrugs. "We weren't right for each other after all." She raises her head, and a ghost of a smile crosses her face. "Guess you were right."

Her smile is fake. It's proof that there's a wall between us, a shield Aly's never put up before. Pain lingers in her eyes, and I want so badly to ask if she's so miserable, why in the hell did she call things off with him in the first place? But I don't. I have secrets I'm keeping from her, too. So instead, I say honestly, "If it makes you this sad, I wish I'd been wrong."

I grab the tray from the end of the line and follow Aly to the cashier. "I'm paying for both of us," I tell the woman, turning to Aly with a nervous smile. "Least I can do for being an ass on Saturday."

"Thanks." She bites her lip and bounces on her toes, darting her eyes around the cafeteria. "You don't have to. But thanks."

"No problem." I tuck my wallet back in my pocket and start walking to our usual table. Aly doesn't follow. "You're not sitting with us today?"

She sets her tray on a floater table and chuckles. "Um, no. I think I'll just sit here and read," she says, lifting her book in a weak wave. "But thanks, Brandon. For lunch. And for apologizing. I overreacted the other day." She sticks out her hand, an authentic Aly grin threatening to grace her beautiful face. "Friends?"

Relief pours through me, followed by a quick shot of disappointment. Friends are exactly what we need to be. I take her small hand in mine and repeat, "Friends. See you at practice later, then?"

Scooting out a chair, Aly nods as she sits. "Yeah, see ya then."

BRANDON
FAIRWOOD CITY PLAYGROUND, 4:05 p.m.

It's our sixth practice and the girls know the drill. They enter the gym, check their names off the roster, and take seats on the front bleacher, waiting for the signal. Once everyone arrives, Aly blows the whistle and we all file out for a ten-minute warm-up jog.

From the beginning, we've made a point of setting an example. Giving as much as we ask them to give. Working hard and playing hard. I don't know if it's made a difference to the team, but today, I'm glad we do it. It gives me a chance to talk to Aly.

I fall in line beside her, our breathing in sync with the pounding of our feet on the rubber track. "Can you believe our last game is this weekend?" I ask between breaths. "It feels like we just got started."

Aly breathes out and gives a small smile. "I'm gonna miss the girls. They've been fun."

I laugh. "Of course you'll miss them. They practically worship you. What will you do without your entourage?"

She giggles, and the tinkling sound makes my pulse race harder. "They don't worship me." She cuts a sideways glance and grins at my disbelieving expression. "Okay, maybe a little. But you definitely have your own underage admirers in the group. Maybe not completely for your skills on the court." She gives a slight shrug, and the teasing tone of her voice is so close to our normal banter that euphoria hits my bloodstream. "But I guess you have to take what you can get."

I jog closer and gently bump her. She pitches forward and then regains her stride, shooting me a playful glare that shows she's not mad. Another hint of normalcy.

We lap the track several times and then single-file it back into the gym. After a quick drink of water, I lead the girls in a series of stretches before Aly begins drills.

"Okay, listen up," she calls from the front of the gym. "We're gonna work on passing. In groups of three, you're going to lie face down on one side of the court. When you hear Brandon call your name, jump up and set yourself in time to return the ball back to me. Got it? First up, I need Baylee, Kaitie, and Britney."

The girls have two turns each at the drill, then we break into groups for a scrimmage for the rest of practice. We dismiss the girls at five-thirty, and while Baylee and Kaitie go to the concession stand for a snack, Aly and I gather supplies to put in the back of my truck.

"Heads up," she shouts.

A ball hits my back, and I stumble. Grabbing a second volleyball, I turn and raise it above my head to lob at her. "You asked for it now."

Aly backs away, crouching and laughing, waiting for me to throw it. But I don't. She stands back up with a questioning look.

"I thought you'd be here," Lauren says, sashaying across the floor. "Surprise!"

I drop my arm and watch as Aly shuts down again. She grabs the two volleyballs nearest her feet and makes a beeline for the bleachers to drop them in the canvas bag. Twirling around, she gives me a tight smile.

"Well, that's everything. I'm gonna grab Kaitie and head on out. See you later, Lauren."

I don't say anything. I just watch her slam into the metal door and throw it open. It bangs shut behind her.

With a frustrated sigh, I fling the canvas bag over my shoulder and fish my keys out of my pocket. Turning to Lauren, I motion toward the door.

This has gone on long enough.

Outside, I toss the bag into the cab of my truck and scan the playground for Baylee. She's a few yards away on a swing, eating a pickle and staring back unabashedly. I lean against the truck and speak to Lauren for the first time. "You wanted to surprise me, huh?"

She presses up against me and says, "That's all right, isn't it?"

I gently push her back and take a breath. Girls like Lauren use me for the same thing I used to use them for. Fun. Excitement. Something to do on the weekends. As captain of the baseball team at a school where the football team sucks, going out with me gives girls social status. It's stupid, flattering, and even embarrassing, but it's the truth. Lauren doesn't care if my heart is in it—hers most certainly isn't—but *I* care.

"Lauren, I think this—" I say, motioning between the two of us, "—has run its course."

She tilts her head and studies me, probably confused. Probably even pissed. It's only been a week, and I've yet to take her anywhere. I never even kissed her. If anything, I used Lauren to look like I got over Aly, and although I have no doubt Lauren was using me too, I still feel ashamed.

She releases a breath and says, "I'm not surprised."

"You're not?" I was completely prepared for a major girl-like fit. She shrugs a shoulder, and I ask, "Why not?"

"I knew this was a long shot. I see the way you still look at Aly." She rolls her eyes. "You *love* her." The sarcastic reply is a lot closer to the reaction I expected.

Popping open the tailgate, I hop up and motion for her to do the same. She hesitates but eventually does, and I turn to her. "Lauren, I'm not saying that I hurt you because I don't know if I did and assuming so would make me an egotistical ass. But I used you this week and you don't deserve that. I'm sorry."

Lauren narrows her eyes. "You're serious?" I nod solemnly, and she laughs. "Damn, Aly did some kinda work on you, huh?" Her lips flatten into a thin line and her nose wrinkles as if she smelled something bad, but before I can give her shit for her attitude about Aly, Lauren continues, "Listen, Brandon, I appreciate the gesture and all, but you didn't hurt me. I pretty much used you, too." She snorts. "Or at least I tried to."

A minivan pulls up beside my truck, and a crap load of hyper kids pours out. They take off for the soccer field, talking smack and taunting, trailed by a set of exasperated parents, and I wait for them to clear out before asking, "What were you hoping would happen?"

I don't know why it matters, and I doubt she'll tell me, but I'm curious. As obnoxious as Lauren's been the last four months, she's not *all* bad. She's hot and smart and amusing in her own way. I never understood why she came after me so hard when she could've had anyone.

Lauren's eyes are on the nearby playground and at first, I don't think she's gonna answer, but then she smirks and says, "You were a challenge." She lifts a shoulder unapologetically. "You've never made a play for me, and you're pretty much the only jock who hasn't. It bothered me. Being popular means being with the best, Brandon, and other than Justin, that's you."

"So it wasn't because you felt a soul-deep connection," I tease with a laugh, and she shrugs again, this time with what looks like a real smile on her face. It's a lot prettier than her usual ones. "Well I appreciate your honesty. To give it right back, if it helps any, I didn't realize I was in love with Aly until yesterday. And I'm almost certain she doesn't feel the same."

Lauren snorts, leaning back to prop herself on her elbows. "You don't know how to read girls very well then."

"Ain't that the fucking truth."

A somewhat comfortable silence stretches between us as we listen to the laughter floating from the playground. After a few minutes, Lauren exhales a breath and scoots off the tailgate. "It's been fun, Brandon. If things don't work out with Aly, you have my number."

"That I do," I say, though we both know I'll never use it. She's a *Casual,* and though I don't believe in love or relationships, I'm officially over that scene. At least for now.

She leans in to kiss my cheek. "Aly's a lucky girl." She wiggles her fingers in a wave, and I watch her walk away, thinking, *I'm the lucky one.*

THURSDAY, SEPTEMBER 23RD
1 week and 2 days until Homecoming ♥

ALY
FAIRFIELD ACADEMY, 12:05 p.m.

The tangy smells of spicy food and nacho cheese waft toward me the moment I open the cafeteria doors. While I've always been a lover of food in general and dessert in particular, Mexican cuisine holds a special place in my heart. I smile, thinking of the yummy goodness that awaits, and walk to get my tray. As I do, I glance at the Beautiful People table, curious if Brandon is there. Things are still weird between us, but they're getting better. I've sat at the floater table all week, but this morning I decided to join them again. It'll be awkward as hell sitting with Justin, too, but I meant what I said. He's a good guy, and I hope we can be friends.

Walking with my head turned, I don't see Lauren coming. Or where *I'm* going. One second I'm thinking about what my opening line will be when I show up at the table, and the next, I'm chest-to-tray with a plate full of nachos. And I'm not the only one.

As the bright-green tray clatters to the ground, Lauren looks at the neon-orange cheese oozing down her shirt. My leg muscles tense, ready to run, as her legion of followers fans off to the side, various stages of outrage and shock on their faces. A flash of cold hits the back of my neck—but this time, I refuse to bolt.

At least not *yet*.

"You skank!" At her enraged shriek, the cafeteria goes silent. It's like the quiet before a storm. A shit storm named Lauren. "You totally did this on purpose!"

I shake my head as she flicks a chip from her shirt. I watch it land on the ground, my pulse thundering in my ears. Never mind that I have globs of radioactive cheese splattered all over me as well; Lauren's evil grin clearly says she's out for blood.

"No," I stammer, like the complete coward that I am. "I didn't."

"No?" she asks, taking a step closer, her lip curling up like Elvis. "Then did you go *blind* in your quest to become a *girl*?"

Her voice twists on the last word, and it echoes in the quiet room.

A hitched breath escapes. The edges of my vision go fuzzy.

On some level, I'm aware of the whispers around us, the gleeful looks from Lauren's minions. I even realize Gabi and Kara have suddenly appeared beside me, no doubt gearing up to kick ass. But it's like I'm removed from it all. Like I'm in a bubble, where the only real sounds are Lauren's hateful words repeating over and over.

Quest to become a girl.

Hell, you actually look like a girl.

Pretty sad you had to resort to all that.

Only way you were able to get him was to change everything about yourself.

It's during that last one that the bubble pops. And I snap. The weight of constantly seeking others' approval, desperately wanting them to like me and fearing I'm never good enough, finally gets to be too much. I don't care if I stumble all over myself or end up giving Lauren more ammo for her maliciousness. I need to say *something.*

Interrupting her snarly griping, I raise my voice to say, "Lauren, for the love of *God*, shut up!"

Her mouth falls open, and she does just that, along with the rest of the room. Then she blinks, as if shocked that I'm standing up to her, and to be honest? So am I.

"All you do is bitch," I continue, throwing my hands in the air, though I have no idea where the words are coming from. It's like I'm on autopilot and someone else is in control of my mouth. "I mean, seriously, you need to get a new hobby. Because terrorizing me and anyone else who dares to shine in your vicinity is getting pretty damn old."

Shaking my head, I realize I'm done. I'm done standing there, waiting for her to come back to life and zap me with another zinger, and I'm done with feeling the need to do the same. She isn't worth it.

Glancing down, I notice my goop-coated shirt.

Well, maybe I'm almost *done.*

Dragging my finger through a particularly thick glob of cheese, I scrape it up and meet her frosty glare. Then I fling it at her. A gasp rends the air, and I spin on my heel.

Gabi's wide eyes meet mine as both she and Kara rush to fall in step beside me. We make it halfway to the back doors before Lauren sputters to life.

"Where do you think you're going? This isn't over. You can't run away now."

"I'm not running," I tell her, glancing over my shoulder. I cover the distance to the double doors and shrug as I push them open. "I'm just tired of talking to you."

ALY

KARA'S DEATH MOBILE, 12:20 p.m.

I'm flying high. And walking on rubber legs. I don't remember the walk down the breezeway, and I have no clue why we're here. Kara presses the remote for her car, unlocking the passenger door and shoving me inside.

"Wh-where are we going?" I stammer.

"Ditching!" she proclaims, sticking her head in. "You totally just handed Lauren Hays her ass in public! That, my girl, is cause for celebration."

She cackles as Gabi hops into the backseat. Pressing her face between the headrests, Gabi lays her hand to my forehead to check for a fever. "Seriously, who the hell are you and what have you done with my best friend?"

I knock her hand away with a laugh—or, rather, an attempted laugh. With my entire body becoming one big shake, it comes out more like a wheeze. "I-I don't know," I admit, still not quite sure what happened either. Kara jumps in the driver's side, guns the engine, and I say, "I-I can't feel my legs."

"Worth it," Kara declares, throwing the car into reverse. "Did you see her face?" She backs up one-handed as she huffs on the fingernails of the other and pretends to polish them on her shirt. "I taught you everything you know."

Gabi snorts. "Yeah, Kar, 'cause *you're* the hard ass of the group."

As we speed out of the parking lot, I lean forward, throwing my head between my legs. Adrenaline is pumping through me so fast, it's like my team just won a championship. I breathe deep through chattering teeth, willing my body to calm down, and say, "Th-that. Was. A *rush*."

Kara whoops again, and I inhale another deep breath, letting it out as I slowly sit back up. And then, I start giggling. Uncontrollably. Tears actually spring to my eyes, but for the first time in what feels like weeks, it's from happiness, not heartbreak.

Kara joins in, propping her chest against the steering wheel as she drives, she's laughing so hard, and through the happy tears, I check my seatbelt, confirming it's secure. Wiping mascara smudges from under my eyes, I turn in my seat, realizing Gabi's suspiciously quiet. Considering how many times Hurricane Gabi has struck and how much Lauren annoys her, it worries me that she's not laughing.

Looking into her eyes, I wince and ask, "Was I *too* bitchy?"

That shocks the weird look from her face. "What? Hell no! If anything, you were still too nice. I just wish I could've gotten a jab in, too," she admits. "You going off like that just had me too damn shocked."

"Yeah, you and me both." The memory plays back in my head, and another giggle-fit shakes my shoulders.

Holy crap, I just told off the captain of the dance team. In public!

As awesome as that is—and it truly is—Lauren was right about one thing: I did try to change everything about myself during this process. And I failed on an epic scale in almost every attempt.

In trying to keep things casual, I realized I *do* like commitments.

In going after Justin, I discovered he's *not* the guy for me.

And in my need to fit this stereotypical mold of what I thought a *Casual* should look like, I reaffirmed my belief that heels are from the devil.

But I also stood up for myself today and faced down the queen of the school, something I never thought I could do. I also rocked karaoke. As terrifying as performing in front of a crowd was, it was also pretty freaking exhilarating. Maybe I *do* have a little *Casual* buried deep inside after all. Maybe I always have. Or maybe it's that we're like that '80s movie, *The Breakfast Club*, where we're all a little bit of everyone.

We're all undefinable.

Kara whips her car into a gas station. "Trust me, Aly, Lauren had that coming."

"Yeah, she kinda did," I say, turning the ring on my finger. "But you know, she had a point though."

Gabi *psshaws* from the back. "Are you kidding me? She acted like you ran into her on purpose. She overreacted, and you rocked. Don't let her steal that away now."

"No, I'm not." I unbuckle my seatbelt and slide a leg under me, shifting my back against the window so I can face them both. "That's not what I mean. I meant with her gunning after me to begin with. She's pissed because Brandon picked me over her, and that *is* pretty unfathomable." Kara opens her mouth to argue, but I shake my head. "Because he didn't. Our whole hookup thing was just another part of Operation Sex Appeal. It was an act."

Kara flicks her wrist, turning off the engine, and the silence speaks volumes. Her eyes are wide and Gabi bolts up. A slideshow of reactions plays across their faces, both ending on bewilderment.

"I don't understand," Kara says, hurt making her voice soft. "Why wouldn't you tell us?"

I hang my head and clamp my eyes shut. "I was embarrassed! I mean, a fake hookup? Who does that, right? When I suggested it, I never thought Brandon would go for it, and when he did, I don't know... I just assumed y'all would try to talk me out of it. Or tell me I was taking the makeover too far. Or that I'd finally lost it. All reactions that, in hindsight, would've been completely accurate." Shoving my fingers through my hair, I squeeze my head as the last few weeks rush over me. "After it was over, I still couldn't admit I lied. Besides, by then I'd fallen for him anyway, so that part was honest. Just the part about him being in love with *me* wasn't."

Gabi tosses her seatbelt aside and slides her folded arms on my seat. Laying her head on top of them, she says, "Aly, I do crazy crap all the time. No matter what stupidity you land yourself in, I'm not gonna judge you. It pisses me off that you didn't know that."

"I do know that," I tell her, putting my hand on her arm. "This was a *me* thing, not you. And I'm sorry. Believe me, it's not gonna happen again. I'm done with lying, games, manipulation, all of it. It's too exhausting."

"So it was all fake?" Kara scrunches her mouth like she is confused. "Even that kiss I heard so much about?"

My lips tingle at the memory, and I feel a blush creep up my neck. "No. Well, it started as fake, just like the rest. Gabi dared us, so we had to do it." I bite my lip. "But then it became very real. It was just that one time, but..." I duck my head and grin. "...it was good."

Gabi snickers, but Kara presses on. "And what about the dance? Those tears in your eyes were real, girlfriend."

The grin falls from my face. "Like I said, I did fall for him. But I don't know, I guess Brandon figured out how I was feeling and it got too complicated for him."

"I don't buy it," Gabi declares, exchanging a look with Kara. "Not the fake-relationship part, but the Brandon-not-falling-for-you bit. I saw the two of you together, and you know I enjoyed watching his reaction to you and Justin hooking up. No one's that good of an actor, Aly. Trust me."

I sigh. "Oh, how I wish that was true, Gabriella."

Kara taps her finger on her lip, like a detective on the hunt for clues. "You said he figured out you were falling for him. Did he tell you that? Or did you just assume?"

"Call it a hunch. My feelings got all crazy-like, things got weird, he freaked, and we called it off." I throw my back against the door, remembering the pain of that night. And every night since. I shrug hopelessly. "It's the only explanation that makes sense."

Gabi rolls her eyes. "Ms. Reed, you are so adorably clueless sometimes."

"And you're so much better?" I ask, scowling at her sudden woman-of-the-world exterior. "Has anything happened on the Carlos front this week?"

That smirk disappears with a quickness. "Actually, we talked this morning in detention."

"And?" I ask, already knowing the answer.

"And it was nice," she answered defensively.

Now it is my turn to roll my eyes. "In other words, you still haven't admitted you like him. To him or yourself." Her cell phone interrupts her growling fit, the theme song to *Jaws* she assigned to her mom, and I smile sweetly. "Saved by the ring."

Gabi yanks her phone from her bag and sends the call to voicemail. If her mom's calling, it means the school is already on to us. It's only a matter of time before Kara and I are summoned, too. Keeping her eyes on the phone, she says quietly. "You do it, I'll do it."

I blink, sure I heard her wrong. "What?"

She lifts her head and repeats, "You do it, I'll do it. If you tell Brandon you want him, I'll do the same with Carlos."

Kara looks at me with eager eyes, so I close mine. "I can't, Gabi. I tried it already freshman year, and it didn't work. Don't ask me to do it again. It hurts too much."

ALY

ALY'S HOUSE, 8:50 p.m.

"*Jenga*, Jenga, Jenga."

Mom fully believes the chant holds magical powers to assist in removing her block. When the tower doesn't fall, she smiles triumphantly. I shake my head and lift my hand for my turn. I slowly tug my block forward, sans chant, and Mom tsks her disapproval.

"That's okay, honey, I believe enough for the both of us." Then she chants again, winking so I know she hasn't completely boarded the crazy train.

A tremor rocks my hand as I slide the last bit of the piece out. The tower wobbles, and the four of us take a collective breath. When it doesn't fall, everyone cheers.

A night with my nut job of a family is exactly what I need. The school *did* call my parents, but when I told them everything that's happened the last month (well, the parent-approved version), they let me off with a weekend on restriction. Considering I no longer have a social life, I figure I got off extremely easy. Besides, this is nice. Dad grilling steaks. Mom forcing us to taste-test her latest creation—a kicked-up Cajun spinach and artichoke dip. Kaitie and I pigging out and pretending we're both traumatized by our parents' flirting. This feels normal.

I miss normal.

The timer for Mom's baked macaroni goes off, and I put my hand on her arm. "I got it. You take my turn. Just don't forget to chant."

Stepping through the back door, the cool air-conditioning hits my warm skin and I shiver. I pad into the kitchen, rubbing my arms, and peer inside the oven. Noticing the top isn't quite as toasty as Mom likes, I close the door and add another five minutes to the timer.

The kitchen is quiet. No hiding in here. I push myself onto the counter, kick my feet, and heave a sigh, giving in to the thoughts that have run through my head for hours.

Operation Sex Appeal was the stupidest scheme in the history of forever. Oh, it succeeded in changing surface stuff, but it never gave me the confidence I hoped for. Probably because the girl getting noticed wasn't *me*. There is some of that girl in me, but I'm also the cute and funny friend, the girl who likes relationships and prefers walking down the hall without feeling like her butt is hanging out of short shorts. I'm me, and that's okay. Actually, it's more than okay. It's pretty freaking fabulous.

Sitting up tall, I announce to the quiet room, "As of this moment, Operation Sex Appeal is officially called on account of stupidity."

The room doesn't respond, but saying the words aloud releases a weight off my chest. I don't even care that Homecoming is a week away. If I can't go with Brandon, I don't want to go anyway. There's still time to wrangle up a just-a-friend date or maybe even a real one, but I want more.

I want a relationship.

And I want it with Brandon.

Well, that ain't happening, kid, so what else you got?

The buzzer goes off again, and I hop down. I slide the bubbling macaroni out of the oven, humming "Summer Nights" from *Grease*, the song I performed with Brandon on the camping trip.

Stepping outside, I sing, "He showed off, splashing around," and Mom claps her hands.

"Oh, I love that movie!" A wistful smile touches her lips, and she says, "I told you I played Rizzo in high school, didn't I?"

"What?!" The image of Mom playing the bad girl of Rydell High doesn't compute. Like, at all. I knew she did some theater when she was younger, and she sings along with the radio all the time, but singing in a musical is a *big* deal.

She nods. "Long time ago." Hugging her arms around her waist, she gets a faraway look in her eyes. "Only time I ever sang on stage, but man, what a rush."

"Yeah, it is," I whisper to myself.

Shaking herself out of her memories, Mom pats my head and scoops a large serving of macaroni onto my plate.

She's right. Singing on stage is a rush—much better than my nightly serenades to my toothbrush. A thought suddenly comes to me, and I bite my lip, wondering if I have the guts to act on it. Maybe this is a sign from the universe that, while I write off the male species, call off the makeover mission, and give up on Homecoming, I can still do one last thing just for me.

Maybe Operation Sex Appeal has one final phase.

I take a deep breath and say, "Hey, did I tell y'all I'm thinking of singing at the Spirit Day Talent Show?"

FRIDAY, SEPTEMBER 24TH
1 week and 1 day until Homecoming ♥

ALY
FAIRFIELD ACADEMY, 12:15 p.m.

Kara sets her tray down and slides into the bright orange plastic chair across from me, taking in the cafeteria's arranged social order with obvious disgust. After yesterday's showdown, I think we all expected a fallout. Some sort of change. We expected...something. Instead, Lauren's pretending like it never happened, and everyone else is following suit.

Shaking her head, sending the ends of her cute bob flying, Kara says, "All these people need to go see Mom for a counseling session. People here need some serious therapy." She forks a cherry tomato from her salad and pops it in her mouth.

I push my mashed potatoes around on my plate, mounding them into a hill and then flattening them out. As I drag my fork through them in a zigzag design, I feel the weight of Gabi's gaze. "What?"

"Nothing," she says, abandoning her steak in lieu of her chocolate cookie. Breaking off a corner, she waves it over my plate. "I was just observing the lovely food art you were creating. Obviously you are fully sane and not distracted at all." She takes a bite and smirks.

"Not distracted," I say, sighing and shoving away my tray. "Contemplative. I made an important decision last night."

This morning, I decided to act on my kitchen declaration, and the result has been surprising. While my inward shift feels monumental—comfort in my own skin is something I've chased for years—the outward change is more subtle. Thanks to the uniform we all wear, I still kinda look like the new Aly my classmates have gotten to know. My hair is down, rather than in a ponytail because I've learned I like it that way, and this morning I found a new balance with my makeup, using lighter, natural colors. So I'm not surprised my friends haven't seen the change. But I want them to know.

Making sure I have their attention, I announce, "Say goodbye to the makeover portion of Operation Sex Appeal. The time for pretending to be a sexy bombshell is over. Clearly, I am the cute and funny friend, and wonders of wonders, I'm finally okay with that."

Gabi smiles—a real one, not a smirk, a rarity for her. She bumps my shoulder and says, "About time you figured that out."

Kara nods. "I agree. I know I aided and abetted the whole thing, but Gabi was right. It wasn't you."

Next to me, Gabi pretends to choke on her cookie. She takes a large slurp of her chocolate milk and looks up with wide eyes. "I'm sorry. Can you say that again? Something about Gabi being...right?"

Kara throws a cucumber slice at her and grins. "But the entire mission thing hasn't been a completely wasted exercise. There were some definite memorable moments."

"Couldn't agree with you more," I say, my eyes tracking a certain boy as he pockets his wallet and heads toward his usual table. "Hey, Carlos!" He straightens in surprise, and I smile. "Can you come here for a minute?"

He strolls over and sets his tray next to Gabi's, darting his eyes between the two of us. "Yes, Miss Aly?"

"Last week, you suggested we pair up for tonight's talent show and I declined," I say, my throat closing around the words. *I cannot believe I'm doing this.* Clearing my throat, I press on with only a slight waver in my voice. "I've been thinking about it, and I was curious if the offer is still on the table?"

Carlos jumps back, looking as shocked by my words as I am. He shakes his head, and the corner of his mouth kicks up. "Hell yeah." He spins the chair next to Gabi's, apparently deciding to stay, and straddles it. "Girl, as long as you're singing, we can do anything ya want. But you don't think it's too late to enter?"

Sneaking a glance at my statue-like friends, I almost laugh out loud. "Nope. You can sign up until the end of school today."

Kara unfreezes first. "Are you serious?" She drums on the table and throws her head back in an enthusiastic *whoop.* "Aly, this is huge! Seriously, whatever you've been having for breakfast this week, keep it up."

Gabi grabs my shoulder, pulls me closer, and slaps the back of her hand on my forehead. "Patient doesn't appear to be feverish. Maybe I'm the one hallucinating. Aly, you just said Operation Sex Appeal's over."

Carlos's head swivels at the words *sex appeal,* and I knock her hand away with a smile. "No, I said the makeover portion is over. This is a new phase, and it's just for me. I'm gonna be scared out of my mind, but I want to do this. I need to try."

Gabi stares at me intently and nods. Then she takes a deep breath and turns to face the high-school boy sitting next to her, who seems thoroughly confused by our conversation. "Carlos, I know it's next week, but do you maybe wanna go to Homecoming with me? No big deal or anything," she adds quickly, shaking her head and fidgeting with her heavy rope chain. "I totally get it if you already have a date or think it's lame or whatever."

Carlos's smile spreads over his entire face. He reaches out, cups her chin, and presses a light kiss on her lips. Gabi's shocked eyes flutter closed, and when she opens them with a dazed look on her face, Carlos answers, "I'd love to." He lifts his head to look at me and announces, "Wow! I don't know what the hell's happening, but I am on *fire* today!"

Gabi giggles and then slaps her hand across her mouth. Kara kicks my foot under the table and flashes a maniacal grin. I attempt to match it, struggling to keep the jealousy at bay. I'm happy for Gabi.

I am.

She manned up, admitted her feelings, and went for it. That's awesome. But there's no way in hell I'm doing the same. Brandon and I are *finally* getting back to some sort of normalcy in our friendship. I'm not about to mess it all up again.

Grabbing my cookie, I decide to forgo lunch and head straight for dessert.

Carlos slips his arm around the back of Gabi's chair and peers around to look at me. "How 'bout you, girl? What lucky guy's taking you to Homecoming?"

"Nah, I think I'm swearing off guys for a while," I say, lowering my eyes and shoving a corner of cookie in my mouth. "And I think this is one dance that I'll sit out."

Kara gasps.

"What?" Gabi protests. "You can't miss your senior Homecoming. Wasn't that the catalyst for the whole freaking makeover?"

"Yeah, Aly, you have to come with us." Kara claws the pearl necklace at her throat and stares at me with pity-filled eyes. "Daniel can hook you up with one of his friends, or Carlos, is there anyone on the baseball team who needs a date?"

Carlos stands to eye the back table, not at all being covert, and embarrassment flames my cheeks. From the corner of my eye, I see Gabi mouth something to Kara, probably telling her to shut the hell up, and when the first lunch bell rings, I bolt out of my chair.

Normally I stay for both periods, but I need to get out of here. I seize my tray of uneaten food and shrug, aiming for blasé but fearing it reads more like a tic. "Guys, it's cool. I don't care anymore. We have tons of dances throughout the year, and really, it's only one night, right?"

I look across the cafeteria and meet Brandon's eyes. If he were my date, it would be more than just one night or another dance. It would be everything. He lifts his fingers in a wave, and tears burn the back of my throat. Blinking rapidly, I lift my hand in return, then quickly make my escape.

ALY

FAIRFIELD ACADEMY, 6:20 p.m.

The stands in the gym are overflowing. Chairs are set up across the floor for the influx of parents coming in for the Spirit Day Talent Competition. The clamor of voices, screeching of chairs along the linoleum, and occasional shouts of "Go Hokies!" don't quite cover the sounds of instruments tuning up backstage where I stand, peering around the dark curtain, having a mild panic attack.

"If you don't *chill* out, you're gonna *pass* out," Gabi says, pulling me away from the edge of the stage. "Breathe. In and out. You can do it. It's an involuntary body response."

The lights dim, signaling the start of the competition, and I wipe my palms on the curtain. Out of the three types of contestants—musical, monologue, and variety—our category is up first. There are five acts—three singers and two instrumental performances—and Carlos and I are in the second slot.

Julie McPherson, a quiet junior most known for her work as a library aide, takes to the stage first. She twists the microphone to the right height, and feedback echoes across the gymnasium.

Carlos holds the program up to his face to read in the dark. "'Somewhere Over the Rainbow.' *Wizard of Oz*, right?"

"Love the song, hate the movie," Gabi whispers. I jerk my head to look at her, and she shrugs. "They totally ruined the book."

The music begins, and Julie's voice cracks on the opening line. After clearing her throat, she timidly starts over. Her voice is feather-soft, and snickers erupt from the rafters, causing her to falter again.

"Assholes," Gabi mutters, glaring through the curtain at the crowd. From the corner of my eye, I see her look at me for agreement, but I'm focused on the stage, my body tense, willing Julie success and feeling every inhalation and note along with her.

When Julie pauses to take a deep breath, I watch her visibly give herself a pep talk. Her spine straightens, her chin lifts, and she puts on a smile of determination. She closes her eyes and loosens her grip on the microphone. With each line, her voice grows steadily stronger, building to the long, drawn-out note that she hits perfectly.

The crowd erupts in applause, and a radiant smile breaks across her face. She bounces, then bows, then runs offstage. I reach out as she scampers past and grab her arm, pulling her into a fierce hug. We don't really know each other, so I'm sure I'm freaking the girl out, but watching the shy junior overcome her nerves and an unfortunate start gives me an extra dose of confidence that maybe—just maybe—*I* can pull off the same miracle.

Julie steps back, her mouth in a small O, and I laugh. "Sorry," I say, now more than a little embarrassed about my enthusiasm. "I'm just happy for you. Endorphins flowing. Fear and adrenaline, you know?"

Julie laughs. "Oh, yeah, I *definitely* know."

The stage manager walks up and interrupts. "Aly and Carlos?" We nod, and she ushers us to the edge of the curtain. "You're up!"

Julie squeezes my elbow. "Good luck!"

I turn to say thank you, but she's already been swallowed by the other performers waiting their turn. Instead, I turn to Gabi and hold out my shaking hands. "I can't feel my hands."

She grabs them, leaning in to say in a strange voice, "Me neither."

I look in her eyes, smiling as I realize she's just as nervous for us as I am. That's how amazing my friends are. Why did I ever think I had to keep the truth from them? Throwing my arms around her neck, I squeeze her tight. "You're made of awesome. You know that, right?"

"I do," she confirms, squeezing me back. Stepping back, she kisses Carlos's cheek, then pushes us both forward. "Now, y'all go kick some ass."

The smile on my face freezes in place as I glide to the center of the stage, barely feeling the ground beneath my feet. Behind me, Carlos grabs a chair and settles in to finger the strings of his guitar. He nods, looking completely relaxed (which drives me a little insane), and I turn to scan the audience.

Shadowy outlines and camera flashes are the only things I can make out in the crowd. For that, I am extremely grateful. My parents are out there somewhere, my sister, too, and maybe even Brandon. I hope he is, because none of this would be happening without him. I adjust the microphone even lower and take a deep breath.

This isn't a makeshift stage at Cypress Lake. This isn't about trying to be anyone else. Tonight is for me, and this time, it's for real.

Carlos strums the opening chords for the song I chose, an acoustic version of my favorite Natasha Bedingfield song, and I close my eyes.

A moment later, I open my mouth.

BRANDON
FAIRFIELD ACADEMY, 6:30 p.m.

"Dude, you need to relax," Drew says, slapping me on the back. "Aly's gonna be great."

I crane my neck to look at the people in the rafters and then scan the crowded floor. Justin catches my eye across the bleachers, and I glance away. I *know* Aly can do it, but this is way different than singing karaoke on a school-sponsored camping trip. The audience alone is enough to have me sweating, and I'm not the one out there.

Julie bows before disappearing behind the black curtain, and Drew sits back down. Everyone else around me follows suit. I can't. With hands slick with sweat, I remain standing, waiting for the first glimpse of Aly.

A jean-clad figure emerges through the dark curtain, and I swallow the lump in my throat. She drifts to the center of the stage, and Carlos follows, setting up behind her. Aly scans the audience and I whistle, but her eyes roam past me.

"It's too dark for her to see us," Drew whispers.

I nod, not taking my eyes off her for a second. "That's a good thing. If she can't see us, she can't see the rest of the crowd either. Seriously, I'm freaking out enough for the both of us."

The opening chords begin, and Aly closes her eyes. I hold my breath, eyes trained on her mouth, waiting for it to open. A moment later, her throaty voice breaks across the room.

I pump my fist and fight the urge to scream. Quickly, I look at all the smiling faces and nodding heads around me, then turn back to watch Aly.

In the spotlight of the stage, she glows. Her hair is loose, but instead of a skimpy tank top or halter like she's been wearing the past month, she has on a bright blue top, the same color as her eyes. It skims over her hips, which I now realize are encased in loose-fitting denim. I glance at her feet and smile at the familiar beat-up Nikes.

Then I narrow my eyes and study her.

Is Operation Sex Appeal over?

Relief pours over me as Aly opens her eyes. She sang the entire first verse and chorus with them squeezed shut, but now, even though I know it's not possible, it feels like she's staring right at me. Her eyes sparkle with excitement.

I forget how to breathe.

Watching her perform is like watching her discover what she was born to do. She chose a song about releasing inhibitions, and as Aly finishes serenading the gymnasium, she loses hers. Her voice rings out strong and clear, and when the last note fades away, the crowd roars to its feet.

Aly's eyes widen and her jaw drops, and I can't help but smile.

She did it.

Amidst screams for an encore, Aly grabs Carlos's hand and lifts it high in the air. They bow together, and then Carlos steps back, giving her one last moment in the spotlight. Aly gnaws on her lip and bounces on her toes in giddy excitement.

There's *my* Aly.

With one final, bubbly curtsy—her face lit up in triumph—she walks off the stage, and I sit, eagerly awaiting the results.

♥ ♥ ♥

After the winners are announced and performers spill out the stage door, I sneak up behind Aly. Her mom looks up from hugging her, and I put my finger over my mouth, wanting to surprise her. Mrs. Reed nods and smiles at her daughter.

"Honey, I'm so proud of you. You were a rock star up there!" Grasping the strap of her purse, she looks like *she* was the one who just killed it on stage, not Aly. Seeing her mom so proud of her makes my chest feel tight, like *I* had anything to do with it. This was all Aly. "I'm sure you want to be with your friends," her mom continues, "so restriction is suspended for the night. And tomorrow before you go to work, we're celebrating!"

Aly raises her nose in the air. "I'll have my people fax my full contract rider in the morning. Now that I'm a famous musician, I demand nothing but green M&Ms and Double Stuf Oreos in the pantry and a fridge stocked with Cokes in my room."

Her dad laughs. "Is that all? Seems perfectly reasonable."

Aly ruffles Kaitie's hair and nods. "I thought so, too."

Her mom subtly squeezes Mr. Reed's arm and shoots me a weighted glance. "We should be going, but I'll need to see two copies of that contract in the morning."

Aly laughs and hugs all of them one more time. Then they turn and walk away, leaving her alone. She tilts her head to search the room, and suddenly, I'm nervous.

Is she looking for me?

I tighten my grip around the stems of the bouquet I hold, unsure of what to say or do next. Are the flowers too much? Not enough? Will she think they're stupid?

Do they say too much about how I feel?

Aly takes a step in the wrong direction—away from me—and I snap out of it. I snake an arm around her tiny waist and thrust the bouquet of daisies in her face. She squeals and, spinning on her heels, jumps into my arms and buries her face in my neck.

It's so naturally Aly, yet so *un*natural for how we've been toward each other lately, that I'm shocked. I pull her closer and lose myself in holding her. Feeling the warmth of her breath on my neck, the soft curves of her breasts pressed against me, the rhythm of her heartbeat against mine. I close my eyes and inhale her delicious cookie scent.

"You killed it up there," I tell her, my voice choked and raspy. I cough and kiss the top of her head. "The judges were idiots. It was totally rigged."

Aly laughs and hops down, looking slightly embarrassed. "I don't care about that. What matters is that I did it. I actually did it!"

She beams at me, and the urge to lean down and kiss her soundly on the mouth is almost overwhelming. Instead, I say, "Yes, you did. But you still should've won."

She lifts the daisies to her nose and sniffs them, then glances at me over the blooms. "We're going to Carmela's tonight for a celebratory dinner. Kara and Daniel, Gabi and Carlos, and me. The lone wolf." She bounces on her toes and scratches the back of her neck. "Um, would you maybe want to come with us?"

Hell yeah.

I'd kill to go with her and our friends, to sit next to her and act as though that's all we are, too. *Friends.* But my mouth can't form the words. Seeing her on that stage, stealing the show and looking so unbelievably beautiful—it did something to me. And if I go with her tonight, I know there's no way in hell I'll be able to keep myself from pulling her into my lap, kissing her senseless, and telling her that I'm in love with her.

And that overwhelming desire scares the crap out of me.

"No, I should go," I say, quickly adding when her smile diminishes, "Bayls is home tonight and Mom has a late shift—who knows what kind of drama that girl will get into on her own. But go have an amazing time. You deserve it. You looked beautiful up there, Aly. Seriously, I'm so proud of you."

Her head tilts, her eyes crinkle, and the dimple in her right cheek pops as she smiles her Aly smile, then reaches her hand out to hold mine. "Thanks for being here tonight, Brandon. It really means a lot."

"I wouldn't be anywhere else."

We stare at each other, so many words in my mouth, options I could take, things left unsaid. I glance up and see Gabi walking toward us, her attention focused on our joined hands. The expression on her face says she is reading way too much into the gesture. She looks at me, and I see it in her eyes. She knows the truth.

Hesitantly, reluctantly, I let go.

SUNDAY, SEPTEMBER 25TH
6 days until Homecoming ♥

BRANDON
BRANDON'S HOUSE, 6:40 p.m.

A light knock raps on my door, followed by a more determined one. After getting the shading just right on Aly's eyes and without looking up from my sketchbook, I call out, "Come in!"

The door clicks shut and muffled steps approach. I quickly cover the sketch with my notebook and glance over to see Mom standing by the bed. "Can we talk for a minute?"

"Sure," I say, pricks of apprehension steeling my spine. A paper crinkles, and I look down to see a sketch in her hands. I jerk my head to the empty space over my desk. It's the before-and-after of Aly I drew weeks ago.

How in the hell did I not notice it was gone?

She holds the paper out. "Why have I never seen this before?" she asks, her voice a mix of bewilderment and awe. "I mean, I didn't even know you had an interest, much less a talent like this." Mom looks at the sketch again wistfully and smiles. "Baby, this is *really* good."

I shrug, drumming a beat on my notebook. "It's nothing. Just something Dr. Foster recommended after Dad died. It helps me figure things out."

Mom nods, sinking down onto my blue comforter. Clearly in no hurry to end this awkward conversation. "That's good. I'm glad you found this outlet. But, Brandon, you know you can always talk to me, too, right?" She places the sketch on the bed and shakes her head. "Baylee said you and Aly acted almost normal again at the match today. I never even knew y'all were fighting. I feel so out of the loop."

Shit.

Mom already battles regret over her hectic work schedule. I refuse to let my issues make her feel worse. Walking across the room, I sit beside her and say, "Really, it's not that big of a deal," I lie, and I hate myself for it. But I'm doing it to protect her. That makes it better, right? "We just decided we're better off as friends."

"Friends, huh?" Mom picks up the sketch again and studies it. "Judging from this, I'd say you're more than that."

I stare at the picture, remembering the night I sketched it, how I blamed the clothes for making everything so confusing. The transformation from track pants and a ratty tee to a bikini top and cut-offs. But as I compare the two again, it seems so obvious. She's the same girl in both pictures. Same signature smile. Same flirty eyes. Same crazy humor and contagious laugh.

It was never about the clothes. The only thing Aly's makeover did was force me to get my head out of my ass and finally see the girl she's been all along.

the back of the row, though, instinct takes over and I raise my head, feeling someone's eyes on me.

On the hood of my car, bathed in the golden glow from the streetlamp above him, sits Brandon. He isn't smiling. In fact, his chest rises and falls in apparent nervousness, but his gaze holds an intensity I'm almost too scared to name. And it's that unnamed emotion that emboldens me. My steps quicken to cover the distance between us, not slowing until my chest presses against his knees and my hands rest in his lap.

"Hi."

"Hi," he answers back, the right side of his mouth kicking up. "Got off early, I see?"

I narrow my eyes and study him, taking note of his spreading smile, twinkling eyes, and finally the wink he adds. My jaw drops. "You? *You* had Gabi get me out of work early?"

Brandon nods. "Guilty as charged." He glides his hands up my arms and along my shoulders, running his fingers through the hair at the nape of my neck. "There's something I need to tell you, and I was too impatient to wait."

Fear and desire mingle in my stomach as his fingers continue massaging my neck. My eyelashes flutter as he plays with my hair, and I widen them, trying to gain a clue to what it is he has to say. Good or bad, as I stare into his eyes and feel his magical fingers, I make a decision. I'm not letting him walk away again without knowing how much I love him. Our friendship made it through one confession; maybe it can make it through another. But even if it can't, after everything I've been through with Operation Sex Appeal, I owe it to myself to take a chance. Brandon is worth it.

But I'll let him go first.

"Whatever it is, Brandon, you can tell me."

He takes a deep breath, hands clenching around my neck. "Aly..." The pain in that one word hits me, and instinctively I clasp my hands around his forearms. "I've *missed* you."

Hope, pure and simple, springs to life in my chest, and I close my eyes at the sensation.

"I miss calling you," he says, and I open them again. "I miss hearing you tell me about every single minute detail of your day. I miss shooting hoops behind your house and playing endless hours of video games. I miss tasting your dessert concoctions and playing board games with your family. I miss studying together and laughing with you and having you call me on my stupid shit."

His breathing spikes, and it's like a storm has been unleashed. Emotions flash and gather in his eyes, turning the grass-green shade to jade. I open my mouth to tell him just how badly I've missed him too, but he shakes his head. He gently slides his thumb across my lips, and they burn with the memory of his.

Brandon swallows so hard I can hear it. "I miss holding you in my arms," he says, his voice noticeably rougher than before. "And even though I only got to do it once..." His eyes flick to mine before returning to my lips. "I miss kissing you. I dream about it, Aly, and I'm at the point where I might just go insane if I can't do it again."

My veins ignite at the image of being in his arms. A bubbling feeling bursts throughout my body as he continues his light caresses on my face, and I struggle to hear my thoughts over the roar in my ears. All I want to do is replay his words over and over, but I know he's waiting, needing to hear that I feel the same way.

"Brandon, you don't know what these last few weeks have been like for me. It didn't just feel like I lost my best friend—it felt like I lost a part of myself." My eyes close briefly at the truth of my words, and I draw a breath, gaining strength for the rest of my confession. "Three years ago, I had a massive crush on you. For the sake of our friendship, I convinced myself I was over it, over you, and I honestly thought I was. But being with you? Pretending we were more and watching you pretend to care about me like *that*? God, Brandon, it was torture."

His forehead crinkles, misunderstanding what I'm saying, and I clutch his arms so tight my nails embed in his skin. "That trivial crush I had in the beginning? Brandon, that was nothing compared to how I feel now."

He stills completely. Not even his chest moves for a breath as he asks, "And how's that?"

My legs start to shake, and my heart pounds so fast I fear it's about to jump out and make an appearance. *Here goes nothing.* "I'm in love with you."

In the wake of my speech, time seems to stop. Brandon has yet to come back to life, still frozen all statue-like, and I wonder if I went too far. Missing someone and wanting to kiss them again is *not* the same as professing love. But it's the truth of how I feel and I'm tired of pretending otherwise. I want him to know.

I release a breath, and as it hits his face, Brandon thaws. His shoulders relax, and a broad smile breaks across his beautiful face as he says, "I wanted to be the one to say it first." He yanks me against his chest, cradling my head in his hands so reverently it's as though I'm made of glass. The gentleness and the meaning behind his words bring tears to my eyes. "I had this whole thing prepared, but then I got selfish. I wanted to hear you say it. But God..." He leans down and presses his lips to the crown on my head once, twice, three times. "I love you, too. So damn much."

Holy cannoli.

Those gathered tears spring out of my eyes. I can't help it. They wet the cotton of his shirt as he tightens his hold around me, and I wish with everything in me that I could pause this moment. Memorize it. The sound of his voice, the way his body feels against mine, the distant sounds of cars on the interstate, and even the not-so-distant smell of the Dumpster. Right now, all of it is so *perfect* it almost hurts.

Brandon loves me.

He freaking loves me!

He places a knuckle beneath my chin and tilts it up. "I was so scared that admitting it would ruin everything. That I'd scare you away or lose your friendship, and you're too important to let that happen. But not telling you, not admitting it even to myself? It destroyed me. I was angry all the time, jealous and hurt." Brandon's eyebrows scrunch at the memory of the last few weeks apart, and I lay my hand against his cheek to comfort him. Under my touch, his tension eases, and with a slight shake of his head, his mouth kicks up. "I'm just no good without you, Aly."

A feeling of floating spreads throughout my body, and I laugh aloud. I wrap my arms around his waist, knowing the moment can't get any better.

"Aly?" The words rumble in his chest, and I look up into his kind, sexy green eyes. "There was one question I wanted to ask you." The smile he bites off belies his affected nervousness, and I wait with curious expectation. "Would you go to Homecoming with me?"

Laughing again, I smash my mouth against his. "Yes, yes, a thousand times yes," I answer dramatically, leaning back as giddy joy surges through every pore.

Brandon doesn't laugh though. His eyes darken again, and his teeth sink into his bottom lip. My laughter dies as I remember sucking on that lip, and this time it's my turn to forget to breathe as my gaze darts between his mouth and eyes. Anticipation skims over my skin, causing it to prickle.

"No offense," he says, the rough sound causing my stomach to flip. "But I've waited entirely too long to kiss you again, and that simply didn't do the memory justice."

Brandon slides off the hood and grasps my waist, lifting and placing me on the car instead. His palms push my knees apart, and he presses his body between them to get closer, but not close enough. Threading his fingers into my hair, he turns my face toward him, and I meet his gaze briefly before my eyes flutter shut, feeling his warm breath fan across my face.

If he doesn't kiss me soon, it's quite possible I'll explode.

Then I feel it—the heat of his mouth hovering just above mine. I tremble, held in what seems like an eternity in the moment of *before*. Before our friendship changes forever. Before our real relationship begins. Then, finally, the sliver of distance between our lips closes.

Our last kiss was hesitant before our instincts had taken over. Not this one. This time when Brandon kisses me, it begins as a gentle brush, but it feels like savoring rather than uncertainty.

His mouth caresses mine, nibbling and sucking. His tongue darts out for a taste before coaxing my lips apart. When he deepens the kiss, my body becomes liquid fire, and I'm grateful for the car's support below me. I wrap my legs around his waist and devour the taste of his mint-flavored gum, fisting my hands in his shirt and tugging him even closer. Brandon growls with approval.

Cool fingers glide across my cheek as he rains light kisses across my jawbone from earlobe to chin. My head falls back and tingles dance down my spine. Scratch that—my body is one *giant* tingle. When his mouth meets mine again, a moan escapes my throat. It's loud and I should be embarrassed, but I'm not. I just want more.

Lifting my heavy eyelids, I sneak a peek and a thrill courses through me. I'm kissing Brandon. This is real, this is happening. And it's blowing every memory of our first kiss out of the water. Smiling against his mouth, I lose myself in his lips, his heavenly scent, and his strong arms.

A whimper escapes my throat as he lifts his head, the sliding and lingering of his dazed eyes as much a caress as those of his fingers and mouth. "I love you, Aly," he says again, the surprise, joy, and tenderness in his voice enough to make my head fuzzy all over again. "So much, it hurts knowing we could've been doing this all along."

He laughs, the sound deep and rich, and I sigh as I grasp his chin between my fingers, bringing his mouth back where it belongs. "Then let's start making up for lost time, shall we?"

SATURDAY, OCTOBER 2ND

Homecoming ♥

ALY

TIMBERLAKE COUNTRY CLUB, 7:30 p.m.

Brandon's truck rumbles below me, and my hand shoots out to stop him from turning off the engine. Frowning, he turns, the fabric of his dress pants softly hissing on the leather seat. "What's wrong?"

"Just give me a moment."

The night I've been counting down to for fifty-seven days is finally here. I have on a beautiful dress, my hair is in a complicated up-do I will never be able to recreate, and I am in love. Even more unbelievable, Brandon loves me, too. At this moment, everything is perfect. The moment I step out of the truck and into the dimly lit ballroom of the country club, it could all change.

Brandon scoots next to me on the bench seat and nuzzles my neck. "I'd be perfectly happy staying in the truck all night. The way you look in this dress, I'm not sure I want to share you."

Chill bumps dance down my arm, and I tilt my head to give him better access.

"But first, we need to get photographic evidence," he continues, his breath warm against my ear. His tongue darts out for a lick before nibbling gently. Moaning, I let my body go limp in his arms. Brandon whispers, his voice a sexy promise, "We'll run inside, take the picture, then come right back here and pick up where we left off."

My eyes close as his mouth traces a path from my ear, across my jaw, to my eagerly waiting lips. I've lost count of how many times we've kissed since that night in the parking lot, but it isn't enough. After a few blissful moments, I pull back reluctantly.

Sighing against his mouth, I mumble, "Let's go get that picture then."

He flashes a grin, and it's all I can do to shove his shoulder away.

"Go," I say, running my hand along the back of my hair and reaching into the glove compartment for my compact. "I need this picture for my wall, and if you keep looking at me like that, we'll never go in!"

Brandon rounds the truck to let me out the passenger side, his laughter floating through the open window. I reapply my lipstick, snap the compact closed, and hold my hand out so he can help me down.

"I love this dress," he whispers, lifting me out of the truck and letting me glide down his body before leaning down to kiss me again.

At the last minute, my hand shoots between us, and I smile. "Picture first," I remind him, smoothing my dress over my hips and looking at my reflection on the side of his newly washed truck. "But thank you. I love it, too."

My emerald-green, one-shoulder satin gown fits beautifully, and I feel gorgeous in it. Finding such a perfect dress a week before Homecoming was nothing short of a miracle.

The door to the country club opens as we approach, and music spills out onto the sidewalk. Stepping inside, Brandon leads me to a round table covered with a dark blue tablecloth, the flame inside the metallic globe centerpiece flickering through hammered shapes of crescent moons and stars. My eyes drift over the dance floor and the handful of couples swaying to the beat, past the DJ booth and monster speakers on either side, toward the photo display set up in the back corner.

The photographer's vision of a "Starlight Fairytale" includes a full moon, a handful of stars, and delicately lit tree branches on a golden background. Considering I'll be standing next to Brandon, the backdrop could be a cheesy Disney castle against a map of the solar system and I would love it.

Brandon rests his hand on my lower back and leads me toward the short line for pictures. We're among the first to arrive, so the line only has one other couple waiting in front of us.

Justin and Lauren.

We step behind them, and Brandon tenses beside me. Slipping my hand into his, I clear my throat. "You look beautiful, Lauren," I say, taking in her asymmetrical one-shoulder top and kimono sleeve. "That dress is...wow."

Lauren glances down, fidgeting with her sleeve. "Thanks." She takes her time giving my own dress a once-over and then, shock of all shocks, smiles. And not her plastic one, either. "You look great, too."

"Ah, thank you," I say, completely gobsmacked. She nods, then glances at Brandon and turns back around.

I squeeze his hand, giving him a pointed look. "Fine," he mouths. Cracking his neck, he straightens his back and blows out a breath before tapping Justin on the shoulder.

Justin's eyes glide over my dress on their way to meet Brandon's gaze. Brandon holds out his hand. "Sorry about the football game last week. I overreacted. I never should've come at you like that."

Justin slowly raises his hand to shake Brandon's, and he gives me a long, appraising look. Smiling wistfully, he says, "Forget about it, man. It looks like everything worked out the way it was supposed to."

I smile gratefully, and the guys drop hands. The photographer calls for the next couple in line, and Justin and Lauren carefully walk across the duct-taped wires to the backdrop, where the photographer poses them in an uncomfortable position meant to look natural.

"Thank you," I say, stepping in front of Brandon and running my hands under the back of his sports jacket. "That was very magnanimous of you."

He kisses the tip of my nose and grins. "Anything for you."

The photographer calls us forward and makes a face at our obvious height difference. He asks Brandon to get down on one knee and seats me on his other one, guiding me to lean into his chest and nestle our faces together. Brandon kisses my cheek as the bulb flashes, and without even seeing it, I know it will be the best picture on my wall.

Being short does have some advantages.

Walking past the umbrella light kit, Brandon smiles wickedly, laces his fingers with mine, and starts pulling me back toward the exit. The sultry beat of the slow song floating from the dance floor wars with the temptation I know awaits me in his truck. Delaying gratification, I force my feet to stop carrying me forward.

He quirks an eyebrow, questioning.

"My last dance with you ended quite abruptly," I say, thinking back to the breakup that cut our dance short. "And with a far-from-happy ending. I want a do-over."

Brandon closes the distance between us and lifts my hand. Pressing a kiss to my knuckles, he smiles. "I'm not much of a dancer, but considering the circumstances, you're absolutely right."

He leads me across the glossy wooden floor reflecting the twinkle lights above to a back corner of the dance floor tucked away in the shadows. Wrapping his arms around me, we take a step as the last note of the song fades. When the next song begins, I smile at the beautiful coincidence.

Adele's "Make You Feel My Love."

The same song we danced to that night. My head snaps up, and I search Brandon's eyes to see if he remembers. He slides one arm up my back and gently tilts my chin back with his thumb.

"I think we got our do-over," he whispers, his raspy voice sending tingles skating down my spine.

His lips meet mine, and I get the dance I should've had five weeks ago.

♥ ♥ ♥

ACKNOWLEDGEMENTS

This part always makes me sappy. It also scares me a bit. See, blame it on my chaotic author/homeschooling mama brain, but undoubtedly, I'm going to "pull a Rachel" and leave out a name of someone vitally important. So for everyone listed below, and for everyone I sadly forgot (and will kick myself over in 3, 2, 1...), please know you rock my socks off.

The Fine Art of Pretending was the first story I ever wrote. After writing what later became my debut novel, I came back and rewrote it again. I kept tweaking and adding scenes during editing, too, determined to make this book the best it could be. Out of everything I've ever written, this book is the closest to my heart. It is the *story* of my heart

Which means, I've got a boat load of people to thank. To Nancy Bowden and Natalie Markey, my first fabulous critique partners, for giving me hope, making me believe I can do this—that I don't totally suck as an author—thank you!

To Trisha Wolfe, who read and critiqued *two* versions of this book, you are my goddess. Shannon Duffy and Victoria Scott, thank you for joining the critique party in round two and totally making this baby shine. Ashley Bodette, your suggestions, listening ear, and rereading of every word in the edit process made all the difference. Paula Stokes, your blurb TOTALLY made me squeal. I'm posting that sucker everywhere (tee hee). You girls rock.

Brooke Troxclair, you probably don't remember this, but you're my baseball-fact godmother. Back in 2010, mid all-nighter, I took to social media for help with Justin's date. You answered the call, even though we hadn't spoken in years, and saved my butt. For the help—and the fabulous rekindled friendship since—*thank you.*

Staci Murden, Kayleigh from K-Books, and Heather Self, I adore you girls to pieces. Kayleigh, thank you for getting this story. For loving it and these characters as much as I do. Heather, thank you for swooning over Brandon and your fabulous friendship. And Staci, thanks for pouring over these words so closely and for all the funny texts. *Mwah*

To the Cool Kids Mafia...secret handshake, chin lift, sly wink.

Cindi Madsen, Lisa Burstein, Tara Fuller, Melissa West, Megan Erickson, Stina Lindenblatt, Caisey Quinn, Rhonda Helms, and Christina Lee, you girls are my sanity. Thank you for being my sounding board, for making me laugh when I feel like crying, and never failing to be there when I need your advice. You girls are foxy, yo!

Cindy Thomas, you're amazeballs. You worked so hard to make this launch the best it can be, and you're a master at Google Hangout. For all the fun chats, the silly laughter, and the fabulous results, thanks girl.

Kelly Simmon, you are my girl. Thank you for all the "outside the box" brain sessions, creativity, giggly phone calls, and most importantly, for your dear friendship. Your constant encouragement never fails to fill me up. You're my ray of sunshine

Lauren Hammond, you were one of the first people to read and fall in love with this book, and because of YOU, it found a home. You are *marvelous*, darling. Keep on dancing!

Patricia Riley, from our very first chat, before there was even a contract, I knew you were the editor for this project. Your enthusiasm and excitement has remained off the charts, your edit letter may be the best thing I've ever read, and your love for Brandon makes me do a bazillion happy dances. Saying 'thank you' isn't nearly enough, so I'll save the rest for a tackle hug at BEA. I ADORE YOU!

A huge shout out to all the copy editors, publicists, and staff at Spencer Hill, particularly those who had their hands on this book. Kate Kaynak, thank you for providing such a fabulous home. Danielle Ellison, you are a title QUEEN. And Dahlia Adler, you are a word genius. You girls complete me (grin).

To the Flirt Squad...seriously, I have the best street team EVER. You girls aren't just readers and fans. You're my friends. Your tireless support and enthusiasm and *love* are unmatched—and a total blessing. I know I've been teasing you with snippets from this book for over a year now. I hope the full thing lived up to your expectations! Love ya hard, girls.

Katrina Tinnon, Jessica Mangicaro, Jennifer Staci, Jenna DeTrapani, Staci Murden, Saleana Rae Carneiro, Meredith Johnson, and Valerie Fink, you ladies go WAY above and beyond. I truly can't thank you enough, and until words are invented to do it properly, my plan is to bombard you with virtual slobber fests. And dozens of happy twirls.

Christine (I Heart Big Books), Crystal Leach, Ali and Ciara Byars, Maliha Khan, Megan Rigdon, Maura Trice, Kathy Arguelles, Heather Love, Amy Logg, Shelley Bunnell, Melissa Casey Lemons, Zoe Miller, Amy Fournier, Wendy Hung, Chelsea Cochran, Vi Nguyen, Cindy Ray Hale, Veronica Bartles, Mindy Ruiz, Shari Drehs Bartholomew, Jessica Baker, Linda Townsend, Bette Hansen, Gaby Navarro, Denice Cordero, and Jas Dela Cruz, you do so much to support me. Countless times, one of you would post a note or message that filled me up. Calmed the storm. Motivated me to dive back in. Each of you is a blessing.

To every blogger, reviewer, and reader of my previous books, a huge, heartfelt thank you. Your emails, messages, blog posts, reviews, and visits to my signings have each touched my heart. Thank you for the support, encouragement, and inspiration to keep on writing.

Finally, to my incredible family. My husband Gregg is my rock. He believes in me so completely, I have no other choice but to do the same. (SHMILY!) My girls, Jordan and Cali, cheer me along, give me ideas, and make FABULOUS fan art. My mom and dad, Rosie and Ronnie, buy books for their friends and clients, listen to my never-ending tales of the industry (when I'm sure they'd rather listen to *anything* else), and offer plenty of free babysitting! My brother, Ryan, gives advice on lingo and all things music. My godmother, Rhonda, lifts me up constantly. And my mother-in-law, Peggy, is my number one fan. Without this solid support system, I'd be toast. And, most likely, still dreaming of someday. I love you more than words can say.

ABOUT THE AUTHOR

Rachel Harris writes humorous love stories about sassy girls-next-door and the hot guys that make them swoon. Emotion, vibrant settings, and strong families are a staple in each of her books...and kissing. Lots of kissing.

An admitted Diet Mountain Dew addict, she gets through each day by laughing at herself, hugging her kids, snuggling with her husband, and losing herself in the story. She writes young adult, new adult, and adult romances, and LOVES talking with readers!